VERONICA'S NAP

Sharon Bially

(sixoneseven)BOOKS
Boston, Massachusetts

Veronica's Nap

(six one seven) BOOKS

ISBN: 978-0-615-47560-8

Gratitude to my husband, Jacques Cohen,
and to our sons, Sam and Alex.

Chapter One

After three years in Aix-en-Provence, Veronica knows why Van Gogh cut off his ear. On sunny days, when the sky glows a shade of sapphire as brilliant, she imagines, as the color of God's eyes, the mistral wind rips apart the beauty, howling with rage, rattling olives from branches and whipping the feathery tips of cypress trees into demented, evergreen whorls. Gates and steel shutters clang madly. The pitch of conversation rises to a scream. It's a wonder that with these gales that batter southeast France year-round and have been blowing relentlessly for three days straight now, he could paint at all. Veronica hasn't cracked open an easel since she moved here from New Jersey.

Of course, Van Gogh didn't have two-year-old twins like Veronica does. Their whiny, high-pitched voices shatter the rare silence between the mistral's gusts, grating on her nerves, setting her on edge, and making it impossible to concentrate, even when they're not around. With twins, Van Gogh would have surely cut both his ears off.

He didn't have a French-Moroccan husband, either— Sephardic, to boot, with a warm heart but a hot, Mediterranean temper—who's been waiting with thinning patience to see some progress in the studio. This alone can kill the nerves, Veronica thinks. Didier rarely voices his impatience, but from the way his gaze has darted away lately when she's tried to meet it, she knows. Just as she knows that his edginess these days over her parenting style has more to do with her painting, or lack of it, than it does with the all-too-American habits she's teaching the kids.

Hearing his footsteps crunching now outside on the gravel walkway to the door, she checks her watch and tenses. He's early. Luc and Céleste, home from a day at their nanny's house down the street, are sitting in twin highchairs in the family room, eyes riveted to the television screen. They've barely touched their dinner.

"Eez Daddy home?" Veronica snorts, joining him in the hall. Even if he's edgy, she can't resist imitating his French accent, thick as a slab of butter on every word.

He nods and lets his briefcase thunk to the ground. Fatigue shadows his eucalyptus-bark complexion, carpeted with five-o'clock stubble as thick as anybody else's two-day beard. Kissing the top of her head, he peers into the living room. His eyes, brown as sun-dried Moroccan dates, slide directly to the television screen where the Wiggles are dancing round in circles, holding hands. "TV during dinner?" he frowns.

"Oh, come on. It's a Wiggles DVD!" She elbows him in the ribs, pretending not to notice his grouchy mood. What else can she do? Complaining, even gently, would only add to his stress. At thirty-five—four years Veronica's senior—he's one of the top ear, nose, and throat specialists in inland Provence. He operates two or three times each morning and sees dozens of patients each afternoon. Veronica may not know how it feels to work twelve hours nonstop each day on top of a session of the synagogue's morning minyan prayer group, but Didier has no idea what it's like to sit at the table alone and feed two squirming kids. Letting them watch TV while they eat keeps them still. It's become their dinnertime routine, at least for now. They're only two. As quickly as they grow, routines change.

"What about forks?" he asks, eyeing Céleste, who's busy swiping macaroni curls off her high chair's tray. Pieces of Shake 'n Bake chicken, which Veronica made using the mix she stocks up on at Aix's Anglo-Saxon grocer, fly off with them. European to the core, Didier believes children should start learning proper table manners as soon as they're old enough to sit.

"You mean those pronged things I've already had to pick up from the floor fifteen times? Don't even bother. The kids are completely wired tonight." It's best just to let these issues slide without giving in.

He walks to the kitchen—a narrow galley separated from the living room by a counter edged with four distressed-bronze stools—and returns with a couple of kid-sized forks. After zapping off the TV, he positions himself between the children, stabs a fork into a lump of chicken and holds it out to Céleste. She pushes it away.

"Do you want Papa to read you a story at bedtime tonight?" he coaxes, glancing from one child to the next. The fatigue in his voice is laced with kindhearted determination.

Céleste nods, peering up at him from beneath her copper bangs. Luc blinks. His eyes, date-brown like Didier's, shine in agreement.

"No dinner, no fork, no story," Didier insists, faking a pout. He raises the fork again to Céleste's mouth, which she opens deliberately, wide as a yawn.

While Didier feeds the kids, Veronica busies herself in the kitchen opening a package of prewashed salad and putting up a pot of rice. Didier hates reheated macaroni. She also uncorks a bottle of wine, which they both could use. She bites her tongue as he insists, "*Allez, allez*, just one more for Papa, open wide." If only she had a painting to show for all the hours she spends alone in the house, she thinks. Better yet, if only she could announce, right now, that she's finished one and is ready to sell it. Then she'd feel more confident standing her ground.

A painting to sell. It sounds so easy, she thinks, and logically, it should be. Veronica came to Provence in the first place to paint. Three years after college—Boston University's visual arts school—she was still living with her parents in Tenafly, New Jersey, working a nine-to-five job her father suggested she take for the income and getting absolutely nowhere with her painting. How could she paint when she worked dawn to dusk and her commute into Manhattan lopped off another hour at each end? Back at her parents' house each night, she barely had the strength to watch a good episode of *Mad About You* before collapsing into bed. So she signed up for a painting vacation in Provence—artists' heaven—to kick her artwork into gear.

Didier, whom she met during that trip, has given her everything she needs to succeed. He made sure they found a home with space for her to paint. After Luc and Céleste were born, he suggested getting them a nanny, full-time. All that vies for her attention Monday through Friday is the detached garage outside that houses her studio, freshly renovated and stocked with easels and brushes, tubes of paint, and canvases of various sizes, glaringly blank.

Over the past few years she's ventured in from time to time to check that everything's still in order, still there. But actually *painting*—choosing a subject, mixing colors, handling a brush—has proven as daunting as the prospect Didier once suggested of finding a job in France, where her vocabulary is limited to the names of fresh produce items and balms for diaper rash and teething pain. Uprooting from Tenafly to settle in a country where she had no history and connections other than her husband left her reeling. Before she had a chance to catch her breath, she was pregnant. With twins. Since their birth, she's taken her mother's advice and cut herself some slack, using the time they spend with their nanny to catch up on her rest and deal with the laundry and the grocery shopping that pile up when they're around. The closet-organizing and the weekly orders to place with the kosher butcher. She's only human, after all. But for each load of bed linens she hangs on the clothesline there's a hamper full of onesies and elfin pajamas to throw into the machine, and for each new shelf she installs in the cavelike nooks that pass for closets in her two-hundred-year-old stone house, another cracks or falls down. With every passing day, the notion of tending to anything more than her children and home grows fuzzier and more intangible, like a perfectly good self-portrait that she's slowly but surely washing over in white.

With Luc and Céleste bathed and tucked into bed, Veronica and Didier sit down to eat at the dining table by the kitchen. This is *their* routine—a few minutes of peace and quiet reminiscent of the months following their wedding. Though only a card table and folding chairs furnished the dining space back then, they feasted every evening on the cornucopia of leftovers that Didier's older sister, Mireille, would send them home with after hosting the extended family's weekly Shabbat lunch: portions of *dafina*, the traditional Moroccan Shabbat stew of meat, eggs, chick peas, and rice prepared with chicken or beef in a broth of curry and cumin, or a sweet and tangy lamb stew called *tagine,* smothered in coriander and olives. Mireille always threw in a few sprigs of fresh mint leaves so that Veronica and Didier could end meals with the Moroccan custom of a glass of sugary mint tea.

If the care package included grapes or plump dates, Veronica would pluck them from the bag after dinner and drop them into Didier's open mouth. "Sultan, I am your slave," she'd giggle, fanning him with her free hand. "Your wish is my command." Didier would grunt, "Off with your shirt." Topless, she'd straddle him, gyrating her midriff in her best belly-dancer imitation and trying not to snort while he buried his face between her copious breasts. When she'd strain to unbutton her jeans, he'd order, "Be still. I am a married sultan. You're just a slave." They'd both end up naked on the dusty, concrete floor.

Veronica spoons some rice and two reheated drumsticks onto Didier's plate. "Big day?" she asks, sitting down. His clenched jaw tells her that he still needs a few more minutes to decompress.

He sighs, humming a tuneless note as he exhales. "The usual," he says, eyeing the drumsticks on his plate and then opting for a forkful of rice. "Too many patients, a secretary who takes lunch from twelve to three and then leaves precisely at six o'clock in the evening even if there is still work to do. And piles of bills to pay." He nods expectantly at Veronica, as though he's just lobbed a ball into her court.

"So what's the bad news, doc?" Veronica kicks him

playfully under the table—a dose of silliness should help him lighten up. She's long since stopped reminding him that if he'd moved to the States as she'd practically begged him to before they got married, he'd have a bigger staff and would get a much bigger paycheck each month. Big enough to make going back to school for a couple of years to pass the U.S. Medical Boards worthwhile.

Didier furrows his inky eyebrows, pushes a hand through the thick slab of hair on his forehead the color of the espresso shots he drinks all day, and shakes his head. "Nothing," he says, twisting his mouth. "How about my *artiste*? Tell me, how was *your* day?"

Veronica's cheeks prickle with heat. She usually maneuvers answers to this sort of question away from herself, highlighting instead Luc and Céleste's new vocabulary words, signs of their progress toward potty training, and the latest tactics in managing Céleste's temper tantrums. With so much to say about them, she can easily pass off the details of their day as the details of hers. Her own days are laughably predictable and include certain things he needn't know. Today, for example, she spent several hours online. First, she found plane tickets for her annual trip to New Jersey with the kids in July. Next, she glanced at CNN.com. The headlines haven't budged in weeks: President Bush wants to send troops into Iraq although the rest of the world, led by France, opposes, claiming weapons inspectors have found nothing to justify war. So she wound up reading celebrity gossip. And every day after lunch, she treats herself to a two-hour nap. God knows she needs the rest: for the past few years, nights have been one enormous blur of stumbling across the hallway in the dark to give a bottle or stick a pacifier back into an open mouth. Didier sleeps right through it all, and the only time she ever asked him how on earth he could block out the sound of their children howling at three in the morning, he answered, "After four straight hours of surgery and eight straight hours looking up people's noses and down their throats, it's quite simple, *non?*" She never raised it again. After all, when Didier's exhausted during the week, he has no choice but to gulp down another espresso and keep going.

Tonight, however, this question is the perfect cue for her to tell Didier about the plane tickets she found. "I reserved flights for July," she says, shoving a forkful of chicken into her mouth and bracing herself for his gaze to dart away. "And the tickets are a steal!"

In past years, a decent deal on airfare was good enough. But now that Luc and Céleste are two, they can no longer fly for free. With three tickets to pay for, getting a steal is as essential as getting tickets to the right destination. Not that Veronica would ever have imagined that as the wife of a doctor she'd need one. Then again, before meeting Didier, she'd never have imagined being the wife of a doctor in France.

"A steal!" Didier looks impressed. "That is remarkable, stealing tickets from an airline. How did you do it?"

"Yeah, I wish!" Veronica laughs. "I just found a great deal, you know, with so much lead time."

"A great deal, meaning what?" Didier peers up from beneath his espresso-colored bangs, a bit too long.

"Meaning the tickets cost less than two thousand Euros altogether. That's about two-thirds of what we'll pay if I wait till next month." Didier's tone is making her tense.

He dabs his lips with a napkin and shuts his eyes briefly, sifting his words. After a long moment of silence, he says, "You know, I have been thinking of your summer trip, too."

Veronica blinks. "You want to come with us for a change?" She hopes he'll just say yes and end the conversation.

"On the contrary. I feel that, with Luc and Céleste being two, and with all four of us still living on just one salary, we must rethink this trip." He slices into a drumstick and then, glancing at the morsel on his fork, puts it down.

"Very funny." Veronica forces her lips into a goofy grin, but her heart thrashes in her chest.

"Seriously, Vero. July is one of the most expensive months to travel. It is difficult enough for us to pay for one expensive ticket. But three? That is impossible."

"You're cracking me up!" Veronica's yearly trip home to spend July in New Jersey is as central to her routine as dinner. Nobody skips dinner. She and the kids spend the month with her parents in the house in Tenafly where she grew up. Taking a break in her parents' spacious, air-conditioned home from the grind of running a household and caring for twins in a country where central air and even clothes dryers are as rare as private jets reinvigorates her like a visit to the spa. New Jersey may look like one enormous strip mall, but at least it doesn't flash constant reminders that she should be painting, as Aix does, with its breathtaking view of the Montagne Sainte Victoire's giant, limestone face hanging like a square cloud over terra-cotta rooftops. And there's no mistral wind. When it's nice out, she takes the kids to her parents' pool club. The air there always smells like chlorine and singed hamburger patties the way it did when she was a kid, and nobody stares at the drawstring shorts she wears over her suit to hide her wide, spongy thighs. She treats herself to a decadent overdose of chocolate chip muffins, bagels and lox, *Mad About You* reruns and lunch dates in Manhattan with her roommate from college, Terry Malone. She lets the rules of keeping kosher slide so she can eat whatever her mother serves, and then some. After stocking up on Gap and Old Navy clothes at the mall, she heads back to Aix with a full extra suitcase, feeling like she's replenished her soul. Forget cruises or Club Med, where you have to mind your p's and q's and look your best. As far as vacations go, this is all she needs.

Didier catches her stunned expression. "I don't mean that you shouldn't go at all," he says, in the even, polished voice of a professional used to reviewing inadequate alternatives. "Why not go, for example, in November, to spend Thanksgiving there, from now on?"

"Are you kidding?" Veronica cries, though clearly Didier means business. "It's freezing in November! I'd be pent up with the kids indoors all day!"

"It would be half the price of going in July. Maybe less."

"But it's not the same thing! In the summer my dad can take time off, we can go to the shore, we can go to the pool." She swallows back a wave of tears.

Didier shrugs. "You can go to the pool club here five months a year."

"No thanks. The women here wear g-string bikinis without tops."

"And so?"

"Compared to them I look like a sausage in my Speedo!" The tears resurge, pushing closer to the surface. "But that's not the point. The point is, I *like* going in July. The year works out nicely that way. July in Jersey with my parents. August on the Riviera with you and the kids. Then in September, back to the usual. It makes sense. Besides, soon the kids'll turn three, and the way things work around here, they'll be in school. Then we'll have no choice."

"At that age, it will be okay for them to miss a couple of

weeks of school."

Veronica's stomach twists into one big sour knot. Didier just underhandedly shortened her trip from one month to a couple of weeks, but in November, even a couple of weeks of vacation just wouldn't compute. Summer is meant for vacation: long, sun-drenched breaks from reality like kids get every year. Growing up, Veronica looked forward to summer vacation all year. The chance to relive it with her own kids is one of the perks of being a mom. It's also one of the perks of living in France, where work schedules include six weeks off each year and adults consider themselves entitled to a long, lazy summer break, too.

"Don't be ridiculous." She pokes at her serving of macaroni, now crusty and cold. "I'm not going in November. I'm going in July. And it won't break the bank. I promise."

"Unless we suddenly earn more money, it will."

"Great. I'll start playing the lottery."

"Good luck," Didier puffs. Softening his voice, he places a hand on hers and adds, "Listen. If a trip in July means so much to you, do you not think this would be a logical time to try, for example, to sell a painting?" He narrows his eyes the way he often does when words can express but a teeny fraction of what he's thinking. "After all this time, perhaps you are not far from completing one that you could sell."

Veronica stands up and paces to the window behind the dining table, wiping her prickling nose with the back of her hand. The window's pair of tall, doorlike panes form twin mirrors against the night's black sheen. Gazing at their reflections of the heavy oak dining table and the bronze chandelier above it—gifts from her parents, Rich and Shirley Berg, just like the matching counter stools, the sofa behind them, and the wide-screen TV—she murmurs, "Not at this point."

Didier rubs his chin. "Ah. Well, then. When?"

She squeezes her eyes shut and rubs her pounding temples. Tacit impatience is one thing. But actually voicing it blows a little problem up into a much bigger deal than it is. Until now, whenever the topic of painting has come up, Didier has reassured her that he knows art takes time: *c'est normal*. He's encouraged her to get involved with other things, too. She's taken French classes. She's learned to drive a stick-shift car. When she first moved to Aix, she supervised the remodeling of the dreary, 1950s kitchen and bathrooms in the rustic stone house she and Didier chose for its proximity to Aix's center and its potential charm. Her parents gave them a generous cash gift so they could afford the renovations right away. At the top of the list: converting the detached garage into a studio by installing a big skylight in the roof and laying a foundation atop its dirt floors.

One evening shortly after it was finished, Didier came home early to find her standing outside, staring at its door. Since art school, she'd dreamed of a studio just like it, all her own.

"Ah!" he sang, looping an arm around her waist and giving it an approving squeeze. "So. You are back on the job?"

Veronica winced. "Not yet. I need to keep an eye on the workers. But I'm getting inspired. I mean, just look at this gorgeous scene, right here." She gestured toward the studio's roof, where wisteria dribbled like bunches of grapes off the scalloped, moss-coated tiles. When Didier said nothing, she asked, "Tell me straight, doc: what's the prognosis? Are you going to write me off as a hopeless case?" Folding her arms over her bosom, she noticed that, like her hips, it felt even fuller than usual since her move, when she'd started binging on chocolate late at night.

Didier brushed his cheek against her forehead, nudging away a strand of her long hair the color of a freshly-paved driveway with his nose. Tilting his head to one side to view the wisteria, he sucked his tongue away from his teeth to make a clicking sound—"*Tchk*"—his subtle way of saying, "No, my love. Not at all."

A few weeks ago, however, she found him peering through the studio's window. When she approached, he pursed his lips and turned away. She understands his exasperation: her artistic inclination appeals directly to his own creative side. When he opted for medical school, he placed on hold an old dream of going into a field like research where he could spend days innovating, pondering problems, and inventing new solutions. He'd take pride in Veronica's success as an artist as if it were his own. He doesn't realize, though, how quickly creativity and the gumption to take on new projects get lost to bottles of milk, dirty diapers, and jars of mashed peas.

Veronica squeezes her eyes shut and rubs her pounding temples. "I don't know when," she mutters.

"A month? Six weeks? *J'sais pas, moi.* Give me an estimate!" He throws up his hands.

"Let's say that I can't make any predictions," she blurts, flinging her arms out. "See, I'm kind of …" How can she possibly explain? She can't seem to latch her attention onto anything other than the swamp of tiny details governing her home and her children's lives. Tending to them gives her a soothing sense of order, an illusion of control. Each day she tells herself tomorrow will be different. That she'll wake up full of vim and vigor, able to zip through her housework in an hour, then shift her focus directly to her art.

Or able to forget her housework altogether, foregoing the instant gratification she gets from scheduling pediatrician's appointments and labeling drawers. But each day turns out exactly the same. And rather than inspire her, the astounding beauty of Provence, offering a full-length catalogue of images to choose from right outside her front door, only rubs salt in the wound. Almond trees in neighboring yards sport tiny, white blossoms right now—an early sign of spring. The wisteria on the studio's roof is starting to bloom. Yet the sun's glorious, amber aura illuminates these potential subjects in such vivid detail that she can't fathom capturing their spirit appropriately, if at all.

"Well, it's like … I'm sort of …" She glances up at him briefly and then hunches her shoulders, her cheeks burning with shame. "In a rut."

"A rut," Didier repeats, looking concerned but not at all surprised. "Tell me. What, exactly, is a rut?"

"You know—when things are going really slowly, and you're not getting very far."

Didier leans back in his chair and studies the ceiling while processing this information. It's hard to tell from the frown lines cupping his lips and the stern furrow of his brow whether he's upset, or deep in thought. "What you are doing is not easy, I know," he says. "It is so hard to create something in a vacuum, to work all alone with no deadlines except the ones you define for yourself. Perhaps you need some."

"Yeah, right. Like a hole in the head. Or another set of twins."

"Yes, Vero," he says, joining her by the window and grasping her shoulders. "In fact, I think that is exactly what you need. And *voilà*! Now you have it!"

Veronica stares at him.

He slides his hands down to her triceps and gives them an authoritative squeeze. "Didn't your sister once promise to buy a couple of paintings from you?"

She shakes loose from his grip and slumps into the window's deep frame. A cold draft licks her back. Yes, her older sister, Stella, did once promise to pay top dollar for some of her art. In fact, when Stella learned that Veronica was moving to Provence to paint, she declared that she was placing an order for not one, but an entire series of lavender and olive-studded landscapes for her Spanish-style villa in Boca Raton, Florida. "Throw in a few scenes of stone farmhouses surrounded by vineyards, too, why don't you?" Stella gushed. "And make the paintings tall. *Really* tall."

Selling to Stella would have been a cinch of a way for Veronica to showcase her work and launch herself doing commissioned landscapes. With Stella's job at the time with the Miami branch of a national law firm and her husband Ray's position as a Wall Street trader, a constant stream of investment bankers and attorneys flowed through their house in Boca and their apartment on Manhattan's Upper West Side. And Stella's promise to buy whatever Veronica produced was as good as gold. During Veronica's first few months living in Aix, Stella called every few days to see how her custom pieces were coming along. Even when Veronica confessed that she was struggling to get started, her sister cheered into the phone, "Just head for the nearest olive grove with your easel!" Veronica could practically see Stella's angular, athlete's jaw clenched with determination as though she were the one who'd have to try to stuff her blossoming hips into a pair of coveralls she hadn't worn since college and get lost driving her stick-shift car down a narrow, bumpy road. As time passed, though, Stella's phone calls became less frequent. When Veronica announced that she was pregnant with twins but still hadn't made any progress, Stella said, "Good thing I've been browsing the galleries."

"That was ages ago," Veronica mutters.

"Yes," Didier answers. "But you know, it is better late than never. Stella, she is your sister. I think she will still be happy to help out." He begins collecting the dishes from the table and clearing them into the kitchen.

"You mean like helping out a charity case?" Veronica scoffs. "Gee, thanks."

Didier shrugs. "Well, it is up to you. But it does make sense, *non?*"

When Veronica doesn't answer, he casts a sidelong glance her way and adds, "By the way, this chicken—" he motions toward the table with his chin. "This, *euh*, Shake 'n Bake? I know you like it, but … maybe you could try making something different next time?"

She salutes limply. She doesn't have the energy to remind him that their deal included kosher cuisine, not fine cuisine. Didier isn't pious, but he relishes the traditions he grew up with, like keeping kosher, attending the morning minyan prayer group, and celebrating Shabbat for the family bonds and the grounding sense of unity between past and present that they create. Until meeting him, Veronica—who grew up in a household where tradition boiled down to using phrases like "*oy, vay!*"—had never even met a person who kept kosher. She went out on a limb in agreeing to a more observant lifestyle and grew to love the way its rituals knit the family together, but she's no cook.

"I must finish up some reading now," he says, removing the last plate from the table and wiping away the crumbs.

As Didier heads upstairs to the office, Veronica hoists

herself from the windowsill and shuffles into the kitchen to finish cleaning up. To her relief, the mistral has subsided to a coarse, intermittent whisper. She can hear swallows, back early from their winter home south of the Mediterranean, circling the rooftop outside, twittering their hypnotic song—*weeet-a-weeet-a-weeet*—as they soar, swoop, and dive. Didier may have a point about Stella, she thinks. Even if Stella has already bought a few pieces from galleries, she's got oodles of space on her walls. And she'd never turn Veronica down or negotiate the price. With the amount Stella would be willing to fork out for one *really tall* painting—or even a short one— Veronica could pay the way for three to New Jersey in July. But if she's going to give it a shot, she'd better hurry. July will be here in a heartbeat.

Chapter Two

At six fifteen Veronica's eyes pop open just as the alarm clock starts beeping. She hasn't used one in eons; Luc and Céleste usually do the job. But today, before she can get to work on a painting for Stella, she needs to clear from the kitchen sink the stack of dishes that she left last night, too weary to deal with it, and to organize the mess of discarded layette clothing she's been promising for ages to pick up from the floor of the closet in the office upstairs. She needs every extra minute she can get.

Across the hall, Luc winces in his sleep as if wired directly to her heart. Veronica jolts upright, pulse racing. Creating a painting is one thing. Getting it done in a month or two verges on insane. It's hard enough to do things quickly when you have small children, who interrupt you constantly and suck up every extra bit of energy and time. But in Provence, time plays by a whimsical set of rules, evaporating as instantaneously as particles of moisture evaporate from the crackling, dry air. Stores shut from noon to four, appointment times serve as rough approximations, and the immense distances to traverse, punctuated only by crags and cliffs and cornfields, can swallow you up like a riptide. Families spend entire Sundays picnicking along the maritime cliffs to the east of Marseille called Les Calenques. Bellies full, they gaze idly at the Mediterranean's indigo waters stretching out to the horizon until the sun goes down. In Didier's family—the vast Benhamou clan—Saturdays are just as lazy, with three generations convening to share a *dafina* that also takes its own sweet time, simmering on a hotplate overnight. The scent of curry and cumin weighs on limbs like the heat of a sauna, and the meal is never over until everybody's sprawled out on the sofa, half-asleep.

When she moved to Provence, Veronica embraced the laid-back pace. It suited her: she never did like rushing or stress. Before taking her job in the art department of a Manhattan children's book publisher after college, she envisioned a future in which she'd spend days dabbing the final touches onto commissioned portraits of children and Oz-like landscapes populated by her trademark unicorns and cherubs.

"I'm going to be a painter, not some office peon chained to the clock and a desk!" she protested when her father, who heard about the job through one of his patients, suggested she send in her résumé.

"If you want to be a painter, be smart about it and make sure you have some other skills to fall back on and an income on the side," Rich answered. His fleshy, pockmarked cheeks jiggled like a Saint Bernard's, taking the edge off his stern gaze and making him look as though, if you offered him a biscuit, he'd wag his tail and give you his paw. Ruffling Veronica's hair and then giving her a noogie the way he used to before dismissing her from a scolding when she was a kid, he added, "Think of it this way: if you have a job, you can start saving up right away for a place of your own. And you won't have to hit your mother and me up for cash every time you want to go Dutch on a date in some fancy-shmancy uptown restaurant, or buy a new pair of shoes."

After a few weeks of sulking and taking stabs at a drab view of the Manhattan skyline that came out looking more like a service station off the New Jersey Turnpike, Veronica agreed that a day job to finance evenings and weekends at the easel wasn't such a bad idea. It would get her out of the house and into the city, where she could grab lunch every now and then with her college roommate, Terry Malone. Terry—skinny, sassy, surly, with nails bitten down to the bone and a mop of black ringlets that matched her all-black wardrobe—had majored in painting and sculpting. Her canvases and brass figurines showed hands in various states of toil or distress. By day, Terry pitched stories to fashion magazines for a PR agency, and over regular lunches at Au Bon Pain once Veronica had started working, she entertained her with snarky imitations of the reporters who hung up on her when she called. "Who cares?" she once said, tossing a short curl off her forehead. "I still get paid." Veronica's job also got her out to happy hour with colleagues. It provided a stream of cash for pedicures and ten-minute massages at the nail salon down the block from her office, and membership at a gym.

When she told her father she'd take the job, she figured that, since she'd be free to paint in the evenings and on the weekends, she had nothing to lose. But racing from the bus to the subway and then down the jam-packed avenue, up the elevator, to her desk, to her screen, to the phone—which she answered as it rang off the hook all day for a taciturn art director named Brenda Gray—frazzled her. So did jouncing around in traffic on the interminable ride home. The oppressive, pungent scent of Brenda's Eau D'Issey perfume and the sight of her pin-thin legs and horn-rimmed glasses as she strode down the corridor, always in a rush, always chasing something urgent yet elusive, gave Veronica a debilitating headache. Why couldn't Brenda—and the phones, and the constant flood of e-mails—slow down? Each meeting she sat in on about page size and cover design left her feeling drained, and depressed from pretending she cared. With her nerves crackling from overload night and day, she could do nothing but veg out in front of the TV when she got home.

By her third year working in Manhattan, the visions she'd nurtured during college of spending days painting commissioned portraits and Oz-like landscapes in a sunny, SoHo loft had become overwritten by mental notes to double-check whether an author's photo was in a .jpg file and to pick up her father's dry cleaning on the way home. Her cheek twitched whenever she recalled her initial plan to sell a painting or two, then quit work. And she rolled her eyes so high up in their sockets that it hurt each time she pulled into the driveway of her parents' house in Tenafly at the end of the day, anticipating another evening of greasy rotisserie chicken from Shop Rite or takeout lasagna that her thighs could do without. When was her salary going to climb out of the twenties so she could afford a decent place of her own? Not that she minded her parents' company or the comfort of granite counters, cedar closets, and dinner on the table every evening. She just wanted her *real* life to begin. After three years of waiting, she was itching for something—anything— to happen. Even a date in a fancy-shmancy uptown restaurant with a man whose future might help shape her own. In three years, she'd met no one she cared to see again. A package vacation to Provence including airfare, lodging, meals, and daily painting classes seemed like a perfect way to carve out the tranquility and peace of mind missing from her frenzied days.

Across the hall, Luc winces again and then whimpers. How ironic that even in Provence tranquility and peace of mind exist only in brief spurts, few and far between. Veronica tugs the window open, and unlatches the shutters outside, inhaling the tangy, organic scent of damp earth and mulch burning in a freshly tilled field beyond the outskirts of town. The sky, often misty in the morning, glimmers behind its sheen of sapphire blue. The feathery tips of cypress trees in a neighbor's adjacent yard reach toward the heavens in mild supplication as though Van Gogh himself had placed them there to study while painting *Starry Night*. Her heart clenches anxiously the way it used to back in school before a test. Against such an illustrious backdrop, even the simplest subject, like the fig tree in her backyard, appears hopelessly intricate. How can she possibly capture the unfathomable complexity of the tension in its gnarled, knobby, branches on canvas—the tree's very soul?

She takes a deep breath. There's no reason to get all worked up over a canvas for Stella, who may have a law degree from Harvard, a live-in nanny, and a house the size of a roadside hotel but still brags to her Boca and Manhattan friends that her younger sister is an artist in Provence.

No time for a shower this morning. Instead, she splashes some cool water on her face, taking a quick glance at her reflection in the mirror. The dark circles that appeared beneath her eyes shortly after the twins' birth haven't faded and probably never will. Her broad chin juts out from her hair's straight, dark frame. On good days, it makes her look confident and determined. Today it makes her look more like a camel.

Another whimper, then Luc sneezes. "Mommmmy!" he wails, sneezing again.

Veronica wipes her face with a towel and frowns. Luc usually sleeps for another hour or so. And while he tends to wake in tears, he rarely cries for her with such gut-wrenching despair. "Is Luc the Duke awake?" she sings out, trying to sound cheerful.

From the room beside Luc's—a niche behind it, really, accessible only through a passageway in his wall—Céleste calls out, "Milk!"

"I hear you, too, princess," Veronica answers with a sigh, entering Luc's room and flicking on the light. Luc's cries must have woken her. So much for getting off to an early start.

Stenciled circus animals—hippos, lions, and giraffes—painted shades of gold and olive-green waltz over the room's tan walls, interspersed with a few unicorns and cherubs. Papier-mâché renditions of each creature dangle from satin ribbons nailed to the ceiling. Veronica designed them while she was pregnant, delighted to imagine the awe and fantasy that her creations would inspire in a child's mind. She crafted the papier-mâché figures by hand, stenciled the images onto the walls and furniture in both kids' rooms and appliquéd cloth versions onto the curtains. While mixing colors and kneading the strips of paper into gluey paste, she pictured herself sitting on the floor making papier-mâché and stencils with her children one day, happy as a kindergartner at craft time.

Luc, sitting in his crib, stretches his arms out and waves his hands, silently imploring Veronica to pick him up. Céleste demands, "Milk, Mommy, *milk*!" in a voice as grating as the alarm clock's beep.

"Okay, okay," Veronica mutters, slipping her hands beneath Luc's arms. She's used to adjusting her expectations according to what's going on with the kids. They need her, and there's nothing more important. That's the job description for "mom." Scooping Luc up, she kisses him on the soft, concave bridge of his nose—one of her favorite spots to place a kiss.

A bubble of mucus billows and deflates at the tip of Luc's left nostril. With her free hand, Veronica snatches a tissue from a box on the changing table and presses it to his face. "Blow," she says.

Luc jerks his head away, leaving Veronica holding the tissue in midair.

"Come on, Duke, you have to blow the snot out," Veronica insists, bracing her hand against Luc's face.

"Mommy Mommy *milk milk milk*!" shrieks Céleste.

"I know, princess, I know," Veronica answers, mustering as much patience as she can. With Luc on one hip, she marches through the arched passageway between the rooms and hoists Céleste from her crib, crinkling her nose and recoiling as she breathes in the distinct, sour-grass smell of urine-soaked clothing and sheets. "But first we've got to change you," she says, shaking her head.

"First milk!" Céleste yells, pounding Veronica's shoulder.

For the next half hour, Luc whimpers each time Veronica takes a few steps away. He refuses his Bob the Builder sippy cup filled with warm chocolate milk and his bowl of dry Cheerios. His brown eyes droop dolefully at the corners, and he sneezes often, expelling a goopy glob of mucus each time. To get dressed, Veronica has to bring him upstairs with her so he doesn't bawl.

"What's with you this morning, Duke?" Veronica asks as she laces up her Reeboks and ties back her hair, which really could have used a shampoo. She lifts him from the floor of her room and presses her lips to his forehead. He doesn't feel feverish or warm. "So much fuss over a silly little cold!" Picking him up, she heads downstairs and sets him back into his high chair beside Céleste's. "If you stay grouchy, you won't have fun playing at Maria's today."

Céleste, hearing her nanny's name, rattles the tray of her high chair and sings, "No *nounou* today, Mommy. No *nounou!*"

Veronica frowns and folds her arms over her chest. It's hard not to lose her temper with such a stressful day ahead, but the situation would only degenerate if she did. She's just going to have to focus on the here-and-now and stop anguishing over what time she'll make it into the studio. With little kids, it's the only way. Curling a lock of Céleste's copper hair around her index finger, she says, "But you love seeing Maria, your *nounou*."

Indeed, Maria's house is like a second home to Luc and Céleste—a spacious, sunny home packed with friends and toys. The twins began spending a few pinch-hit hours there every day at the age of three months, after the departure of Veronica's mother, Shirley Berg, who had come for an extended visit from New Jersey after their birth. Their daily stays with Maria lasted just long enough for Veronica to catch up on some of the housework that her mother had been doing until then, and a little sleep. It was a good compromise between having her mother come over every day—which Shirley swore she would have done in a heartbeat had Veronica lived anywhere in the tristate area—and having no help at all. "You've got twins, for crying out loud!" said

Shirley. "Twins! Nobody in their right mind should have to chase twins around alone all day!"

Around the time Luc and Céleste turned one, Didier suggested signing them up with Maria full-time so that Veronica could not only keep up with laundry and groceries, but also, finally, paint. The decision was easy: in France, government subsidies make high-quality child care affordable to all. Most parents take advantage of the sturdy network of day-care centers called *crèches* or the certified nannies like Maria, who watch small groups of children in their homes. Moms who don't work enjoy the convenience of public, hourly drop-off centers known as *halte garderies*. In the pediatrician's waiting room, at playgrounds, and at Halloween and Valentine's Day parties organized by the godsend club of local, English-speaking expats called the Anglo-American Group of Provence, Veronica has met more young mothers than she can count who don't have jobs but who guiltlessly drop their kids off so they can shop, take a yoga class, prepare dinner parties, or get their legs waxed. Didier supports it wholeheartedly, just as he supports Veronica's painting. "*C'est normal*," he's often said. "Every mother needs time to be a woman."

By then, the twins had become so accustomed to Maria, to her flashing black eyes, her bubbly, Mediterranean warmth, her Portuguese-twanged accent and toy-filled family room that they barely seemed to notice the difference between their own house and hers. Even Veronica had come to view Maria's place as an extension of home built at the end of a very long hallway: the road. Enraptured by the swing set in Maria's front yard, the company of the two other toddlers Maria watches and her two school-aged daughters who come home for lunch every day, Luc and Céleste rarely, if ever, protest going. Of all the days to start. Maybe, Veronica thinks with a pang of regret, they sense her urgent need to focus on something else and feel insecure.

Luc frowns at the Cheerios scattered on his high-chair tray and brushes them aside. "No *nounou*," he echoes.

"Oh, come on, you guys!" Veronica says in her best cheerleader's voice. "I'll tell you what: we'll go out for a little treat, like Nutella *crêpes*, when I pick you up."

Quickly, while the kids' moods are still dappled with visions of licking melted chocolate from their hands, she dresses them and zippers them into the new nylon windbreakers she bought for the spring. The temperature's already above fifty Fahrenheit. On such a gorgeous day they may not even need them, but better safe than sorry.

Outside, she snaps open the double stroller, a train-style contraption with one seat behind the other that she chose on the misguided assumption that she could negotiate it fairly easily through Aix's narrow sidewalks. Since she can't, she rarely takes it—or the kids—into town.

Seated and strapped, Luc gropes continually for her hand. Veronica has to pause often as she walks to let him grasp her fingers lest he howl. Most days, this would drive her crazy. By this time of the morning, she's usually ready for a little peace and quiet.

Today, though, her heart lurches with each glance at Luc's sorrowful eyes. At each squeaky whimper he emits, she hunches over him, crooning, "Sshhh, sshhhh," more to soothe herself than to soothe him. Though less grating than Céleste's shrill demands, Luc's cries convey such profound, unbearable desperation that they invariably leave Veronica feeling desperate, too. As she approaches the wide stretch of gravel before the gated entrance to Maria's yard, a sudden, overwhelming urge seizes her to keep both kids home so she can spend the day coloring and papier-mâchéing with them, painting mouse whiskers on their cheeks, playing duck-duck-goose, and blowing Luc's nose.

Chapter Three

Finding a man to marry and have kids with wasn't exactly on Veronica's mind when she signed up for a painting vacation in Provence the year she met Didier. Sure, she hoped that one day she'd settle down and start a family with a husband she loved madly, a soul mate with a solid profession like medicine to balance out the uncertainties of art. But first, she'd establish herself as a painter.

Not the brainy type, she'd long since ruled out other fields—particularly if they required years of studying or long days in an office wishing it were time to go home. In high school, she'd struggled to keep up with Spanish, chemistry, and Shakespeare, but she drew impressive doodles of unicorns and cherubs in the margins of her notebooks. At home, she'd clip out the doodles, watercolor them over in various pastel shades, and paste the finished products onto elaborate collages that her mother would frame and hang on the living room walls. "Such talent shouldn't go to waste," Shirley would say, stepping back to admire them. Shirley also made sure that Veronica took plenty of art classes outside of school.

Shirley's praise helped Veronica shrug off her glaring differences with Stella, who excelled at history and calculus, held the Tenafly High record for the 400-yard dash, and had received a plaque of honor for brokering mock compromises at the Model UN. At family events such as weddings and Bar Mitzvahs, Shirley would elbow both girls in the direction of relatives they hardly knew and boast, "This is my Stella. She's a straight-A student. And this is my Veronica. She's got gifted hands." Her chest would puff as she spoke. Her hair, dyed ruby-red and sprayed into the shape of a wavy cycling helmet, would tower over everybody else's like a crown, making Veronica feel short, somewhat self-conscious about her own sturdy string of Bs, but very proud.

After receiving a letter of acceptance to BU's School of Visual Arts, she gloated for weeks. Clearly, her talent outshined her indistinct transcript. The admissions committee had even liked the dozens of unicorns and cherubs in her portfolio, which her advisor had suggested she take out. As soon as her parents sent in the deposit, she imagined getting phone calls from galleries around the world offering to buy her art. She'd wrap bridges with Christo. Critics would compare her with Georgia O'Keefe. In her mother's generation a woman's identity boiled down to the accolades her children collected and their watercolors framed on the walls, but Veronica, like her peers, expected to forge a bold identity of her own. With the desire for a family in mind, art—flexible, work-at-home—seemed ideal.

By the spring of her third year working in Manhattan, however, Veronica no longer knew what to imagine or expect. Her publishing day job and life with her parents in Tenafly kept dragging on like a chronic cold. She tried to reassure herself each morning while sorting through Brenda

Gray's e-mails over a Starbucks caramel latte—her little treat to herself for having gotten up at five forty-five and schlepped into the office via car and bus and subway—that she was, in fact, making progress. Her new skills for judging illustrators' portfolios at a glance, distinguishing between amateurish and adept brush strokes and sensing palpable emotions in a composition, would surely make her a better painter herself as soon as she got started. But the more time went by, the harder it became to imagine getting started at all. How could she, when her job sucked up her most productive hours? Watching *Mad About You* and going on weekend excursions with her mother to the mall weren't lazy procrastination tactics, as her father insisted whenever she lamented that at this rate she'd never paint again, but rather, relaxing breaks in her hectic schedule.

"If you ask me, it would be smart to skip lunch and happy hour Monday through Friday and hightail it home early to paint, before you're too wiped out," Rich Berg once suggested. "Chip away at it a little every day. How else do you think I made it through dental school at your age with a wife and a full-time job?"

"If you ask *me*—which you never did—it would be smarter to quit my publishing job and wait on tables a few nights a week," Veronica retorted. "Then I could wake up and paint first thing every morning. And the pay would be exactly the same."

"I can just hear your mother now, sputtering, 'This is my Veronica. She's a cocktail waitress.'"

One rainy April morning that year, as Veronica sat at her desk at work sipping a caramel latte and browsing the Web, Brenda tapped at her cubicle wall. Brenda, who preferred instant messaging to face-to-face conversation, rarely stopped by in person. She hardly ever looked up when Veronica arrived in the morning or left at night, and during the long hours she worked, studious concentration magnified by the forbidding tortoise frame of her horn-rimmed glasses rumpled her brow. What a shame, Veronica often thought when she glimpsed her. She's so young—midthirties, max— but takes her work so seriously that her heart has hardened into a knot of dried-up wood.

Seeing Brenda's angular silhouette in the threshold of her cubicle, Veronica straightened her back and put her latte down. "I was just finishing up your e-mails," she said, swiveling her chair to face her boss.

"There's no rush." Brenda's platinum-blonde bob with a hint of honey-colored roots glinted in the light of the fluorescent bulbs overhead. Dropping her eyes to the floor, she said, "I just wanted to share some news with you. Some news I'm excited about." Her lips curled into a tender smile.

Brenda, excited? Veronica thought. She must have gotten a really big promotion.

"My first children's book will be coming out in the fall," Brenda whispered.

Veronica stared hard at her boss, whose pale blue eyes oozed joy that Veronica hadn't felt in years, if ever. She stood tall and straight as a dancer in the cubby's threshold, chest lifted beneath her navy, cable-knit sweater, her pin-thin legs anchored firmly to the ground. Clearly she didn't mean one of the books she pushed daily through art and editorial to publication, which she churned out without a blink. That left only one other option, improbable as it seemed. "Wow. You wrote a children's book?"

Brenda beamed. "I wrote it and illustrated it. It's

taken forever—nearly two years. But I finally brought the manuscript down to editorial last week, and they liked it. They liked my art, too. So it's a deal."

Veronica jumped to her feet. "Oh my God!" she blurted out. "Congratulations!" She opened her arms and leaned toward Brenda, who responded by hugging her with astonishing warmth and force.

"Thanks," Brenda murmured. Her hands trembled as she pulled away. Behind the harsh tortoise rims of her glasses, her eyes brimmed with tears. Catching Veronica's dismayed expression, she let out a chortle that sounded like a stifled sob and added, "It's been a really long couple of years."

Veronica watched in stupefied silence as Brenda slipped down the hall to spread her news. The host of assumptions she'd constructed about her boss had proven dead wrong. More than a wooden rung on the corporate ladder, Brenda was an artist and a writer juggling dual lives. For years she'd plugged twelve-hour days at the office and then returned home to work some more, on a project with an uncertain future that she'd nonetheless devoted herself to, against all odds, one word and one brush stroke at a time. She'd probably risen early every weekend, skipping brunch or a jog in Central Park with her labradoodle, to slave away at her drafting table or computer. The anxiety of it, the strain and the fatigue, must explain why she looked so pale and thin—not obsessive weight control as Veronica had always suspected. She'd probably subsisted for years on stale coffee and leftover Chinese takeout while drafting and redrafting, tearing out pages, starting them again. And all the while, Veronica was spending lunch hours bitching about day jobs with Terry before going home to watch TV.

She reached for the latte on her desk. The whipped cream

had deflated into a disgusting, viscous blob, and the cup was cold. She needed another. She needed some chocolate to go with it—an espresso brownie from Starbucks, or a couple of those Lindor truffles from the Korean grocer down the street. She picked up her bag and glanced out the window across the hall. Rain streaked its pane. Deep puddles dotted the tar rooftop across the street while streams cascaded down chimneys and antennae. On second thought, a cup of Folgers and some Oreos from the office kitchen would do. In fact, forget the coffee. Forget the Oreos and the chocolate. What Veronica needed was a vacation. A good, long vacation ASAP, someplace she'd never been, someplace where she could disappear into the woodwork, an anonymous stranger free from all assumptions, including her own. Maybe then she could shake off the cobwebs of a stale routine and muster the energy to hunker down and do something like Brenda had to jump-start her life.

Sitting back down, Veronica stared at her computer. Her latest screen saver showed the sparkling white cliffs of Cassis in southern France plunging into the Mediterranean's turquoise shallows. The deep green caps of umbrella pines sprawled across the background, and the sky shimmered in the precise shade of sapphire blue that Veronica imagined whenever she pictured God's eyes. She'd downloaded this image the previous autumn after getting a postcard just like it from Stella, on her honeymoon with Ray at the time in the south of France. The postcard had read: "This place is unbelievable! It makes me wish I could paint!"

Yeah, right, Veronica had thought when she read it. Studious, Cartesian Stella, painting. How absurd. What really disturbed her, however, was that, slapped with this emblem of Stella's good fortune, she felt like she was twelve again for a brief but agonizing moment, wondering, Why Stella and not me? Petite, sculpted, athletic Stella had the fluke blonde hair of the family, eyes shaped like blanched almonds, and a gymnast's toned triceps and calves. Had Stella been a stranger, Veronica—with a figure her mother described as "voluptuous," her camelish jaw, and limp hair the color of a freshly-paved driveway—would have avoided her like the plague. After high school, Stella had breezed from U Penn to Harvard Law, where she met Ray. She'd since traveled to Tokyo and Sidney for business and tacked on vacation days in places like Borneo and Phuket. Meanwhile, at twenty-five, Veronica had never set foot outside the continental United States, except for a few spring break trips with her family to the Bahamas. She'd have given an arm or a leg to spend an afternoon gazing at the coast of Antibes, or sitting at an outdoor café shaded by olive trees and white canvas parasols in a village with a famous name like Gordes or Roussillon. Just the thought of it made her skin prickle with impatience. But after taxes, retirement plan contributions, gym membership, pedicures, lunches at Au Bon Pain and the token monthly fee she paid her parents for utilities and food, Veronica was left with an annual vacation budget that could barely cover a week in Miami with Terry. And unlike Stella, she hadn't just married a trader. The Mediterranean coast taunted her from her screen like a jewel in Tiffany's Fifth Avenue window.

In the wake of Brenda's announcement, however, this perception shifted as a silent revolt flared in her chest. The south of France? It was just another place on earth, accessible by credit card and plane. Getting there would require nothing more than a good package deal. To hell with her budget and Miami, Veronica thought, jiggling her mouse until the screen saver gave way to her Internet browser. To hell with waiting.

If she needed to take an exotic, adventuresome vacation to get her life rolling, she would. Surely in the south of France—artist's heaven—she could find a painting class for English-speaking tourists like the cooking and wine-tasting classes she'd seen ads for in the travel section of the *New York Times*. With sparks flying the way she expected they would the day she'd meet her soul mate, she positioned her cursor in the search bar and typed "painting tours Provence."

Chapter Four

So many rules to keep track of in a kosher kitchen, Veronica thinks, elbow deep in last night's dishes after dropping off Luc and Céleste. Meat has to come from certified animals, raised and butchered in a certain way. It can't be eaten in the same meal as any of the creamy, satiating dairy products like cheese and butter that she still longs to melt onto burgers or slather onto every slice of bread. Since meat and dairy products must never touch, they require separate sets of dishes, washed in separate sinks. This complicates the simple chore of scraping Shake 'n Bake crumbs off plates crammed into the narrow "meat" side of the divided sink—a prospect that Veronica laughed off as trivial back when she and Didier were dating.

"To keep kosher, you must make sacrifices," Didier said during one of his many trips to see her in New Jersey after they met. "Just like with any commitment." They were standing on line for a table at the Cheesecake Factory, where Veronica had insisted on taking him for *real* American cuisine—forget the snooty, overpriced restaurants in Manhattan. He had just reminded her that he couldn't share her all-time favorite appetizer: popcorn shrimp.

"No popcorn *shreemp*?" she laughed, poking him in the ribs. "How cruel. But it could be worse. At least chocolate's not out."

Months later, when they got engaged, Didier told her that marrying him would mean not only moving to France, but also keeping kosher. "Sultan, I will indulge your crazy whims," she giggled, bending into a curtsy so deep that she almost fell over. What did a few minor dietary restrictions—or even a move to France—mean compared with the promise of a husband, a family, a future? Who knows, she might even lose a little weight. Besides, Didier's commitment to keeping kosher didn't stem from an impulse to go blindly through the motions of a habit he'd picked up from his parents. *Au contraire.* He'd given it careful thought over time. He'd even rebelled for a while in his twenties, dating a Catholic woman from Madrid who taught him to cook and savor garlicky langoustine and calamari tapas. He'd gorged on everything from prosciutto to mussels and enjoyed the crisp, greasy skin of a wild boar roasted whole over an open pit fire at a party on a farm near Lyons. When he told this to Veronica, he'd curled his lips downward and said, "Looking back, that was a very empty time. It was all about ourselves. Our desires and our pleasure. But without sacrifice, it is hard to sustain devotion and love."

During the period of mourning following his mother's death a few years later, he ate kosher meals out of respect for her memory and solidarity with his father and sisters. He also prayed daily. It helped assuage the pain. Like the fibers of an ancient tapestry, the simple, soothing repetition of these familiar customs wove Didier and his family together, connecting them with one another, with countless others sharing the same customs, and with something far greater,

Didier sensed, than the sum total of history and humanity's parts. He realized how lonesome he'd felt in his rebellion and vowed not to let this loneliness return. "Who knows," he said the night he gave Veronica her ring. "If I had not started observing the holy days, praying and keeping kosher again, my life might have taken quite a different direction, and I might have never met you."

He was right, Veronica thought. Of course he was; he was smart—a doctor. Not just any doctor, but *the* doctor—the soul mate—she'd always figured abstractly into her future. And he wanted to marry her! She'd be a fool to look such a gift horse in the mouth. So what if he happened to keep kosher and live in France? In France, she had learned, the vast majority of Jewish families kept kosher, especially among the hundreds of thousands from Morocco, Algeria, and Tunisia who had immigrated as recently as the 1960s and 1970s. These *pieds noirs*, or "black feet"—nicknamed in loose reference, some say, to the black-booted French colonists in Algeria—had never faced pogroms or deportations or concentration camps. They'd kept kosher right through the twentieth century, unlike the surviving European Jews, forced to abandon their traditions as a matter of life and death, and unlike their American counterparts, who'd let tradition slide because it was too easy to resist. Didier was a Moroccan Jew in France, a *pied noir*. Fate—or God?—had brought him and Veronica together. Keeping kosher came with the package, sacrifice or not.

Next chore this morning before Veronica can start painting: the layette mess she's been promising for ages to clean up from the office floor. But when she steps into the office, her heart plunks to the bottom of her stomach. The doll-sized onesies and footsy pajamas she's left strewn across the floor for months have been sorted, folded, and stacked in a hamper. Beside the computer on the desk sits a stack, just as neat, of medical journals and thick textbooks. From the multicolor Post-its earmarking their pages, it's clear that Didier not only organized the layette after Veronica went to bed but also did a good deal of reading.

It amazes Veronica how Didier always manages to accomplish so many things in so little time. Simply cleaning up the layette mess might have taken her an entire day. Her sluggish pace irritates Didier, who whizzes around the house picking up the dirty pull-ups and empty juice boxes that she and the kids leave scattered in their wake. As he does, he mutters, "*Mais comment peut-on être si bordelique?*" meaning, "How on earth can a person be so sloppy?" This leaves Veronica painfully aware of her flaws, which suddenly seem like mountains that cannot be moved.

The mountains double in size when she unlocks the studio door. A pool of sunshine pouring through the skylight illuminates every object in stark detail: the spanking new drafting table without so much as an erasure clinging to its surface; a set of crude wooden shelves lining the back wall, stocked with a dozen canvases of varying sizes, all perfectly blank; and two easels, one empty, the other sporting an old sketch pad half-filled with drawings Veronica started years ago. She's kept it there, open to a sketch in progress, in case Didier should come snooping, even though he's promised to respect her need for privacy and stay out.

How careless of her, she fumes silently—how disgraceful— to have neglected this precious space. Since her days in art school, she's dreamed of having a studio just like it. So what if it's not in the sunny SoHo loft she once imagined? Like marrying Didier, it was a gift horse. In fact, the studio and Didier came hand in hand. After they got engaged, he told her, "Do not worry, Meess Popcorn Shreemp. If you move to France you will have the possibility to leave your job and paint. We will buy a house with space for a studio. You can paint every day. I will be proud to support you and see you succeed."

Yet all this time, Veronica has been staring this gift horse right in the mouth. Even worse: she's been kicking it in the foot. She's let her studio go to waste, and with it, her talent—the very thing her mother always warned her not to do. After a while, waste disintegrates. Like the sound of a tree falling in a deserted forest, it makes you wonder: did it ever exist at all?

Maybe if she'd had a chance to clean up the layette mess, to ease slowly into a productive frame of mind, the studio wouldn't look so daunting. But now she has to dive in cold. And she has no idea what to paint. Her incomplete sketches propped on an easel don't inspire her at all. Flipping through them, Veronica gawks at how immature and awkward the lines appear. The sketch she started of the famous Fountain of Four Dolphins in the heart of Aix during her painting vacation five years ago looks more like an upside-down merry-go-round than a stone obelisk rising from a shallow basin supported by four ornately sculpted dolphins spouting water. She remembers abandoning it for a *pastis* at the café *Les Deux Garçons* with a couple of the other students from her class. Her depiction of potted geraniums spilling over the ledge of a window framed with wrought iron railings bears an embarrassing resemblance to a stenciled mailbox, and the study she began the day she met Didier, of a lionesque gargoyle spurting water into a fountain carpeted with centuries of moss, looks cartoonish. Distracted by romance from that day forward, she never got around to finishing it.

I'm going to have to do better than that now, she thinks, turning to a blank page and warming up by doodling a couple of unicorns pawing anxiously at the ground. And I'm going to have to paint a scene that Stella will love, something colorful, something fanciful and floral.

Wandering outside, she surveys the panoply of choices in her yard. A rustic composite of uneven, ash-colored stones forms the studio's exterior walls. On one side, an old rose trellis left over from previous owners is covered with vines that neither Veronica nor Didier has ever tended, yet whose deep green leaves are beginning, today, to unfurl. Tight buds an astonishing, edible shade of tangerine poke out from the leaves. With the sun radiating a glorious amber aura and the sky a perfect shade of sapphire, even this simple scene would make a stunning canvas. It could be titled, *Artist's Atelier, Aix-en-Provence,* Veronica thinks, wiping her hand on the leg of her coveralls. And when she's famous, the plaque beside it on the museum wall can read, "Veronica Berg Benhamou, circa 2003."

Her stomach lurches. She'll never be able to get so much as an abstraction of this scene right. It's too complex. Same goes for the view of the paved walkway in the front yard leading to an iron gate flanked by ceramic tubs of lavender in an early stage of bloom: too busy, too multidimensional for a first day back at the easel. Jasmine tendrils curl their way around the bars on the gate's upper half, adding a tricky element of detail. Better stick with something simple, like a still life, which she can do indoors.

Dapper red poppies, the first of the season, speckle the narrow band of grass between the studio and the walkway. They look surprisingly cheerful for a bunch of weeds.

Hastily, before she can change her mind, she plucks a few and arranges them into a sparse bouquet. Then, returning to the comfort of the contained space indoors, she lays the bouquet on the sill of the studio's single, original window. Square and stout and wedged right beneath the ceiling, the window looks out onto a section of the peach stucco wall of the house, a few yards away. The edge of an apple-green shutter is visible against the wall. She steps back to inspect the scene. *Poppies and Provençal Windows.* Not the greatest, but under the circumstances it'll have to do.

Feeling mildly nauseous, she pulls her stool up to the easel, lifts a pencil from its shelf, and strokes it across a blank page. The line she produces looks more like a squiggle than the outline of a windowsill. She turns the page and begins again, thinking of her old boss Brenda, who spent two years drafting and redrafting twelve simple illustrations and a five-hundred-word story. Producing art requires trial and error and time. After stroking her pencil just so, she steps back to examine her second line. No better. She turns the page once more and tries it from a different angle. Still no better. How many trials will it take? She wonders, tracing lines across page after page, over and over, frowning. How many errors? How much time? Almost an hour has passed, and she's still taking stabs at this damn windowsill. She hasn't even drawn a single poppy, and they're starting to wilt. There are seven altogether. At the rate she's going, it would take a miracle for her to get them all down on paper by the end of the week. Once the initial sketch is done, there's no telling how long it'll take to complete the final canvas.

After about a dozen more botched attempts to draw the windowsill, she wants to scream. She's rusty and out of practice—a fact she didn't consider when she decided to whip together a painting for Stella. The windowsill is grimy, the bouquet of poppies is meaningless and ugly. It was a bad idea. On top of it all, her stomach is growling, making it impossible for her to concentrate. It's a little early for lunch, but maybe a break and some food will settle her nerves so she can begin again calmly.

In the kitchen, she slices open a baguette and fills it with a few thick slabs of brie. Taking her sandwich to the sofa, she sinks into its inviting cushions and flicks on the TV. The midday news shows France's president, Jacques Chirac, behind a podium. His dripping, jowly cheeks, punctuated by the brown bump of a mole beside his nose, barely move as he speaks. From what Veronica can make out, it sounds like Chirac is saying something about using a veto to block UN approval of military action in Iraq. It wouldn't have surprised her. Everyone in France opposes a war. A few days ago, on February 15, 2003, nearly fifteen million demonstrators marched through six hundred French cities, including Aix and Marseille, to protest military action. Veronica was glad that day that she didn't have to go into town.

Her eyelids grow heavy. Most days, she's got a good hour or so of energy after lunch before her body downshifts into neutral like a car and groans with fatigue. But the roiling emotion of attempting to paint, on top of a difficult morning with Luc and Céleste, has sapped her. The comforter on her bed upstairs, its duvet crisply ironed by Maria, beckons like the linens in a luxury hotel where room service has just turned down the covers and placed a mint on the pillow. Chirac's face blurs into a sleepy smudge. His words blur, too, until they're unintelligible, soft as the intonations of a lullaby.

Chapter Five

Veronica has always napped. In college, she indulged in a little snooze between classes most afternoons, especially when the winter temperatures in Boston slipped below twenty and the mere thought of venturing outside numbed her toes. While working in Manhattan, she looked forward to a two-hour nap on Sundays—her trick for stocking up on energy for the week ahead. A special treat as scrumptious as a slice of chocolate cake, the promise of a couple of hours cocooned in bed while the rest of the world muddled along helped her through countless drowsy lectures and meetings. Everybody has their vices. At least this one's harmless, and much healthier than drinking tons of coffee or taking drugs.

During her pregnancy, napping evolved from a treat to an insurmountable need. From the day she began feeling queasy and sensing the powerful presence of life in her womb, exhaustion overcame her, so deep and so pervasive that even the simplest tasks—brushing her teeth, darting from the sofa to the toilet to throw up—seemed as onerous as swimming against a strong ocean current with a weight belt on. As if the new life inside her needed to drink every ounce of her strength in order to thrive, and she had no choice but to let it. All she could do was sit on the sofa, forget about painting, forget about housework, shut her eyes and, inevitably, doze off. Didier would come home after work to find her slumped into the couch, blinking as she drifted in and out of cat naps so intense that she drooled.

"I just can't help it," she'd murmur when she saw him, wiping the corner of her mouth with the back of her hand.

"Don't," he'd say, patting her tummy and kissing her soppy mouth. "The first trimester, it is the hardest. When it passes, your fatigue will pass, too."

When she learned that she was carrying not one child, but two, she moved her lengthening cat naps upstairs to bed. Some days, it was easier for her just to stay there. Not only had her body become thicker, heavier, and slower by then, but the immensity of the news of impending twins weighed on her like two hundred pounds of lead. She had agreed giddily with Didier's suggestion, shortly after their wedding, that she stop using the Pill and let Mother Nature take her course. But she'd assumed that getting pregnant would mean conceiving *one* baby. A baby—one—would feel as delicious squirming around in her belly as Didier's hard, stout penis felt whenever it slid toward that space that only a baby could fill. One baby would make a delightful playmate and companion to lock eyes with, to coo nonsense syllables at, and wear in a Björn while window-shopping in town. With one baby, Veronica could paint while her son or daughter slept during the day. But two babies—*two!*—would mean crazed days stuck in the house waiting for one to fall asleep or the other to wake up. It would mean endless reams of laundry, of dirty diapers and bottles, and two infants for Veronica to rock and bounce and burp alone in a country where she barely spoke the language and had no family of her own. Coming to France had been hard enough, but she had chosen to do so. Having twins would be even harder, yet she never would have chosen it in a million years.

Napping while pregnant, she discovered the brand-new sensation of drifting into delectable nirvana, free from her cumbersome body, free from the irritating awareness of her sore breasts, her aching lower back, or the disgusting, amplified smell of dirty socks in the hamper. Buffered and unencumbered, she seemed to float, like her babies, in a sac of amniotic fluid.

During the months of twenty-four-seven nursing following the twins' birth, a daily nap remained as essential to her life as that amniotic fluid had been to theirs. Nowadays, their continued night wakings are reason enough to crawl into bed for a couple of hours each afternoon. And she can't resist. Alone in an empty house all day with nothing urgent to do, her pace becomes all the more sluggish. It's easier to succumb to the urge to drift away than to force herself to stay alert. As a mother, though, Veronica wakes more easily than before, receptive even as she dreams to noises signaling that the kids might need her. Like the hum of cicadas in the summer reminding her of their cries, or the whiny buzz of the phone.

The phone. She jerks awake and blinks. Squinting, she checks the clock on the night table. Half past one: too early for her mother to call from New Jersey, six hours behind. Didier never calls at lunchtime—he's always too busy racing through a meal at the same pizzeria where Veronica first noticed him while vacationing in Aix. And at Maria's house, it's nap time, too. The kids should be fast asleep, safe and sound.

Unless something has happened. She rolls over and gropes for the receiver. "*Allô?*" she says too loudly, to compensate for the sleepy hoarseness of her voice.

"*Allô, Madame Benhamou? C'est Maria.*"

Veronica's pulse races and her veins flood with fight-or-flight adrenaline. "*Il y a un* problem?" she asks, sitting up.

"*Luc est malade,*" Maria answers, enunciating these three simple words with intentional, pointed clarity. "*Il a de la fièvre.*"

"Luc is sick, with a fever?" she echoes in English.

"*Oui.*"

"Okay. *Je viens.*" Veronica answers. As she hangs up the phone, she realizes with embarrassment that the best way to say, "I'm on my way" is "*J'arrive.*" "*Je viens*" can also mean, "I'm having an orgasm."

Clumsily, limbs still numb, she opens the shutters, steps into her Reeboks, and smoothes the covers back over the bed. She's only napped for about an hour—half her usual time. Her temples throb. The crown of her head burns unpleasantly, as in a bad case of jet lag.

No more painting today, she thinks. An anxious burning sears her chest as she unfolds the empty stroller and pushes it out the front gate. How absurd to have thought she could plan her time or control its outcome with two young kids: something like this seems to happen every time. That's why setting deadlines makes no sense when you're a mom. Lucky thing she didn't take her easel and head out to an olive grove an hour's drive away. Luc needs her, right here, right now. When she gets him home, she'll lie down beside him, stroke his hair, and read *Barnyard Dance*, belting out her best neighs and moos.

The stroller's plastic wheels clack over the sidewalk as she curves to the left, past a neighbor's almond tree decked in clusters of tiny, white blossoms, past a row of linden trees fragrant as honey, also set to bloom. No need to ring the buzzer at the gate of Maria's house in the cul-de-sac at the end of the street: Maria is standing behind it, waiting, with Luc in her arms.

"*Voilà Maman!*" Maria sings to Luc, stepping back as Veronica enters the yard. Her voice chimes like a bell, and her black eyes flash with warmth. She nuzzles Luc's head with her nose, rocks him side to side. "*Pauvre chou, elle va te ramener à la maison.*"

Luc peers up at Veronica and holds out his arms.

Veronica takes him. "That's right, sweetie, I'm taking you home." She says, placing a kiss on the bridge of his runny nose. She glances around at the teak table and sturdy wooden swing set in Maria's manicured yard and her squat, rectangular house with stucco walls painted a uniform, mellow shade of peach. Maria's parents, who moved from Portugal when Maria was a child, built it themselves and still live there, now in a two-room annex in the backyard they added when Maria got married. They still share a kitchen and meals with Maria and her husband, Manu, and help her out with her own daughters as well as with the four toddlers she watches during the week.

Pressing her lips to Luc's forehead, Veronica notes that he feels barely warmer than he did this morning. He's probably had a fever all along. She should have listened to her instincts when seized with the urge to keep the kids home. "I'll make you feel all better, Duke, I promise," she whispers, nose prickling.

"*Il a à peine trente-neuf,*" Maria says with deliberate slowness. Her words end in the melodic "euh" typical of a

Provençal accent, making each sentence sound like a happy song. *"Dans deux ou trois jours il ira mieux, c'est sûr."*

Veronica nods. Thirty-nine Celsius is about a hundred and two. He'll probably need to stay home for the next few days. Her chest constricts. She can forget painting for the rest of the week.

Maria motions for her to follow her inside for Luc's lunch box and binky. Her wavy, ebony hair cropped to the ears and bell-shaped denim skirt swing mirthfully as she turns, tiptoes toward the front door, and ushers Veronica in. In the foyer, she puts a finger over her lips. The lights are off, and the shutters are closed. An odor of sautéed carrots and something fruity and buttery, home-baked, fills the house. Veronica can make out the shadows of the living room to her right and the distinct shapes of three toddlers asleep on crib-sized mattresses spread out across the tiled floor. A fourth mattress, Luc's, is empty. By the wall behind the mattresses stands an open ironing board draped with a man's button-down shirt. On a table beside the ironing board, the hem of a flowered sundress cloaks the plate of a sewing machine. These are the tools of Maria's second job mending and ironing strangers' clothing—including Veronica's and Didier's—which she does while the children she watches are sleeping or playing at her feet. In the evenings, when Manu comes home from the convenience store he owns on the outskirts of Aix, Maria leaves for her third job running the shop until it closes at nine. And she still manages to care for her own two daughters, both under ten, to sauté carrots, have a sit-down lunch with her family every day, and bake.

Veronica shifts her weight and scans the floor. Céleste, as usual, lies supine with her arms sprawled to the sides, clutching her furry stuffed whale named Baleine in one hand.

Her soft, rounded lips are parted slightly, like the almond blossoms down the street.

"*Je la chercherai …*" Veronica pauses, fitting together the words to explain that she'll get Céleste at the end of the day. "*A cinq heures.*" She taps her watch.

"*D'accord,*" whispers Maria.

Céleste's eyes pop open. "Mommy!" she exclaims, sitting right up.

"*Chut,*" Maria hushes, beaming at Céleste like an enamored bride. She swoops down, lifts her, and carries her out of the living room so she doesn't wake the other children.

Veronica sighs. Yet another example of why deadlines just don't work. Home alone with Luc, she might have had a chance to sketch for a couple of minutes if he fell asleep. Or she could have relaxed in the yard, harnessing her wherewithal to try again another day. Now she may as well take Céleste home, too. She'll spend much of the afternoon rocking Luc in her arms while dutifully trailing her daughter as she toddles through the house asking questions and opening drawers.

Chapter Six

At home, while Luc sleeps upstairs and Céleste watches the Wiggles, Veronica paces in the yard. She's used to things not quite turning out the way she'd hoped, but it still hurts. Today is Tuesday. The earliest Luc will be able to go back to Maria's is Friday. With a good chance that Céleste will catch whatever he has, Veronica probably won't make it back into the studio until the middle of next week. Her fragile momentum will have petered, her bouquet of poppies will have shriveled into compost.

Worse yet, after years of having no particular time frame, now she's in a rush. She'll need to complete and sell a painting in about six weeks if she wants to get a decent deal on airfare for July. This ultimatum hanging over her head makes her tense. It's probably one of the reasons she was so klutzy and inept while sketching. Art takes time, and an artist needs to be relaxed. How can anybody create something beautiful under pressure?

She checks the baby monitor on the porch and glances through the sliding glass door at Céleste, still entranced by the TV. Being under pressure's no way to raise children, either.

Usually, when Luc and Céleste stay home on a weekday for whatever reason—a fever, a rash, a holiday, or just a spontaneous day off to rest and regroup—Veronica watches videos with them and leads them through art projects, which is a lot more fun than sequestering herself in the studio alone. She paints mouse whiskers on their cheeks, makes salt dough that she shapes with them into dragons and serpents, traces their bodies on large sheets of paper, and helps them color them in. At nap time, she lies down with them on her bed. She's happy to share these simple, silly moments, to watch their faces light with awe as their salt dough creatures come to life or get lost with them in a goofy medley of sing-along songs. Having the freedom and flexibility to do so is priceless. If her own mother hadn't been there to offer her watercolors when she was small and applaud each streak of color she splashed onto the page, she might never have had the guts to try her hand at painting as an adult. Even back when she assumed she'd launch her painting career before marrying and having kids, she relished the notion that being an artist, free from the schedule and constraints of the corporate world, would be the ideal way to balance family and work. Now here she is, home with her two kids on a gorgeous afternoon and too stressed out over a deadline to be fully present. This morning she was so distracted by her goal that she didn't even notice Luc's fever.

Wiping her nose with the back of her hand, she gazes at the sky. Her religious beliefs may be as sparse as the annual trip to the synagogue she used to take with her family on Yom Kippur and the single Passover Seder they held each spring, but often—like now—it reassures her to think God exists. Not the amorphous, mystical god Didier believes in—a sort of vast, unifying spark of light—but an omnipotent humanoid of a being capable of making things turn out for the best even when the odds are against it. The notion makes her feel safe and snug, the way she does when she curls up on the sofa in her penguin slippers with a warm cup of tea. If true, it would also help explain events that have seemed nothing short of miraculous, like getting into art school on a portfolio full of unicorns and cherubs, and meeting Didier. And the painting vacation that brought them together, which was far beyond Veronica's reach but fell into place like some sort of a divine plan.

Once Veronica decided to visit the south of France in 1998, it took her all of five minutes to locate a Web site advertising a two-week painting getaway in Aix-en-Provence. The package included round-trip airfare from New York to Marseilles, a shuttle bus to Aix, twelve nights in a three-star hotel, and daily meals. It also came with ten half-day painting classes by a local, English-speaking artist named Guylaine LeMaître, free use of Guylaine's studio in the afternoons, and field trips to coveted artists' destinations like the Montagne Sainte Victoire, Picasso's mansion in Vauvenargues, and the cliffs of Cassis featured on Stella's postcard. Altogether, it cost a little more than Veronica's credit card limit. She had just paid her latest bill and had a couple of thousand dollars sitting in her savings account. After a quick calculation of how much interest would accrue if she emptied her savings account and charged the balance, she went ahead and booked a trip for June.

That evening, she brought home bagels and lox and fancy cream cheese with chives from Zabar's, told her mother she'd taken care of dinner, and hummed while setting it out.

When her father emerged from his end-of-day run on the treadmill in the basement, he eyed the spread on the table, including a heaping bowl of exotic fruit salad and tortellini al pesto. "What's all this?" he asked, wiping his brow with a towel balled in his fist and cocking his head toward Veronica. "Did you get a raise?"

Veronica just smiled and poured him a glass of wine—a Pouilly-Fuissé that the salesman in the wine shop next to Zabar's had suggested when she asked him for something good, something French.

Shirley, sipping wine beside the broad, stainless steel fridge, shot Rich a triumphant, knowing look. "I've been trying to pry an answer from her since she came home. I'll bet she's in love."

Veronica plucked a papaya cube from the fruit salad and popped it into her mouth. "Wishful thinking," she said, motioning for her parents to sit down. "I'm just going on a little vacation."

Rich raised a bushy eyebrow and crossed his arms over his chest, ignoring his wine. Circles of perspiration drenched his undershirt, making it cling to his Brilloish mass of chest hair. His thinning gray and auburn curls stuck to his head, matted like a wet shag rug. "All this for a little vacation?" he asked.

"A *painting* vacation," Veronica clarified, taking her seat at the table and spreading cream cheese onto a raisin bagel. "To get the ball rolling with my artwork."

"Now there's a smart idea!" Shirley declared, nodding at Veronica with satisfaction. Her ruby hair glinted in the light of the stained glass chandelier above the kitchen table and her plus-sized bosom swelled beneath her velvet zip-up sweatshirt the same shade of aqua as the pool water at the club. "Here's to a painting vacation," she said, raising her glass.

"Wait a minute, wait a minute," Rich said. He frowned, dabbed his temples with his towel, and shook his head. His pockmarked cheeks were taut. "Where is this painting vacation of yours? And how much time off, exactly, are you going to take?"

"I'm just taking my vacation days for the year." Veronica replied with a shrug. "Two weeks. And I'm going to the south of France. I found a class there. There's no better place in the whole world to paint."

"The south of France," Rich repeated. "Did you rob a bank?"

Shirley put down her wine glass. "Don't be such a grouch. This is the best news I've heard in ages. Now come eat."

"For your information," Veronica said, "I did not rob a bank." She could feel her face turning pink and the tip of her nose starting to prickle. What a relief it would be when she could move into her own apartment. "Between my savings and credit card, I'll be fine."

"Your savings?" echoed Shirley through a mouthful of lox. "Isn't that supposed to be a nest egg for when you move out?" She glanced at Rich, busy pacing back and forth the length of the granite counter, eyes fixed on the bay window behind the sink and its view of a dogwood tree encircled with mulch. Like everything else outside, it was dank, soggy, soaked with rain.

"Look," Veronica said, putting down her bagel. "Isn't it true that sometimes you just have to do the right thing at the right time without worrying about the future? Well, this is the right thing for me at the right time. Who knows, it could change my life. Believe me, I could use a change. And if it helps kick my painting into gear, I might not need to worry about my savings account so much anymore. But if I don't take the risk, nothing will happen. Nothing."

"That's for sure." Rich stopped pacing. "But what makes you think this painting vacation is going to help any?"

"I just have a feeling. It's hard to explain."

"It's called intuition," Shirley piped in. "And Veronica's right: nothing ventured, nothing gained."

Rich gazed past the table at some unidentifiable spot on the wall. "So the kid's got spunk," he said. "That's good. And her painting—it sounds like she means business." He frowned, turned to Veronica. "But enough to blow a hard-earned savings account?"

"Would you sit down already?" Shirley said, pulling back Rich's empty chair. "It's not Veronica's fault that she's underpaid. And there's no reason that she should *have* to dip into her savings." She shot Rich another knowing look.

Rich tossed his towel over a shoulder. "Aren't there any of these painting vacations someplace closer, like, what's it called, the Berkshires? Or the Hamptons? There are lots of artists there."

"It's not the same," Veronica said.

"Vermont?"

"I'm going to the south of France."

Rich studied the wall as though he'd just discovered something—chipping paint, a water stain—that required immediate repair. Then he walked to the table and peered down at Veronica. "You're just like your mother: stubborn as a mule." He sighed, shook his head with resigned dismay. "Well, the right dose of stubbornness can be a virtue, I suppose."

"Amen," said Shirley, helping herself to some tortellini.

"But the south of France," Rich muttered. "Of all the places. You're sure about this?"

Veronica lifted her chin, hoping it made her look more confident than camelish right then. "It's done. I'm going at the end of June. And I've already paid."

Rich nodded and ruffled Veronica's hair. "All right. But you shouldn't have to blow your life's savings. Just tell us how much it cost. We'll write you a check."

Veronica was so surprised that she sprang from her chair and gave her father a hefty bear hug, sweaty undershirt and all. If there was such a thing as miracles, this was one. "I'll pay you back, just like I would have paid off my credit card, I promise," she said, breathing in the sweaty scent of her father's rough skin and silently, fervently thanking God. But Rich just dismissed the conversation with a wave and sat down.

Veronica has since imagined a benevolent, supernatural hand smoothing over other situations, like getting settled in her house in Aix. She and Didier had had a hard time finding the kind of house they wanted, one close to the center of town with more than one bathroom and space for a studio, but in the end, they'd set their hearts on the one where they live now. The trouble was, for each of its merits—its yard filled with prolific fig and persimmons trees, its detached garage with wisteria cascading from the tiled roof, its proximity to the center of town—there was a downside, like the dreary, outdated kitchen and bathrooms, a dysfunctional plumbing system, and the faux bamboo paper peeling off warped stone walls.

The only way Veronica and Didier could afford the renovations was to tackle them one small portion at a time. It would take several years, a disappointment that Veronica had needed weeks to digest. Not wanting to worry her parents, she raved about the house to them on the phone after signing the mortgage. "It's a diamond in the rough," she gushed. "Little by little we'll rebuild it and fix it up really cute. Just think Peter Mayle: *A Year in Provence*."

The next day Rich and Shirley called back and offered to pay to have the house renovated right away. "Consider the money part of your wedding gift," said Shirley. "We'd have given it to you eventually anyway."

During their biannual visits, Rich and Shirley also showered Veronica and Didier with housewarming gifts like the living room sofa, the dining set, the chandelier above it, the stools at the kitchen counter and a state-of-the art TV. They even bought the furniture for the kids' rooms, since double cribs, double dressers, and double changing tables were more than any young couple should be expected to buy.

Didier had accepted the money for the renovations with humble gratitude. But afterward, each new appliance or piece of furniture from Rich and Shirley sparked an outburst of protest. "Your parents have done more than enough," he'd mutter to Veronica when they were alone. "Please tell them to stop. We are adults. I'm embarrassed. Aren't you?"

Veronica would answer, "My parents would be insulted if we turned them down."

Fortunately, or perhaps by miracle, Didier always acquiesced.

A swallow swoops low across the sky, dips behind the roof, and resurges like a phoenix, its pointed black wings tilting side to side. It would be nice if miracles existed, she thinks. But who knows? They could be nothing more than serendipity or plain old good luck. Which is why, if you really want something to happen, your best bet is to give your luck a little nudge in the right direction. Veronica's painting vacation was a little nudge. So was introducing herself to

Didier. Nudges are risky and frightening to give. They may get you nowhere, or—worse yet—get you laughed at. But when they work out, they're worth it. And with Luc sick, a pathetic bouquet of poppies wilting in the studio, her self-confidence swirling down the gutter and a summer trip to New Jersey at stake, she'd better give one. Never mind if it brings a flush of shame to her cheeks.

She climbs the steps to the porch, crosses it, and pulls open the sliding glass door. After checking on Céleste, still entranced by the Wiggles, and on Luc, still fast asleep in bed, she picks up the phone and dials her parents' number.

Chapter Seven

When Veronica introduced herself to Didier during her painting vacation in Aix-en-Provence, she was a foreigner in a foreign country. Nobody knew her. Nobody cared. Putting herself on the line, exposing her hopes at the risk of embarrassment or disappointment, felt much easier than it would have at home. She could produce an atrocious self-portrait with a bunch of strangers peering over her shoulder and laugh at it with them. She could go braless in a sundress, breasts jiggling, oblivious to whether the mustached man selling her a basket of strawberries at the market talked directly to her chest. She could get tipsy on *pastis* before noon, sit at the same table at a sidewalk café for three hours at a time, and strike up a conversation about the difference between an espresso and a *noisette* with the couple beside her who, moments before, had been necking. So the notion of striding into a young doctor's office to introduce herself seemed no more intimidating than asking somebody she'd never see again where to find *les toilettes*.

She hatched the plan over lunch one day at a cozy pizzeria on rue Clemenceau with her painting teacher, Guylaine

LeMaître, and the other students in the class. The group—eight people in all, including a quartet of white-haired retirees who had traveled together from Santa Barbara and an outspoken British set designer named Eve—had just taken seats at a cluster of tables-for-two pulled so close together that Veronica's shoulder stuck like Velcro to Guylaine's. Guylaine arranged her napkin on her lap, scanned the dining room, and nodded stiffly at a man rising from a table in the corner.

By this time, her fifth day in Aix, Veronica had figured out how to use the hoselike shower in her hotel room without spraying the bathroom walls and had learned her way around the maze of cobblestone streets bustling with jewelry, clothing, and pottery stores in the heart of town. She'd grown accustomed to the daily wake-up call of swallows twittering, of shutters banging open, of plastic-bristled brooms swooshing water over sidewalks, and delivery vans too wide for the streets beeping as they backed halfway into place to deposit cases of tomatoes, eggplants, leeks, and legs of lamb. She'd discovered that the sun sets at nearly ten o'clock in the south of France in June, and that the tepid evening hours between six and eight are considered the late afternoon: a time for window-shopping and gathering in cafés to drink *apéritifs* accompanied by little dishes of potato chips, olives, and peanuts. She'd noticed that strangers tend not to make eye contact with each other unless they must but that friends and family kiss each other systematically on each cheek to say hello. More distant acquaintances greet each other by shaking hands.

The man from the corner table—a young thirty-something—nodded back at Guylaine, who stood up and briefly clasped his hand. A hint of stubble accentuated the dusky, eucalyptus-bark tint of his skin, the espresso color of his shaggy hair, and the hue of his eyes, rich as two dark chocolates in a bowl. Fresh rumples streaked his beige linen blazer and tan silk tie, lending them an aura of frenzied intensity amplified by the documents splaying from the top of his supple leather briefcase. He clutched it so tightly that his knuckles gleamed pearly white. His jaw, square and staunch, twitched as he scanned the group of students, then allowed his gaze to linger for a couple of seconds on the spot where Veronica's hair touched the side of her neck, as if fixating on a necklace she wasn't wearing or simply her skin's sunburned veneer.

"*Bonjour, Madame,*" he said, shifting his regard to Guylaine.

"*Bonjour, docteur.*" Guylaine released his clasp and sat back down.

Veronica's neck pulsed with heat. If she had understood correctly, this man was a doctor. Smoothing her hair with her fingertips, she peeked at his left hand: no ring.

"He's cute!" she whispered as the man exited the pizzeria, alone, and disappeared into the street.

Guylaine bobbed her head in acknowledgment, with her usual brisk, no-nonsense air.

"Is he really a doctor?"

"He's my ORL." Guylaine jerked her head. Her stark, angular bob, dyed shoe-polish brown and hardly attractive in isolation, nonetheless formed the perfect frame for her broad cheek bones, her rectangular, horn-rimmed glasses, and tiny, pointed chin.

"ORL?" Veronica snorted. "What the heck is that? An operating room lighting technician?"

Guylaine unsnapped her oversized, calfskin shoulder bag and pulled out a pack of Marlboro Lights. "ORL means *otorhinolaryngologist,*" she explained, in the same matter-of-fact tone she used in class, whether pointing out the light's refraction off a chipped Roman amphora arranged on folds of silk or prodding the buttocks of nude models and using adjectives like "bulbous" and "elliptical" to describe their shape. "You know, the nasal passages, the sinuses, the inner ears. He operated on my polyps last year."

"Oh! That's ENT in English—for ear, nose, and throat. Wow. What a complicated job. He must be the brainy type."

"I suppose," Guylaine huffed with mild exasperation, her lips parting to expose a chipped, yellowing front tooth. She tapped her cigarette pack against the table until one slid out and then offered it to Veronica.

"No thanks," Veronica said.

Guylaine held the cigarette pack out to Eve, the British set designer, seated on her other side.

"Oh, please, no," Eve said, in a lofty London accent that clashed with her dreadlocks, wound around frayed strips of quilting cloth, and her baggy, tie-dyed tank top and peasant's skirt.

"So what have you ordered?" Guylaine asked Eve, cigarette perched between her lips. Hand cupped over her lighter, she flicked it and inhaled.

Eve raised both arms above her head in a languid stretch, exposing generous tufts of curly black armpit hair. "Pizza, *bien sûr*. The Marguerite. Plain old mozzarella and tomato sauce. No meaty bullocks like prosciutto on top for me. And you?"

"Meaty bullocks." Guylaine exhaled a thick cloud of smoke that made Veronica's eyes water. "Duck pâté to start with. Next, lasagna Bolognese."

"Sounds delish," Veronica piped in, not yet ready to let

the conversation meander off to food. "In fact, everything here looks really tempting." She paused as a waiter placed two pitchers of wine on the table and Guylaine filled up everyone's glasses. Then she took a couple of long, thirsty sips. The immediate, tipsy tingling in the back of Veronica's head, intensified by the dusty-smelling, surprisingly inoffensive smoke fumes, helped the words simmering in her chest burble out like a giggle: "Especially that cute doctor who just left."

Guylaine sucked on her cigarette and exhaled again. "Forget him." Her words formed warped smoke rings that hung in the air for a moment before disappearing. "He is a waste of time."

"Oh, really?" said Eve with a devious smirk. "Sounds like you know a bit about this doctor." She winked at Veronica.

"Yes," breathed Guylaine, casting Eve a sidelong glance. "I agree that he is cute. I tried to flirt with him once, after my surgery."

"But?" Eve prodded, leaning onto Guylaine and pushing her a few inches closer to Veronica. If it weren't for the wine making Veronica's brain lilt or for Bill, a retiree from Santa Barbara, seated on her right, she would have edged in that direction for a little breathing room. As it was, if she and Guylaine so much as looked at each other, they'd be practically making out.

Guylaine put out her cigarette and cocked her head toward the waiter, now returning to the table to serve plates of goat cheese salad with walnuts, tangy celery *remoulade*, and thick slabs of pâté. "But nothing. Our first course is here. *Bon appétit.*"

"I'll bet he sent you off saying that you were too old for him. Is that it?" Eve teased, prodding as if she, too, had some stake in this conversation. Or perhaps for pure entertainment.

Guylaine picked up an olive from her pâté dish, sucked at it for a moment, and then slid the pit out her lips. "Absolutely not. The doctor just has some old-fashioned ideas about who he will date and is a bit of a snob. Imagine, for example, that he will not consider dating a woman whose religion is different than his."

"Oh," said Eve, crinkling her nose—the entertainment having taken a solemn turn—and winding a finger around a fuzzy dreadlock the color of a cup of Earl Grey tea with a twist of lemon. "That *is* quite old-fashioned, isn't it? Indeed, a waste of time." She glanced at Veronica and raised an eyebrow that could have used a good plucking. "Wouldn't you say?"

Veronica could feel her cheeks turning as red as the tentlike awning shading the restaurant's front terrace and the oilcloth covers draping its tables. The bizarre new twist to this conversation struck a tender chord very close to her heart. What was wrong with a man wanting to date somebody of the same religion? she wondered. Most people dated because at some level they were thinking about marriage, right? Otherwise they'd go for a fling or a one-night stand. And traditions of all sorts, including religious, were important in marriage. How many times had she imagined herself on her wedding day, standing under a chuppah the way her parents did, watching her groom smash a wine glass with his heel as the rabbi called out, "*Mazel tov!*"? She longed for the day when she'd perpetuate the Berg family ritual of organizing an impromptu scavenger hunt for the *afikomen* during Passover Seders. The Bergs may not have been religious, but colluding with Stella to leave a telltale trail of matzo crumbs for Rich to follow and eat off the floor at the end of each Seder, his fleshy lips curled in feigned disgust as he sniffed each one and grumbled, "Do I hafta put this in my mouth?" always sent her into gales of sidesplitting laughter. Just thinking about it, a quick spasm tickled her abdominal wall. Of course she'd want to share the experience, the memories, with her own kids.

Maybe here in Europe, where Amsterdam's red-light district and its coffeehouses and the topless beaches of the Riviera are never far, these sorts of traditions had lost their meaning and came across as outdated and politically incorrect. Guylaine had three children with a man she'd never married. All of France, it seemed, held former president Mitterrand's illegitimate daughter by a long-term mistress on a pedestal. But to Veronica, traditions meant a lot. They grounded you, reminded you who you are. Apparently, the cute doctor who had just shaken Guylaine's hand felt the same way. This evoked an intriguing sense of familiarity, as though, nationality and language gaps aside, he and Veronica might actually have something powerful in common. And it begged a question that Veronica was bursting to ask now, no matter how old-fashioned or politically incorrect:

"So what religion is he, anyway?"

Guylaine glanced around the table, clearly annoyed at having no choice but to answer. "*Israélite*," she muttered. "That is … you know, Jewish."

Veronica slapped the table so hard that a walnut flew out of her plate. "What?" she squealed. "I've *got* to meet him!"

Conversation around the table and in the broader dining section packed with an eclectic mix of office workers, students, and tourists stopped cold. The waiter, now bearing an enormous, round tray of thin-crusted pizzas exuding a garlicky mist, turned and glared. But Veronica didn't care.

Why should she have, when she was as anonymous as the fly on the wall behind her, as free as the wind? In the company of total strangers unabashedly flashing chipped teeth and hairy armpits, a little squeal of delight seemed as harmless as dribbling some extra olive oil onto an already oily pizza. Which, mimicking Eve, she did, as she added, "Can you introduce me?"

Guylaine pursed her lips.

"Oh, c'mon!" she insisted, slapping the table again. "In ten days I'll be gone. It's no big deal."

Across from her, Bill's wife, Helen, pinched the sides of her wine glass to stop it from sloshing. "Bill and I were introduced by a mutual friend," she interjected, tilting her head toward Bill and turning up her thin lips into a nostalgic smile. "Twelve years ago." She squeezed his leathery forearm.

"It is quite a coincidence," Eve said, her voice tinged with amusement. "I mean, Veronica has something this doctor claims he's seeking in a partner. And it sounds like she's seeking a partner herself. A husband, that is." She winked at Veronica, eyes glinting as if she'd uncovered some juicy secret about her. "In fact, I suspect that's what this journey's all about for her, really. So what harm would a little introduction do?"

Veronica didn't know whether she should smack Eve's presumptuous, round-cheeked face or give her an enormous hug. The urge to connect with this doctor was as fierce now as a nasty mosquito bite's itch. Of course she'd like to meet somebody. Who wouldn't? So far, her painting vacation had yielded very little promise, if any, of changing her life. Her self-portrait and paintings of nude models and Roman amphorae had come out sloppy and halfhearted. She'd tried sketching scenes of Aix's produce and flower markets, its fountains and clock towers, but the town resembled a dense, jam-packed outdoor mall and the allure of window-shopping and people-watching distracted her too much. Nor had anything she'd seen or done so far given her that elusive feeling of exhilaration, of inner strength and rapture that she'd imagined when gazing at her screensaver showing the gleaming white cliffs of Antibes. Granted, she hadn't gone to the coast yet—the trip to Cassis was scheduled for next week. And she'd only been in Aix for five days. But five days of vacation behind her meant there were only nine left to go. Nine days could fly by awfully quickly.

Not that nine days would suffice for a romance, either, she thought, peeling an anchovy off the artichoke pizza the waiter had just placed before her. Or that she should expect a romance with a man who lived in France. But back home, she had yet to meet an eligible doctor, cute or not. Her forays onto Jdate.com—the one step she had taken to try to break her dreary stalemate—had led to dinners out with a willowy accountant and a grad student in the NYU film program. Both men had been nice enough, but no sparks had flown. Now this intriguing ENT had crossed her path, in such close range that if she'd been standing, she would have tripped on him. It could be a sign of something—who knows. At the very least, meeting him could make this trip a whole lot more eventful. And fun.

Veronica shot Eve a cunning look, as if to suggest she was just going along with the game. "So?" she asked, turning to Guylaine. "How about it? What's his name?"

"*Docteur* Benhamou," Guylaine huffed, shrugging to emphasize the triviality of this data. "Didier. That is all I know."

"Didier! That's so French! I love it! What about his office? You must know where that is."

Guylaine dipped her fork into her lasagna Bolognese and rolled her eyes. "Yes, of course."

"Well?" Veronica pressed. The entire class was listening now, their polite curiosity edged with expectation.

"It's right around the corner. Rue Espariat, number seventy-three."

Veronica repeated this aloud and then studied the anchovy between her fingers. She'd never eaten an anchovy before but popped it into her mouth. It was salty, a little mushy, but good. She surveyed the dining room, where conversation had resumed in the wake of her noisy outburst, now forgotten, and swatted at the fly humming about her ear. "Okay," she said, suppressing the urge to gloat. "*Merci!*"

The next morning, Veronica skipped class and browsed the shops in the center of Aix. After picking up some snakeskin sandals made in Italy to match a pair of Capri jeans with slits up the sides she'd bought a few days earlier, she returned to her room and tried it all on in front of the mirror. The jeans fit snugly and rode low on her hips, accentuating the curve of her waist. They went well with a form-fitting halter top she'd brought from home that exposed her neck from every angle, revealed the voluptuous length of her cleavage, and pressed it together into a deep, suggestive valley. She brushed her pavement-colored hair so that the shorter wisps in front formed an arc around her face like the edges of an open fan. It shimmered in Aix's dry air. She'd never looked this good.

At three o'clock—a good time, she hoped, to catch a doctor in his office—she left her room and headed for the rue Espariat. The address was easy to remember: Espariat sounded like the Spanish word for hope, *esperar*, which she had miraculously remembered from high school, and '73 was the year she was born.

The building, a dignified, six-floor stone edifice, circa 1700, boasted a grandiose door: tall, heavy, fashioned from molded, varnished wood, with a polished bronze knob in its center. Veronica's heart clenched. A similar uneasiness had gripped her the day she'd boarded her flight from Kennedy to Marseille via Paris, alone with a brand-new passport, a duffel bag on wheels, and no clue what to expect when she landed. But the trip had turned out to be a cinch. She'd slept for most of the trans-Atlantic leg and later enjoyed an intoxicatingly strong coffee with breakfast while flying over the Loire valley. In Marseille, a driver awaited her, holding a sign that read "Studio Guylaine LeMaître." The first time she sat down alone at a sidewalk café, the first time she'd ordered an *éclair au chocolat, s'il vous plaît* in a *patisserie,* and the day she'd approached the saleswoman in a fancy boutique to try on her new Capri jeans, she'd also experienced an instant of panic and utter self-doubt as she faced a foreigner with a stern, somewhat forbidding demeanor whose unsmiling face conveyed absolutely nothing she could to relate to or understand. Yet everybody she'd spoken to had replied in decent English. A few people had asked where she came from. When they heard she worked in New York City, they'd raised their eyebrows and exclaimed, "*Ah, bon!*" with unmasked awe.

She had overcome her fear of ridicule then and could overcome it now, she told herself. If this doctor—Didier—seemed uninterested, indifferent or, worst case scenario, inconvenienced by her unscheduled visit, she could invent an earache, let him examine her, and then leave. She'd heard Bill and Helen raving one day in class about how, thanks to universal health care, a visit to the doctor in France cost just about 120 francs—twenty bucks. If it came down to faking an earache, she'd pay cash and skimp on dinner that night.

A polished bronze plaque on the building's façade read *Docteur BENHAMOU Didier, Otorhinolaryngologist, 1ère Gauche*. Otherwise, the building looked strictly residential. Veronica scanned its intercom until she spotted the matching button and pressed it. The door clicked open to a cool, dark foyer where a stairwell encircled an open elevator shaft as narrow as a phone booth. On the first flight up, two unassuming doors appeared to lead to apartments. One bore a smaller version of the bronze plaque outside. In the upper right reaches of its threshold hung a ceramic mezuzah no bigger than a peanut shell. Swiftly—before she could change her mind—Veronica rang the bell, cringed at its loud, strident buzz, and then sucked in her breath as the door swung open.

The office, too, looked residential. Its waiting room had the distinct feel of a fancy, upper East Side apartment in Manhattan, minus furniture and other accoutrements. An antique fireplace occupied the better part of the far wall; it would have looked stunning, she noted, with a distressed-glass mirror above it. Original cornice molding edged the eggshell walls, and a pair of six-foot-high French windows, both slightly ajar, faced the street. With the walls lacking art, the windows screaming out for curtains, and the original hardwood floors in need of a buff, this otherwise beautiful space felt somewhat sad and neglected. It could use a woman's touch.

In the far corner of the waiting room stood an empty wooden desk that seemed to be made for a secretary. Four black, plastic office chairs lined the back wall, one occupied by an elderly woman holding a cane across her lap, eyes shut. Aside from the woman's raspy, irregular breath, an eerie silence prevailed.

Could this doctor be some sort of second-rate quack? Veronica wondered. Or do physicians' offices in Provence typically have such a sleepy, anachronistic feel? Just as she was debating how long she should wait before scrapping this ludicrous plan, a door behind the desk creaked open. A young mother pushing a stroller emerged from what appeared to be the consultation room, crossed the waiting room, and left. After a couple of long minutes, Dr. Didier Benhamou stepped out.

He eyed the empty desk, checked his watch. After muttering a few words in French that sounded angry or contemptuous, he surveyed the waiting room. When his gaze reached Veronica's, it sharpened as though zooming in on something important that he'd suddenly remembered. After resting for a moment on her face, it slid down to her nonexistent necklace, then traced it with delectable slowness like an index finger exploring the elevation of her tendons, the depth of the indentation at the base of her throat. Goose bumps peppered her neck: no need for an earache.

"*Je peux vous aider, Madame?*" His neutral, professional tone did nothing to conceal the glimmer of fascination in his eyes.

Veronica lifted her chin, dug her fingernails into her palms, and recited the line she'd prepared using a French phrasebook and had practiced over and over before the mirror in her hotel room: "*Je suis Veronica. Je suis américaine.*"

"*Ah.*" He raised an eyebrow, reining in a smile. "And you need a doctor? Who speaks English?" His delightful French accent softened his words, spread them into the air like butter on a slice of warm, fresh bread.

Veronica's cheeks burned. *Yes, I do!* she wanted to bellow.

You have no idea! Her eyes wandered down the thick tubes of his creased linen sleeves to his hands, where tufts of hair dusted his knuckles and fingers: strong, stout. "I—I wanted to meet you. I'm one of Guylaine LeMaître's students."

"Yes, yes." He tipped his head to one side, no longer restraining his smile, and shook Veronica's hand, as clammy as his. "Didier Benhamou. *Enchanté.*" His regard dipped to her cleavage. "Is there something in particular, or …?"

Veronica's heart turned somersaults and cartwheels. Back home, she would have been put off by any man who dared take a blatant peek at her cleavage. Peeking was okay, but politely, without letting it show. Here in France, though, she'd noticed that people didn't bother peeking subtly. They just stared. Maybe it was a compliment. She certainly hoped so, because from up close she could see that Dr. Didier Benhamou was not only cute but also totally her type! His broad chest and well-padded shoulders, hunched ever-so-slightly, beckoned her to sidle up, snuggle in. His hair, a tad too long in the front, appeared disheveled—a sign that he wasn't pompous or vain. And though clearly sensitive enough to have clammy hands, he remained composed and courteous, in control. Veronica could just see him kissing her with wanton abandon, right in the middle of town, as she'd seen French lovers do. Her nipples rose to attention. She could just as easily picture him standing under a chuppah, smashing a wine glass with his heel.

She cleared her throat. "My last name is Berg. You know, as in Goldberg, Rosenberg, Spielberg. No relation there, but …" She squelched a sudden urge to turn and run. "When you bumped into our class at lunch, Guylaine mentioned that, well—"

Didier threw his head back and opened his mouth. "*Ah,*

ah, I see!"

Veronica nodded, thankful that he'd spared her the embarrassment of having to finish her sentence.

"So, you are visiting Aix and would like, perhaps, some company for Shabbat?" He crossed his arms and resumed studying her face, now searching it, too, as if combing the lines of a suspenseful text for a key word that would presage its conclusion.

"Some company would be great. For Shabbat, or … whenever." Veronica hadn't even heard the word *Shabbat* since her Bat Mitzvah twelve years ago.

His eucalyptus-bark complexion darkened to sepia. "*Ah*, of course," he responded, shooting her a coy look. "At the moment, though—" He glanced at his watch and motioned with his chin toward the elderly woman dozing in her seat. "I must unfortunately get back to work. My secretary, well, she is late as usual returning from lunch, and more patients will arrive soon, so I must take care of them and also the phone. Could we meet another time? Perhaps for a coffee?"

Veronica's pulse beat in quick, liquid thumps. "Sure!" she managed, hoping the perspiration accumulating at her halter top's seam beneath her arms didn't show. "I'll be in town for one more week."

"Well, then," he said, his coy look becoming more resolute. "Let's meet today."

That afternoon, after attempting to sketch a lionesque gargoyle dribbling water into a stone fountain's concave, lateral niche, Veronica packed away her sketch pad. Already concentration eluded her. With just a few hours to go before meeting Dr. Didier Benhamou for coffee, it would be useless trying to force it. Instead, she circled the streets of Aix until their rendezvous, stopping before an occasional store window to inspect her reflection, reapply a coat of lip gloss, and brush her hair.

As promised, Didier stood waiting in the street outside his office at quarter past six. Tie gone, white shirt unbuttoned to reveal an impressive tangle of black chest hair at the pinnacle of his sternum, he smelled of a fresh dose of lime aftershave and something minty—mouthwash or toothpaste. When he spotted Veronica, his gaze brightened. "At last," he said, scanning her head to toe as if trying to reconcile a vague figment of his imagination with its sudden incarnation in flesh and blood. "This afternoon, it went by very slowly."

Veronica's skin tingled as the surprising candor of these words worked its way across it like fingertips gallivanting beneath her clothes.

They strolled for a while with no particular destination, pausing before the fountain near the top of the Cours Mirabeau known as *La Moussou*, a bulging stone pilaster coated in a layer of moss as thick as crabgrass spouting water from various, random locations. "Touch," Didier said, guiding her wrist toward a cascading rivulet. "See how it is warm?" He paused to gauge her reaction. "Aix, it is built on natural thermal springs. That is why the Romans founded a city here when they arrived, about a hundred years or so before the birth of Christ. The name "Aix," it comes from the Roman word *aqua*, for water. The hot waters of the Bagniers spring, they flow right through this fountain."

"Pretty deep, doc." Veronica giggled, wiggling her fingers and flicking a few wet drops, tepid as a feverish cheek, at Didier, who beamed as one might at endearing child.

From the Cours Mirabeau they turned into the maze of cobblestone pedestrian streets in the heart of town, where stone and stucco buildings glowed in varying shades of peach, mauve, and gold in the predusk sunlight. In an ardent, hurried tone, as though preoccupied with other topics he was eager to move on to, Didier pointed out the landmarks of Aix's gradual metamorphosis from ancient water source to city, from Roman province to French territory in the Middle Ages, and later, to a hub for wealthy aristocrats and magistrates administering the multitude of courts established by King Louis XIV. He interspersed this narrative with questions, just as hurried, like items in a medical history that needed filling out before more fundamental issues could be probed: "New Jersey: your family lives there, too?" "Berg, it is an Ashkenazi name, yes?" He replied with a humble shrug to Veronica's questions about his own background and family, as if having moved to Aix with his parents and two sisters from Casablanca, Morocco, when he was six, at a time when Jewish families were departing in hordes for fear of clashes with their Arab friends and neighbors in the aftermath of Israel's Six-Day War, was as banal as pausing at a souvenir shop to pick up some postcards.

At the Place de l'Hôtel de Ville, a spacious plaza that, weekday mornings, transformed into an outdoor produce market, they took seats at a table beneath one of the myriad poppy-red and daffodil-yellow canvas parasols proliferating outside a café. The residual scent of raw tuna fillets and squid carcasses long since removed from their display beds of crushed ice still lingered in the air along with whiffs of rosemary, garlic, and dried sausage. Bells clanged from a tall, stone clock tower above. The dissonant song of swallows overhead faded beneath the din of clinking wine glasses, olive pits dropping into porcelain plates and voices bubbling like champagne.

"So," Didier said, knocking back an espresso, a glimmer of fascination creeping back into his gaze. "You are an *artiste*, yes? A painter?"

"Nah." She chuckled. The intensity of Didier's gaze riveted upon her provoked an inexplicable tickling in her abdomen, the kind that often presages deep-belly laughter and a delicious loss of control. "I'm just a wannabe."

Puzzled, he shook his head.

"You know, I just *wish* I were an artist." She told him about college, about the tedium of her job in Manhattan, and her class with Guylaine. "I came here to give myself a push and try to make it happen."

"Yes, yes." Didier placed a hand on her forearm and leaned forward as if about to whisper something confidential. "I know exactly what you mean. It is often tedious, being a doctor. There is no true creativity—just reasoning, decision-taking, and, well, quite a bit of manual labor. I have some ideas to create something, a few of them in fact are very clear, but …" His voice drifted off as he drummed his fingers on Veronica's arm.

Holding herself as frozen-still as the baroque statuette of the goddess Cybil embossed into the amber facade of the former corn exchange building to the left, she eyeballed Didier's furry fingers. Was their position upon her arm an incidental, platonic gesture typical in France? Or was it indeed—as the chills running up and down her spine suggested—filled with innuendos? As a foreigner four thousand miles from home, it was hard to know. And with only nine days left in her stay here, it was just as hard to know which of these possibilities to hope for.

"Lemme guess," she blurted out, preempting a lengthy silence. "You write poetry." She could easily picture him pacing late at night, notebook in hand, scribbling down words, crossing them out.

"*Tchk.*" He shook his head.

"Fiction?"

He lifted his hand and plunged it into the slab of hair dripping over his forehead, smiling. "No, no, I'm not a *real* creative. Not in the artistic sense, that is. Not like you."

"C'mon! What, then? The suspense is killing me!"

He inhaled, chest rising, nostrils flaring like a tiny pair of wings about to open. "Research. I would like to do medical research. Perhaps come up with some new tools, better ways to do certain things."

"That's not so far-fetched," Veronica said, plunking a sugar cube into her cappuccino. "Life's short. You should try."

Didier observed the stone edifices flanking the plaza for a few long moments, their amber facades now basking in a halo of mellow, tangerine light presaging the sunset's finale. Turning to Veronica, he gave a small but sharp nod, sucking in his breath as he uttered, "*Oui.*" After another few long moments he added: "It is good that you came to my office today."

"Oh, please! I made a total fool of myself!"

"No, no, you did not. You were very courageous. I am impressed. And, you know ..." He lowered his voice, perched his forearms on the table, and leaned over them toward her. "It is funny, but I was really not so surprised. I have always thought that I would one day meet somebody—a woman, that is—who was not from France." His complexion darkened again for a moment, and he flashed a complicitous smile. "Because my true identity, I feel, is more Jewish than French or even Moroccan. Like yours." His eyes lit with a sudden, devilish glint. "Well, *Sephardic* Jewish. So not quite the same thing."

The clock bells chimed eight. Earlier, Didier had told her that he'd have to leave around that time for dinner with his father. Veronica's stomach tightened. The evening had flown. "Hey," she said, eager to have it end on a light note. "Speaking of Jewish: what's with the microscopic mezuzah on your office door? I practically needed a magnifying glass to figure out what it was!"

"Ah, yes," he sighed, lifting his empty espresso cup, examining it briefly and dropping it with a resigned clank back into its saucer. "France, it was a logical choice for my family. But it is far from being a perfect place to live."

For the remainder of her stay in Aix, Veronica left her sketchpad in her room and skipped Guylaine's class, spending mornings sleeping off late, wine-drenched dinner dates with Didier. She opted out of the class excursion to the cliffs of Cassis and instead went hiking with him along the dusty, thyme-covered slopes at the base of the Montagne Sainte Victoire. Who needed a painting teacher when the gruff voice tinged with urgency, the stout hands, and wet embrace of a handsome young doctor could open her heart to the beauty of the russet dirt, rich in ochre, accumulating on their shoes and shins? If Guylaine had explained how ochre, abundant in Provence's soil, had inspired Cézanne, the lesson might have gone in one ear and out the next. But when Didier took off his shoes after their hike and banged them together, too absorbed in the earnest execution of this task to notice the dust settling onto his eyebrows, his lashes, and the bridge of his nose, a giddy spasm shot through her abdomen, erupting into an uncontrollable whoop of laughter. Didier stopped banging and inclined his head toward her, his grave expression melting into one of incredulous gratitude, as if her laughter had liberated him from a crushing burden. This expression, a tribute to virtues she'd never realized she had, became engraved in her memory as if immortalized on canvas, as luminous and stirring as its backdrop of blood-red dirt.

One evening, while strolling through Marseille's Vieux Port district after dinner, Didier stopped, turned to face her. Emotion pooling in his eyes, his features soft with vulnerability as raw and unguarded as a plea, he told her about his mother's death following a painful battle with bone cancer. It had brought an uncanny mix of despair and relief, he said: despair that excruciation and suffering could strike so randomly, last so long, and culminate in nothing but loss and grief; and the bizarre, paradoxical relief that with death, pain ends.

"But now, I am beginning to see—how do you say?—the silver lining." He took her hands and stepped so close that she could feel the bump of his erection straining behind his pleated khakis. "After my mother's death, I returned a bit to traditions. Praying again, keeping kosher again, it helped me feel rooted, reconnected with my family and, well, with myself. And it made me want a family of my own."

Such intimate conversations—unlike any Veronica had had before—were as thrilling as peeling off layers of clothes. They made her crackle with impatience for more, causing a sudden, dramatic shift in her vision of the future. Although she'd always imagined that she'd settle down, get married, and have kids *after* establishing herself as a painter, it occurred to her now that that events could take shape in a different order. As the final days of her vacation in Aix flew by, she stopped thinking of painting altogether and daydreamed instead about a life with Didier.

It made no difference whatsoever that Didier lived in France. His remark on their first coffee date about France not being such a perfect place to live had resonated as clearly as the clock bells in the Place de l'Hôtel de Ville. Just as Veronica's position as a foreigner in a foreign country had given her the guts to stride into his office and introduce herself, this simple comment had stripped away her remaining inhibitions— the ones that would have shielded her from the sparks that flew whenever she was with him and would have prevented her from getting carried away, falling in love. By the time she left Aix, her mind was reeling ahead to the day Didier would move to the States and apply for a Green Card. It was swimming with visions of a suburban house complete with a swing set and a garage filled with minivans in New Jersey, or Boca Raton.

Chapter Eight

Shirley Berg's morning routine hasn't changed in years. She wakes around eight, swallows a handful of vitamins with breakfast, throws on a terry cloth sweat-suit, and heads to the pool club to catch the nine o'clock water aerobics class, thermos of coffee in hand. After a sauna and a shower, she continues to the hairdresser, where, every day, she has her hair washed and blown dry. Next she runs errands, stopping at the grocery store to pick up a salad-bar lunch.

Veronica usually calls her soon after that, chatting about the kids and the weather in Aix while Shirley eats. Dialing now, Veronica checks her watch: quarter past eleven Jersey time. A little early, but it doesn't hurt to try.

Shirley picks up after nearly a dozen rings. "Are you okay?" she pants. She must have just gotten home and bolted in from the garage.

Veronica swallows hard. Her mother's familiar voice trumpets like the shofar heralding Yom Kippur's end: loud and strident, but such a relief. "I'm fine, Mom," she squeaks, blowing her nose.

"You don't sound fine. And you're calling so early.

Shouldn't you be picking up the kids?"

"They're already here. Luc's sick. Céleste isn't. Not yet, that is."

"Anything serious?"

Veronica can hear Shirley opening a door—a cabinet or the fridge—and puttering with paper bags and plastic take-out cartons, the kind with two snaplike buttons in the front that make a crunching sound when they open. She pictures her with the phone tucked between her shoulder and her ear, her head of freshly coiffed, ruby-tinted hair the shape of a wavy cycling helmet bent to the side as she unloads groceries.

"Just a bad cold," Veronica says. "His nose is like Niagara Falls."

Something clanks on Shirley's end of the line. "Maybe it's an ear infection. Or strep," Shirley says, mouth full.

Veronica sniffs and then smiles. Her mother has probably just torn off a piece of a bagel or muffin to nosh before lunch. How nice it is to know that some things are predictable and never change.

"If it's strep or an ear infection, he'll go on antibiotics for a couple of days and end of story," she says. After a brief pause, she adds, "Everything should be so easy."

"I knew it," Shirley declares. "You're not fine. Are you taking heat for what's going on in the Middle East? I've heard the French are all bent out of shape that we've lined up troops in Kuwait."

"Oh." Veronica hasn't checked the news since yesterday. "Well, nobody's mentioned it. Don't worry."

"So what's the matter?"

Veronica sits down at the dining table and takes a deep breath. Though she's carefully scripted her end of this conversation, she feels as clumsy as a kid in a school play who has just stepped out onto the stage and forgotten her lines. She clears her throat, chest bloated with shame. "Nothing major. Just a little glitch in my travel plans for this summer. I never would have thought that there'd be a downside to the twins getting bigger, but get this: now that they're two, we have to buy them full-fare tickets to Jersey in July. Can you believe it? That means peak-season airline tickets times three. It's a real stretch, so Didier thinks I should wait until November, around Thanksgiving, and—"

"We'd love to have you home for Thanksgiving!" Shirley exclaims. "Stella will be coming up with the kids, and we can all be together for a change. I'll order a gigantic bird with your favorite cornbread sausage stuffing, and a pecan pie."

Veronica blinks back a deluge of tears. She's not sure whether they're springing from the idea of Thanksgiving dinner, which she hasn't had in years, or the emotion of telling her mother about her dilemma. Shirley has a remarkable, yet exasperating, way of seeing only the bright side of any situation, no matter how dismal, and of putting such a positive spin on everything that she could probably sell the Brooklyn Bridge. When Stella, at seventeen, totaled the family's new BMW, Shirley said, "It's just a car. We'll buy another. Thank goodness Stella's okay." When Rich split with his dental partner of twenty years while Veronica was in college, Shirley said, "Now we'll get to keep every cent your father earns." It never occurred to her that Rich would lose clients and have to work twice as hard. Later, Veronica nearly called off her wedding just a few weeks before the date. She just couldn't see herself vowing "*Oui*," instead of "I do," in a reception hall in Marseille before three hundred guests from France and Morocco. The idea of tattooing her hands and feet with henna at a noisy bash before the ceremony and of women ululating like wounded hyenas after the rabbi pronounced Didier and her man and wife made her cringe. So did the reality of moving to France. "You have a classic case of cold feet," Shirley told her. "Every bride gets cold feet. Just think of the honeymoon you'll be taking to Eilat. I, for one, would die to go to Eilat. And moving to France? The *south of* France? It's a dream just about anyone would kill for. Even Stella." That Veronica would move halfway across the world and only see her parents a couple of times a year seemed to Shirley like a solitary thorn in a vast bed of roses.

"Mom." Veronica raises her voice a half a notch. "I don't want to come home for Thanksgiving. I want to come in July."

"Come at Thanksgiving *and* in July!"

"I can't."

"What do you mean, you can't? It's not like you'd have to take the kids out of school."

Veronica glances at the television screen in the living room, where the Wiggles are singing "Fruit Salad." Céleste, getting antsy, climbs the back of the sofa and then slides down. "The airfare for July alone is too much. That's the whole problem. Coming in July means a lot to me. So I'm wondering if, by any chance … could you and Dad help out with the tickets?"

"Don't be ridiculous! Of course we can help. Come on home—it's our treat."

"Thank you, thank you," Veronica gushes, her shame dissipating into a wave of relief. She's glad her mother didn't ask, as she often does, why money should be an issue when Veronica is married to a surgeon. With her rose-tinted view of the world, Shirley tends to forget certain facts, and Veronica has had to remind her a thousand times that, due to the universal health care system, most doctors in France earn about as much as college professors in the States.

"We're always happy to treat you," Shirley says. "You're our daughter. And you're raising twins. Twins! What a handful! You deserve every treat you can get."

Veronica thanks Shirley a few more times and jots down her parents' credit card number and expiration date. Forget taking antibiotics for strep: *this* is how easy everything should be.

For Shirley, everything is. What a gift. Right now she's probably humming as she sets out her lunch, thinking ahead to installing car seats for the twins' visit in July and ordering a gigantic bird with cornbread sausage stuffing for Thanksgiving whether Veronica comes or not. That's the upshot of positive thinking, the power of the self-fulfilling prophecy that comes from presenting everything—everything—sunny-side up.

Chapter Nine

Half-asleep on the sofa, Veronica rubs her eyes at the sound of the door creaking open long after Luc and Céleste have gone to bed. Sinewy shadows of fig and persimmon branches beyond the window scrape the darkened ceiling like claws, intruding on her trance. Her skull burns in a painful reminder of today's aborted nap.

"Hey," she croaks, hoisting herself to a seated position and stretching out an arm as Didier trudges past the sofa.

He brushes her fingertips and continues walking, gaze milky and unfocused. "*Ciao, artiste.*"

"You can call me 'Doc' today. Luc's sick."

Didier lifts his eyes to the portion of ceiling beneath the kids' rooms. "*Ah bon*? What does he have?" He sounds too exhausted or preoccupied to think straight.

Veronica stretches, wiggling her feet in the soft, oversized penguin slippers, complete with wings and a pointed orange beak, that her parents brought her on their last visit. "Runny nose, fever—you know, all the signs that something bigger is brewing. Like an ear infection. Or strep. I picked him up around three."

"And Céleste?"

"She's fine. Great, actually. A real monkey—bouncing off the walls as usual all afternoon. I picked her up early, too. You know, may as well." She shoots him a meaningful look, a silent reminder of her crucial role holding down the fort while he's out of pocket all day.

Didier's eyes cloud over with wistful tenderness. "I missed seeing them today," he says. He drops his gaze to Veronica's slippers, which he stares at for a moment before heading upstairs to change and kiss the children's inert cheeks.

Meanwhile, Veronica mixes a jar of spaghetti sauce into a pot of leftover noodles and reheats them. Didier might grumble that her slippers look grubby and unfeminine, like the sweatpants and sweatshirts and roomy Gap overalls she likes to wear around the house, but he never complains about how her skin feels underneath when he peels them off. She uncorks yesterday's wine, which she hopes will lubricate the discussion she's forced herself to stay awake for about her summer plans. About a year ago—once the house was furnished—she promised to stop accepting gifts from Rich and Shirley. Breaking the news that she's bent this rule calls for a relaxed mood and just the right sunny, lighthearted touch.

She pours herself a glass, takes a few sips. Fifteen minutes tick by.

"Didier?" she calls out, padding up the stairs. "Where'd you go? Dinner's ready." She pokes her head into the kids' rooms, verifies that they're both out like lights and then crosses the hallway to the master bedroom to check for Didier. She finds him sprawled out on the bed, one hand wedged beneath the fringe of thick hair on his forehead as though frozen in the act of wiping away a bead of sweat or an imaginary mountain of worries and the other dangling over the bed's edge. His shoes are on, and his eyes are shut.

"What's the matter?" She presses her palm to his forehead. He doesn't feel feverish. "Don't you want dinner?"

"What did you make?" Didier asks without opening his eyes.

She tells him.

"*Tchk*." He shakes his head. "This afternoon, a Moroccan patient—an old guy from Fez—brought me a platter of homemade *cornes de gazelle*. You know—those crescent-shaped almond cakes that we served with the tea at our wedding. They were so delicious I could not stop eating them. I must have had a dozen. Maybe more."

She sits down on the edge of the bed and prods his tummy. "Yeah! I can feel them! Right here." If she can get him to crack a smile, their discussion might turn out short and sweet even without any wine. Goofiness and laughter at little nothings have always proven the best remedy for the dark, often anxious, moods he tends to get lost in. She remembers the first time he came to see her in New Jersey. Shuffling through the customs area at Newark, his face was dark with skepticism, as if he were wondering what on earth had possessed him to travel four thousand miles for a woman he hardly knew. When he spotted her, wearing the fitted, knee-length skirt she'd had on at work that day and a pair of glaring white Reeboks with tube socks bunched around her ankles, he balked. "Get over it!" she teased, glancing in the direction of two women milling beside them with lips fat from silicone and green eye shadow up to their penciled, overplucked brows. "At least I don't have big hair."

His gaze brightened. Looping his arm around her waist, he kissed her with moist, open lips and said, "I might find you sexy even with big hair."

Since then, it has rarely taken more than a goofy grin or a well-timed wink for Veronica to get Didier to lighten up, even want to make love.

She slides her hand down his side now and presses a spot just above his left hip. "Wow, check it out! I'll bet you had at least twenty of those gazelle things. No dinner for you for a week."

Didier opens his eyes and blinks, his expression conveying a mix of indifference and sharp irritation. "What I really need is one full week of sleep."

It would be pointless, she knows, to ask him for the umpteenth time why he doesn't slow down the pace a bit at work. One of the only ENT surgeons in inland Provence, Didier never turns a patient away. First, he says, because it is his duty to help people. Second, because it is also his duty to support his family, and more patients means more cash.

"You got home after nine. No wonder you're zonked. But if you ask me, it's pretty outrageous that patients would be hanging around so late."

"They were not. I stayed late because of Madame Carcasse." He rolls his eyes to the ceiling in disgust.

Her hopes for laughter plummet. Nothing sours Didier's outlook like his secretary, whose real name is Madame Caracasse, but whom Didier refers to at home as Madame "Carcasse." This nickname, once a private joke he and Veronica shared, has become more of a rancorous solo these days, and once he gets going with it, there's no stopping him. Madame Carcasse behaves like a factory worker, punching her hours in and out and barely going through the motions of work. She takes excessively long lunches and cigarette breaks and gets around to checking phone messages about twice a week. So on top of surgeries, rounds, office consultations, and hospital staff meetings, Didier has to pick up her slack. Veronica has told him countless times that he should just fire her and find somebody new, but he insists that that would be far more complicated and costly than it's worth. In France, employment comes with a lifetime contract, and employers get slapped with stiff penalties for letting workers go.

"Maybe it's time you called her by her first name," Veronica suggests. "You know, act friendly and casual in the office. Make small talk on slow days. Let her come to the office on Fridays in jeans. She might be happier and more motivated that way."

He rolls his eyes back in Veronica's direction. "There are never any slow days. And we are not in not America, where people believe that using first names makes them automatic friends. She would be shocked and insulted."

"Then who knows, she might quit!"

"Tonight I came back to the office after rounds and saw that the pile of patient's folders that has been growing on her desk all week was about as tall as Céleste. An office is no different than a house or a person's mind: it cannot function productively when there is clutter and confusion. Carcasse would have probably filed the folders sooner or later, but when? So I stayed late and filed them myself."

As if by a knee-jerk reflex, Veronica pictures the layette clothing that Didier cleaned up from the office floor upstairs. Clearly she's wasting what's left of her energy trying to perk her husband up or talk to him tonight.

A sudden, cavernous hunger usurping her fatigue, she returns to the kitchen and polishes off the noodles, cold, straight from the pot. She may not have managed to parlay her art into a lucrative career, but she holds a full-time job tiptoeing around the minefield of Didier's constantly shifting moods. Who would have imagined, back in the days of falling in love? After her painting vacation ended, she could call him anytime she had the urge, to say she missed him desperately, that the Atlantic Ocean dividing them felt like a barbed prison wall, and that she couldn't concentrate on work. Even at two in the morning, he answered. He stayed on the line, he talked. And there was no such thing as a touchy subject, one that would cause him to purse his lips, huff disapprovingly, or clam up. During one of their many extended weekends together that year in the Manhattan hotel that had come to feel like home, Veronica gazed in awe at François Boucher's *Toilet of Venus* while standing in the grand halls of the Met and confessed that its baroque doves and cherubs doting over a nude, portly, and fantastically serene rendition of Venus was exactly the style she wanted to emulate in her painting. Emboldened by the increasingly real prospect of sharing a life with Didier and giddy with the notion that if she did, she might never have to worry about finances again, she blurted out, "Nobody would buy that sort of thing today, but who cares? I should paint what I love. Isn't that what the artist's life is all about?"

He smiled, tipped his head to the side, rested it on hers and contemplated the painting. "In my opinion, it looks much better from this angle," he said. "The cherubs are less prominent. And as for your artist's life, well, that is a *dreamer's* life you have described."

"Then I'm just a dreamer," she giggled.

"It is good to dream," he replied.

Walking through Central Park a few days later munching hot pretzels and kicking up piles of crackly, copper leaves, he confided that being a doctor had little in common with his own dreams, though he'd realized this too late. Some days, he said, he felt like a postal clerk, rubber-stamping people instead of papers. Other days he felt like a butcher cutting meat. Even though he reaped satisfaction from seeing patients' conditions improve over time or witnessing the immediate results of a surgery he'd masterminded, he often wondered how he'd ended up in a profession where he was constrained to examine a single person and a single narrow problem at a time. "When I was younger, I always thought that I would someday find myself examining greater issues, fundamental issues. For example, why do disease and malformation exist in the first place, and how can we eradicate them? In medical school, I used to imagine that I'd prepare a doctorate and become a researcher. I would make some great discovery, help millions of people, become famous and rich. But of course, like everybody else, I became bored with living in a studio apartment and borrowing money from the bank all the time. So I took my exams when school was finished and started working." He paused to stare briefly, with bewilderment, at the sky. Then he picked a leaf from Veronica's hair, took her chin between his thumb and forefinger, and lifted it so their noses nearly touched. "Your artistic dreams, your enthusiasm, and your optimism, so American, have inspired me to dream again. They make me feel that perhaps anything could be possible." His eyes glimmered as he regarded her with palpable intensity. "And there is an idea I have had for a very long time, for something that I could invent. It is a surgical device, one that would facilitate the type of procedures I do. I used to believe this was a crazy idea, crazier than trying to build a time machine. But recently, I have been thinking that in fact, it would not be so complicated to design it, to write a proposal, and try to sell it, perhaps to a pharmaceutical company. Of course there would be a *brevet*—that is, a patent—and other details to resolve, but I now believe that it is at least possible to try. When I get home, that is what I would like to do. Try." He blushed, dropped his eyes to the ground, and then raised them to Veronica like a child seeking praise yet half-expecting a reprimand. "What do you think?"

Veronica hesitated, wondering if Didier planned to work on this device in his spare time the way her boss Brenda had with her children's book, or whether he'd throw caution to the wind, quit practicing medicine, and take his chances. "You should definitely go for it," she said. "But don't risk what you have. Being a surgeon's a pretty amazing job."

Didier slipped his arm around Veronica's shoulders and gave them a squeeze. "Do not worry, love," he said. "It will always be my priority to support a family."

At Christmastime that year, he bought her tickets to visit him in Aix. He introduced her to his father, his two sisters, his brothers-in-law, and his gaggle of nieces and nephews at a Hanukkah party hosted by his older sister, Mireille. Veronica felt like she'd just landed on Mars. The two-bedroom apartment in central Aix that Mireille shared with her husband, Uriel Sarfati, and their three young children, basked in the fumes of home-fried donuts called *sufganiyot* and couscous with chunks of fried chicken. The dense aroma of hot cooking oil made Veronica's head spin. So did the clamor of voices prattling off incomprehensible words followed by bursts of hearty, visceral laughter. For all she knew, the laughter could have been directed at her. Aix looked nothing like it had in June. Its skies and streets had turned a damp, chilly shade of gray, its geranium planters were empty, and its majestic plane trees had morphed into a painful display of naked branches pruned to stubs resembling the rounded, puckered stumps of amputated limbs. Mireille had opened the windows in her overcrowded apartment, where an awkward space to the left of the kitchen passed for a living room, and a glass-topped dining table for eight in its center was set for twelve. Every now and then an icy gust of mistral wind rattled in. The tall, silver menorah on the living room console held oil lamps instead of wax candles. The lamps reminded Veronica of the Yahrtzeit candles her parents burned on Yom Kippur to mourn the deceased. Aside from the yarmulkes capping the men's heads, she could associate nothing in the scene with Hanukkah. Did this have something to do with Didier's comment the day they met about the differences between Ashkenazim and Sephardim? she wondered. Or could she blame it on jet lag? "I want to go back to your place and sleep," she whispered to Didier before dinner was served.

He observed her for a moment and then nodded. "This is perhaps a lot for you at once." He gestured for her to stay put and then strode to the dining table, where Mireille was setting out dishes.

Side by side, the two looked remarkably alike, sharing not only the entire family's date-and-chocolate coloring that forgave all flaws, including Didier's slightly hooked nose and Mireille's untamable, frizzy hair and overlapping front teeth, but also an elegant stylishness. Didier wore sleek, navy wool slacks and a crisp, expensive dress shirt the same shade of mauve as his yarmulke. Mireille had on lime-green, quilted gauchos that Veronica could have sworn she'd seen on a mannequin in the window of a Kenzo boutique. Maybe she had: Mireille was a designer for Kenzo's *prêt-à-porter* division. With the gauchos, she wore a long-sleeved, butter-colored spandex T-shirt, and dangly, multicolored crystalline earrings shaped like bunches of grapes. The T-shirt hugged her abundant bosom and her belly, round as a basketball with her impending fourth child, like a leotard. Together, she and Didier looked ready for the Oscars, while Veronica, in her sensible black skirt, white blouse, nude nylons, low pumps, and the strand of pearls her parents had given her as a graduation gift, was dressed for an uneventful day at work. She may as well have had on her Reeboks and tube socks.

Didier whispered something in Mireille's ear. Mireille pumped her head up and down, her chin broadening into the shape of a half moon. She cleared her throat, cupping her hands over her mouth bullhorn-style and sang out, "*Mesdames, mesdamoiselles, messieurs. Votre attention s'il vous plaît.* This evening, in honor of our guest from America, we shall all speak English. *Hien?* No exceptions." She wagged a finger.

A hush fell over the small cluster of adjoining rooms. Didier's father, Jacques Benhamou, seated on the black leather sofa opposite the dining table, removed his bifocals and tipped them at Veronica like a hat, bowing his bald, yarmulked head. The children whispered among themselves. "*Cchhut,*" Mireille hissed, hushing them; after a few moments, the oldest, Didier's eight-year-old nephew Alain, replied, "Yes, *Maman.*" A girl a few years younger echoed, "Yes, *Tata* Mireille."

Mireille set down a salad bowl and waved Veronica over to her side with exaggerated urgency, as though trying to paddle a vagrant canoe with her hand. "So what do you eat during Chahnookah in America?" she asked, the raspy "ch" emerging straight from the back of her throat. "Not couscous, *non?*" Her accent was delightfully thick, much more so than

Didier's, yet the fact that she was speaking a foreign language, with all eyes riveted upon her, didn't seem to faze her in the least.

Veronica glanced at Didier, her face hot from the unwanted attention and the effort of suppressing the urge to curl up in a corner and sleep. "I don't know." She shrugged. "Potato latkes, maybe?"

Mireille clapped her hands, then squeezed Veronica's forearm. "Ah, yes, that is correct!" she declared, as if Veronica had just given the winning answer on a TV game show. "*Les gallettes de pommes de terre*. They are easy to do. We have some potatoes and eggs in the Frigidaire." She nodded at Didier and ordered him to make latkes, which he did.

Seven months later, he encountered a chillier atmosphere in Veronica's parents' house but rose graciously to the occasion, accommodating other people's quirks without a flinch. He'd met Rich and Shirley a few times before. The first time, over an autumn dinner at America, a restaurant the size of a warehouse in Manhattan's Chelsea district; the second time, in the spring, at a Yankees game Rich had insisted on taking him to with Veronica and Shirley so he could get a *real* taste of America. On both occasions, Rich and Shirley had treated Didier politely, eyeing his well-cut clothing and polished leather shoes only when his back was turned, speaking slowly and pausing often to ask him whether he understood. Shirley had offered her opinion on everything from America's outrageously overpriced menu ("Can you believe this? Twenty-five dollars for a plate of spaghetti marinara that I could probably whip together for next to nothing at home. Manhattan's so overrated.") to the length of Veronica's hair ("Don't you think she'd look smashing if she cut it up to her chin?"). Rich had provided detailed explanations of the differences between a ball and a strike, a slider and a curve ball, and the art and science of stealing a base. At the end of each evening, Shirley gave Didier a hug. Rich thudded him on the back and said, "Look us up when you move to this neck of the woods."

Visiting Rich and Shirley at their home in Tenafly, however, a year after Veronica's painting vacation, was a whole other ballgame, so to speak. Veronica and Didier had just agreed to get engaged. Didier had not proposed. Rather, that very evening, while riding the New Jersey Transit's Pascack line out to Rich and Shirley's place, he and Veronica had reached the conclusion that trans-Atlantic flights had lost their luster, that long periods apart had become a serious drain, and they wished they could spend more time together. A lot more time. "It's almost like we should be moving in together at this point," Veronica ventured, in a voice barely audible over the train's self-important, metallic groan. She was merely testing the water, dipping in her big toe to see if it was warm or cold. She didn't expect it to be scalding.

"Yes, we should," he agreed. "But first, we should get married."

"What?" She sucked in her breath, recoiling from the shock of the heat. "Are you serious?"

"I'm always serious." He sandwiched her hands between his. "You know that."

"Oh my God!" she cried. She flung her arms around his neck and squeezed him hard, fighting the urge to pound the murky, vinyl cushion of the train's seat with her fists and shout out at the passengers reading newspapers and poking text messages into their cell phones, "You want news? Here's news: I'm getting engaged to this gorgeous hunk of a doctor from France!" Instead, she dug her nails into the palms of her hands and dipped her toe back in the water, a little deeper. "When?"

"As soon as possible," he murmured, squeezing her back. "Don't you agree?"

She nodded furiously, fumbled for a Kleenex in her coat pocket, blew her nose, and said that she couldn't wait to tell her parents that night.

Rich and Shirley reacted with a silent exchange of looks followed by a barrage of thorny questions. Shirley bobbed her ruby head at Didier with authority and said, "So you're moving to the tristate area?" Rich ground his teeth as if trying to remove a crumb from the crevice of a molar, the tendons in his neck bulging like taut wire cables. Fixing his gaze on Veronica's left hand, he demanded, "Where's the ring?"

Veronica opened her mouth, but to her relief, Didier spoke first. "This decision, it is very new," he said, glancing from Rich to Shirley and unfolding his arms to his sides. "Veronica and I, we have not yet spoken about where we shall live or whether we shall buy a ring."

"What do you mean, *whether* you'll buy a ring?" Rich balked. His bushy eyebrows slid together into a stern line. "A man asks a girl to marry him, he gives her a ring." He shrugged, defeated in advance but satisfied that he'd stated his case, and shot Veronica a look that meant, "Right?"

"Dad!" Veronica piped in. "Get with the program! This isn't 1965! Didier didn't even *ask,* if you really want to know. We made a decision—a mutual decision. What does it matter about a ring?"

Rich raised his hands in surrender. "Forget I mentioned it."

"No, no," Didier intervened. "You are right." He dropped his head. "Traditions are important. In France, this tradition of a ring, it is quite different. For example, it is a man's parents who usually offer a ring to the fiancée at the time of the *fiançailles*—that is, the party to celebrate the engagement. Often, the ring belongs to the man's family and has been worn by somebody like his mother or his grandmother. My mother gave her ring to my older sister, Mireille, before she died, but I will very be happy to purchase a new ring for Veronica myself."

For the second time that day, Veronica flung her arms around Didier's neck and squeezed him hard. "You're amazing," she whispered, so moved by his reaction that it didn't even matter whether or not he followed through with his promise to buy her a ring. Of course, she'd love to wear a diamond and surely would. But more important, she was going to marry Didier, a prince of a man. Even the question of where they would live paled in comparison. For all she cared, they could move to Timbuktu.

Nobody's perfect, though, and all honeymoons inevitably end. At some point—was it the day she asked him not to mention her painting unless she raised it first? Or the day the twins were born?—Didier began lowering the curtain, in subtle, finite motions, on his inner complexities, the intricate bundle of sensitivities, needs, opinions, and principles that drive his outlook and moods. For instance, his obsessive, practically frantic commitment to work, which makes him tense and inaccessible most of the week as his mind darts from one unsolved problem to the next. And his frequent thirst for solitude and silence, space to ponder problems. He's excessively fastidious and expects the same of everybody else; as a result, just as his generosity is deeply rooted and flows sincerely, he's easily disappointed. His disappointment can turn to grouchiness, finickiness, and tacit rage.

Together, these attributes form a sort of maze that, over time, Veronica has learned to navigate. She knows now that when Didier eludes her gaze or answers "Mmmm," aloofly, to something she says, he's deep in thought, and she should leave him alone. She knows better than to call him at work if she has no urgent news, to leave the TV on after she or the kids have been lounging in front of it, to talk about the things she didn't get around to doing in a given day, or to leave the bed unmade after her nap. She refrains from interrupting Didier's heated debates in French with his sisters and brothers-in-law when they gather for lunch on Shabbat to ask, "What? What are you saying?" More often than not, they're arguing about politics: the French government's attempt to impose a thirty-five-hour work week, and the blatant anti-Semitic bias of the French press corps, whose coverage of incidents such as the bombing of a synagogue in Marseille and the discovery of handmade explosives at a Jewish school in Paris tends to cater to the underlying, potentially volatile frustrations of the four million or so Muslims living in France. Such incidents, Veronica has learned, easily set off by tensions flaring between Israel and the Palestinians or its neighbors in the Middle East, are exactly what Didier was referring to when he said, the day they first met, that France is not an ideal place to live. But Veronica also knows better now than to remind him that they could have avoided all that by moving to the States. As long as Didier is bringing home the bacon (or the kosher pastrami) and she is not, the case is closed.

Veronica once insinuated to her mother over the phone that daily life with Didier is not the breeze she imagined it would be. Shirley just laughed. "Welcome to the dance floor, hon!" she said. Marriage, according to Shirley, is like a never-ending waltz: you have to follow the beat, watch your step, and be careful not to tread on anybody's toes. "Mind you, that doesn't mean yours won't get trampled from time to time, but don't fuss about it," she advised. "Forgive and forget. Keep dancing. When you get it right, it can be a real ball." Even Stella, whose marriage to Ray—complete with two posh homes, a live-in nanny, and a personal masseuse—looks like a fairy tale come true, has divulged that she and Ray cross paths about twice a month and that they practically have to schedule time for sex. So Veronica feels reassured that in marriage, negotiating everything from moods and calendars to the need for space to ponder problems is nothing new.

In the end, it's worth it. The alternative would be to flounder, like Terry, in the no-man's-land between dating and celibacy, flip-flopping from the delirious illusion of having found the perfect partner at last to irate resolutions about permanently renouncing men. Some people may thrive in that sort of wilderness, but Veronica would come unhinged.

Chapter Ten

Insistent noon light bathes the deck outside the family room, bright as a summer solstice in New Jersey, though the sun has yet to peak on this late February day. Didier, just back from playing tennis with his sister Anne's husband, Gilles, climbs the deck's steps and tugs off his sweatshirt, tossing it onto one of the teak lounge chairs Veronica removed from the storage shed last week. His cheeks, slick with perspiration, radiate burgundy heat. His eyes brim with triumph: he won.

"Good game?" Veronica asks, her chest billowing with hope. For nearly two weeks she has kept her news about July locked up in her heart like a secret, patiently awaiting the right moment to tell him. She's used every trick in the book to improve his relentless foul mood, from preparing the Benhamou family's favorite roast chicken recipe with garlic and roast potatoes one evening to slipping into a lacy camisole the next night at bedtime and massaging his feet. The chicken elicited only a lugubrious scowl followed by complaints that it was undersalted and overcooked. The camisole sparked a short round of petting, but while halfheartedly fondling her breasts, Didier fell asleep.

"Not too bad." He sinks into the lounge chair's white canvas cushion and fixes his gaze on Luc and Céleste, busy shepherding toy animals through the Lego farm Veronica built with them this morning in the grass.

"The way things have been going lately, that's worth a celebration!" she chimes. On top of his foul mood, Didier caught Luc's fever last week. He sequestered himself on the pull-out sofa in the office for seventy-two hours, missing work and groaning that, with the backlog piling up in his absence, he'd be better off slipping into a coma than going back. Battling a fiery throat and a postnasal drip of her own, Veronica snapped into action at each of his cantankerous demands: "Can you get me more broth? With lots of lemon this time? And those Propolis drops, do we have any left? Ah, then you must go get some in town." If patience paid off in dollars, she'd have raked in millions by now.

Didier shrugs, reclines, and shuts his eyes. At least he's not scowling.

"Hey—speaking of celebration—" Her mind whirs with a thousand silly phrases she might begin with to transform his blank, unreadable expression into a receptive smile. But the sentence that's been simmering in her chest all this time beneath dutiful small talk about grocery lists, surgery schedules, and the kids is about to boil over. After weeks of playing nurse and single mom, she has the right, at least, to speak her mind. "My parents said they'll cover airfare for July," she blurts out, a moment too soon to rearrange her anxious expression into one that's sprightly and sunny-side up. "Isn't that great?"

Still reclining, eyes still shut, Didier doesn't flinch.

"Hello-o!" she says after a couple of seconds. "Anybody there?"

"*Tchk.*"

"Whoa. Interpreter, please. Does that mean 'No, nobody's there?' Or 'No, you don't think it's great that my parents will fly me and the kids to Jersey in July?'"

"You know exactly what it means." Didier opens his eyes, fiery with impatience to speak *his* mind now that this chance has come up.

Veronica approaches the lounge chair, balls a fist, and knocks it on his head. Sunny-side up, she reminds herself. Sunny-side up. "Yeah, I think it means nobody's there! You must have been bopped on the belfry by a tennis ball. I can see just the headlines: 'Brilliant Surgeon Wins Tennis Game but Loses Marbles.' Who in their right mind would scoff at free airfare?"

"Marbles?" Céleste pipes up, climbing the steps to the deck and bucking her toy horse against Veronica's leg. "Neighhh. Horsey wants some."

"*Lost* marbles," Veronica corrects her. She opens her hands, which tremble with shock and fury. "See? Nothing." She leers at Didier.

"It's true," Didier tells Céleste. "No marbles." Turning to Veronica, he adds, "Just dignity and common sense."

"Oh, please. What kind of common sense would make a person sneeze at an offer that's too good to refuse?"

"The kind that tells me we are adults and must solve our problems on our own."

"That's absurd! This isn't even a problem. My mother offered to fly the kids and me to Jersey in July. I accepted. End of story."

"Horsey's bored without marbles," Céleste whines, waving the brown plastic horse.

"We'll go hunting for marbles in the house in a minute,

princess. I'm sure we have some there." Veronica narrows her eyes at Didier as though to say, "Drop it. We have more important things to do."

Didier ignores her glare. "This story has no end. Your parents' gifts are like cocaine: each sniff makes you feel good for a while but is never enough."

"Oh, so now I'm a junkie! Thanks, Doc." Veronica tries to smile but manages only an ill-disguised sneer. She figured Didier might purse his lips at her news, blow an annoyed puff of air from his lips or, in the worst of cases, give her the cold shoulder by retreating to his office after dinner for a day or two. But take such a hard line? Maybe now wasn't a good time to tell him, after all. She paces to the deck's edge, down its three sturdy steps, and over to the tall, mossy stone wall enclosing the yard, breathing deeply to gain control of her tone. A calm, confident demeanor is the only leverage she has. "Seriously, how can you say that? How can you even think it? Without my parents' help, we wouldn't have this deck where you're enjoying soaking up the sun!" She waves at the deck's concrete base extending from the sliding glass door, topped with a mosaic of Italian tiles in various shades of sienna. She designed the mosaic herself, spending weeks sketching out a pattern of renaissance medallions and supervising the custom cutting of the tiles, to add a little pizzazz. It all cost a bundle, but, thanks to Rich and Shirley, she and Didier didn't pay a cent.

"You know that I thought your parents were too generous in paying for us to remodel the house," he says.

"Yeah, like we really had a choice."

"Of course we had a choice." Didier jerks forward and perches his forearms on his knees, tapping his left foot with agitation. "We could have done the remodeling little by little over time. We could have chosen to live in a place less expensive, like an apartment, or a place in perfect condition, like a newer house outside of Aix."

"In other words, we could have either sucked up living in a house that looked like a bunker, moved to the boondocks and gotten a couple of goats, or crammed ourselves into a two-bedroom apartment like Mireille. Now that's what I call a plan."

"That's called a compromise, Vero."

"Just look who's talking about compromise," Veronica snaps, blinking back a deluge of tears. What an asinine, insensitive thing for Didier to say. And she hates it when he abbreviates her name to Vero. It reminds her of the Spanish word for "true," but the way he pronounces it—"Ver-O"—it sounds more like a joke, an arrogant mockery of the truth and of her.

"I know you have made many compromises." His voice is steady and neutral, clinical. "That is why I accepted your parents' help with the renovations, and with furniture. But the renovations are done now. We are comfortable in our home. And so, we are done with gifts. Gifts are the fruit of other people's work. We must do our own work now to build our future."

"The future. Great. So, like, I'll be able to spend July in New Jersey in what—ten years? When we've practically paid off our mortgage, and the kids are hitting puberty?"

"It all depends on us. For example, many things about my work could evolve." His lips part briefly and then clamp shut again as if he'd been on the verge of some announcement that, on second thought, he decided not to make. "And you, your painting career has not even started. Perhaps staying here in July will give you more time to complete a painting for Stella—or even several paintings." He studies her hard, as if combing the pages of an open book in which no nuance, no cryptic meaning, escapes him.

Veronica's cheeks tingle. "Either that, or the thought of not going to Jersey this summer will throw me deeper into a rut."

"Part of an artist's job is knowing how to climb out of a rut," Didier replies. "*Non?*"

Céleste tugs at the leg of Veronica's overalls and wags her plastic horse. "Mommy, can we find the marbles now?" she begs. "Can we? Neigghhh! Neigghhh!"

Luc, snapping together and then detaching the same three Lego pieces beside the mock farm, announces, "Me, I'm wet."

Veronica glowers at Didier, silently commanding him to drop this, surrender, and move on. Squatting, she slips a finger inside the elastic band of Luc's elfin jeans. "You're wet all right, Duke. Soaking wet. We'd better change you."

"I'll do it," Didier says. He carries Luc inside.

While Didier diapers Luc upstairs, Veronica leads Céleste on a hunt for the bag of rubber superballs she intends to pass off as marbles. Real marbles are out of the question: God knows, Luc and Céleste would probably insert them directly into their mouths. She stomps over to the compact wooden toy chest in a corner of the living room, which she hand-painted last year with the same pattern of gold and olive hippos, lions, and giraffes that she created for the kids' curtains and walls. After amassing its contents on the floor, she makes her way to the paltry corridor that passes as a kitchen. "Comfortable in our home?" she hisses, banging her knee on a cabinet door. She might be if she were a skinny French woman who'd mastered the art of well-timed self-effacement and could fit into skinny jeans.

No superballs in the toy chest. None in the kitchen cabinet that Veronica has stocked with beat-up pots and pans and other makeshift toys for the kids' to entertain themselves with while she puts together meals. Céleste, delighted to rediscover the toy chest's contents, has forgotten her quest for marbles and bangs instead on a xylophone's rainbow of metallic keys. Veronica, however, pursues the search with a vengeance, flinging open drawers, crouching to inspect the dust-ball-infested underside of the hutch by the dining table, determined—driven—to accomplish this one small feat and fulfill her promise to her daughter.

Marching toward the stairwell, she barges past Didier, Luc in his arms.

"Shall we have a quick lunch and meet Gilles and Anne at Les Calenques?" he asks, confident enough that he'll prevail in their dispute to put it aside. "Gilles invited us to take a walk with them. Maybe Mireille's family will come, too. It is a beautiful day for walking by the sea."

"No thanks," she snaps.

"*Allez.*" He grips her arm. "You should not get so upset over a simple change of plans. November is a fine time to travel. Perhaps by next year, you will be able to go in the summer again."

"What change of plans? I'm not changing my plans. I just don't want to have to fight with you about them."

Luc wriggles from Didier's arms and steps toward the mound of toys in the living room, a veritable kingdom waiting to be conquered, fortified by his sister's vigilant guard.

"This is not a fight, Vero. It's a discussion. About things that are important—for us, and for you."

Veronica regards her husband. He hasn't showered yet.

Locks of dark hair cling to his forehead, and his stubble resembles a layer of embedded dirt. Even disheveled and perspiring, he's infuriatingly handsome. And that look in his eyes—that gleam of lucidity subdued by a modest, downward tilt of the head—it turns Veronica's heart into a lump of putty.

"Oh, one of those," she says, toughing up the lump. "An Important Talk. Capital *I*. Capital *T*. The last time we had an Important Talk you convinced me to schlep the kids to a Kol Nidre service at the synagogue. I had to banish myself with them to the women's section upstairs so you could pray, or meditate, or basically replenish your soul with the men while I read them stories and fed them clandestine gummy bears to keep them quiet. Well, to hell with Important Talks. What's the point? If we disagree, we disagree. I'm done giving in. You want to take a walk at Les Calenques, go for it. I'll stay here with the kids."

Usually, Veronica looks forward to the Benhamou family's fair-weather ritual of taking a lengthy, Sunday stroll atop the inlets in the cliffs along the coast between Marseille and Cassis. Yellow-studded gorse and fragrant, wintergreen thyme bushes edge a network of hiking paths, their surface knobby from the roots of Aleppo pines and Mediterranean oaks drilling past copper-colored gravel into dust. Oak branches twist into peculiar, sinewy filaments resembling lengths of petrified rope, or, as Veronica often imagines, the invincible muscles of God's arms. Leaving the men to crack their usual litany of bad jokes while pushing jogging strollers and carrying tired children up ahead, she joins Mireille and Anne at the rear of the pack, where they chat about the kids, the weather, or the supposed provenance of a boat on the horizon. At first she found these conversations frustrating, always skimming the surface without evolving into the kind of gritty girl-talk she might have had with Stella about how to look and feel sexy when your breasts are leaking milk, or with Terry, on the pros and cons of online dating services or whether holding down a corporate job is tantamount to selling your soul. The few times she ventured to ask Anne how she manages to concentrate on her demanding job as a software engineer without her thoughts wandering to her house and her children, Anne ran her fingers through her long veil of midnight hair and answered, "*Bof*"—the verbal equivalent of a shrug. When she quizzed Mireille on the hassles of raising four boys in a small apartment, Mireille replied, "We are lucky for what we have." Over time, though, Veronica found herself craving the simple yet reliable connection these exchanges fostered, the effortless bond of human contact immersed in wild nature, free of judgment and pretensions. Gritty girl-talk could be saved up for the monthly gatherings of the Anglo-American Group of Provence's mom-and-kids playgroup, where Veronica has befriended a handful of young expats like herself from the United States, Canada, Great Britain, and Australia, or for phone calls with Stella and Terry. And while both Stella and Terry can prattle on about the soft underbelly of relationships and the ins and outs of every imaginable choice, neither of them is likely to devote an entire, lazy Sunday afternoon to family or friends.

"Stay if you want," Didier shrugs. He clearly knows she's cutting off her nose to spite her face. "But I will take the kids. The fresh air will be good for them."

Her stomach tightens. If she's going to skip the Calenques, she may as well roost with the kids at home. She likes spending downtime with them. The minute-to-minute concerns they raise now that infancy's behind them—a punctured juice box to replace before it dribbles or a palliative Band-Aid to apply to a black-and-blue mark— keep her mind busy without bogging it down. They spare her from agonizing over more daunting problems, such as the bouquet of poppies disintegrating in the studio or what, if anything, to paint instead.

"Don't bother." She glances at Luc, a few feet away. He has infiltrated the kingdom of toys on the living room floor, despite his sister's guard. In a rare moment of détente, the two sit back-to-back, Céleste still banging a xylophone, Luc rolling the fat, rubber tracks of a Tonka bulldozer against his palm. "It doesn't look to me like these guys are in the mood for the Calenques today, either."

Didier purses his lips. "Luc and Céleste are two years old. Their moods change more quickly than the wind. You, on the other hand …" He walks into the kitchen and begins removing Tupperware containers of leftover *dafina* from the fridge: sulfurous hard-boiled eggs and chunks of beef floating in congealed stew. "You are very predictable. You will help them play Legos for a little while longer and then watch TV with them for the rest of the afternoon."

"Well, if that's what they want to do, we will!" she snaps, wondering why the hell she should have to defend herself for volunteering to stay with the kids.

"So tell me," he says. His voice has an icy edge, so acute that it seems to have been produced by a stranger—the type Veronica would not want to bump into in an alley, dark or light. "Is that what *you* want to do?"

"It's Sunday. Why not?"

"And what about on Monday? And Tuesday? And all the rest of the week, when the children are not with you?"

Heat rips across her face like a slap. Of all the times for

Didier to raise this. On top of feeling as helpless as a dog tethered to a leash, she now has to take a beating for having disappointed Didier—and herself.

"I'm sorry, Vero. I do not mean to sound so … vicious. It is just that, this rut you are in, it seems to me to be very long. I do not find you—*comment-dire?*—very, well, enthusiastic about your art. So I wonder: do you want to continue? And if not, what, exactly, do you want to do?"

The microwave emits a long, shrill beep. A whiff of cumin and paprika mingles with the house's embedded, powdery scent of diapers and Johnson's baby shampoo. Numbness creeps through Veronica's body like morning fog. She backs into the armchair by her side, sinks into its overstuffed cushions. Can't Didier see that she's wounded and in no state whatsoever to talk about her art? Why should she have to time potentially thorny conversations with surgical precision if he doesn't do the same? She has the right to remain silent and to ignore his expectant gaze. She has the right to shut her eyes, to let her thoughts wander off to the slopes of the Sainte Victoire, to the glorious day years ago when his grave expression while banging ocher earth from his shoes brightened at her outburst of laughter. This moment, like so many others in a marriage, will pass. It must. They will have lunch. The children's chatter, their clamor, will drown out the echoes of this conversation which, eventually, will drift away like a letter in a bottle lost at sea.

Chapter Eleven

Veronica sits at the dining table, which Didier cleared and sponged with a halfhearted swipe before leaving for the Calenques with Luc and Céleste. She'd remained silent through the meal, picking at her food, avoiding eye contact lest their conversation resume. She didn't budge when he packed a diaper bag with the snacks and wipes and various other accoutrements the kids would need during the walk. When he asked her one last time to join them, she pursed her lips and sucked her tongue away from her teeth, reveling in the satisfaction of having just the right answer pop into her mind: "*Tchk.*"

She hasn't seen Didier look so sullen and disarmed since the day she tried to cancel their wedding in July of 1999, with just two weeks to go. At the time, having spent countless sleepless nights reviewing the amplitude of the changes she faced once the initial excitement of quitting her job, shopping for a gown, and taking trips to Aix to pick out the world's most decadent parve chocolate cake had fizzled, she called Didier from New Jersey one morning at three. "This isn't for me," she sobbed. "I'm a Jersey girl, not one of those Euro-chic types who spent a semester in Paris smoking cigarettes in cafés and going weeks without washing my hair. I never even knew that people in Morocco spoke French until I met you. Now I'm supposed to get my hands and feet tattooed with henna at some Moroccan bash before the wedding wearing a bead-spangled caftan and a hat the size and shape of a soufflé? A gazillion women are going to ululate at the top of their lungs and carry me around on cushions like some Arabian princess being offered up as a sacrifice to the gods! After which I'm supposed to uproot completely and spend the rest of my life overseas! What was I thinking? I can't!"

"Vero, *mon amour*," he started, his voice gruff and sexy the way it is when he first wakes up.

"Stop," she pleaded. "You've talked me into enough already." When she'd begged him during their engagement to move to the States and get married there, he'd explained with flawless logic exactly why that made no sense: he couldn't relocate his medical practice, but Veronica could easily transport her art. What better place to paint than Provence? And his guest list for the wedding was twice the size of hers. How would they organize a delegation of two hundred guests from Casablanca, Paris, and Marseille in New Jersey? He'd even convinced her that news stories about the impending Y2K bug threatening to destroy travel routes, break down communication lines and leave her stranded, alone, incommunicado, in France after the move, were nothing but hype. But as the date approached, she found her lungs clamping shut every time she took a breath. She couldn't eat. She couldn't sleep. She spent nights pacing through her parents' house in a T-shirt and underpants, fanning away the blazing flashes of heat that rose from her gut like lava. How could she have shrugged off four thousand miles? Her children would grow up in a foreign country and speak a foreign language. Raised in a kosher household, they might never have a birthday party at McDonald's or know the pleasure of chomping into a salty-greasy morsel of popcorn shrimp. "I just can't go through with it," she murmured. "The wedding is off."

After a very long silence punctuated only by the muted pounding of two hearts, Didier said, "Stay right where you are. I will catch the next flight to Newark."

Eighteen hours later a taxi pulled up in Rich and Shirley's driveway. Shirley, who had woken at four to the sound of Veronica weeping in the kitchen, bolted to the door. Garments rustled. A bag thunked to the ground.

Oh my God, Veronica thought, her chest constricting when she glimpsed Didier. His cheeks were sallow and sunken, lost in not one, but several days of mournful stubble. His shoulders slumped and his espresso-colored hair, sucked dry by hours of travel in a pressurized airline cabin, clung limply, flatly, to his head. His eyes, red-brimmed and as sunken as his cheeks, lolled in their sockets like two glass buoys cut loose from their ship, bobbing hopelessly at sea.

With visible effort, he reined them in, lifted them to focus on Veronica. Never before had she beheld such a wounded, defenseless expression—not even on the face of a stray dog begging for a scrap of food or a pat on the head. Where was her strong, hardheaded Didier? Seeing this stranger, this inadequate substitute, made her heart gape with unbearable longing for the man she knew and loved.

"I'm so sorry," she breathed, lunging toward him, throwing her arms around his neck. The faint, stale-lime scent of his Eau Sauvage aftershave surrendered to the residual smell of an airplane cabin, economy class. "Will you hold this against me for the rest of our lives?"

She rises now and paces to the kitchen. How could her silent brooding today at lunchtime and her refusal to join him at Les Calenques—childish, she knows, but harmless—have made him look as stricken, as abandoned and transformed by despair, as he did that day, she wonders. If anything, it is she who got hurt. Not so much by his reaction to her parents' offer: though it is a hard pill to swallow, she can understand. Instead, what made her skull burn with rage even as she tried to put their argument behind her was his thoughtless slap of a question: "*What, exactly, do you want to do?*"

In the kitchen, she pours herself a cup of bitter, black coffee left over from breakfast and forces herself to swallow it cold. What she *wants* to do has become practically irrelevant now that she's a mom. From the instant Luc and Céleste were born, their piercing voices cut directly to a tender spot in her heart that she never knew existed before, commanding her total, undivided attention. Ever since then, their needs have shaped her desires. What she wants—what she feels compelled to do—is to make sure their bellies are full so that they're satisfied and complacent, a delight to rock or read stories to, play games with, tickle and tease. She wants to bathe them at the end of the day so their silky skin smells healthy, fresh, and clean. She wants to take them to the doctor when they're sick and to make sure they go to bed on time at night, before they become overtired and finicky, setting her on edge. When they ask questions, she wants to answer so they won't repeat themselves a thousand times, and when they point out something new they have discovered—a neighbor's cat, a ladybug crawling across the kitchen floor— she wants to look so they don't feel ignored. And while they're at Maria's house on weekdays, she wants, above all, to fold laundry, tidy closets, label drawers, plan meals, and catch up on some rest so that when they return, order and serenity will reign.

So where do art and a career fit in? Perhaps her attempts to get back to painting have failed so because, quite simply, they do not. Of course, she *would like* to paint. She *would like* to succeed. But just as she's not one of those Euro-chic types who can sit at cafés smoking and go weeks without a shampoo, she doesn't feel comfortable juggling too many things. Back in art school, Terry used to nag her to get involved in activities outside of class: write for the school paper, join the rowing team, or help start a club. Each time, Veronica would whine, "Quit stressing me out!" That's why Didier's advice after the wedding, "Take theengs one at a time," struck just the right chord. Today the kids are that one thing she's able to focus on, whether she planned on it or not. They hijack her mind and take precedence over all the rest, including painting—a project as huge yet superfluous right now as starting a club. In fact, now is probably a better time to have another baby than to try to paint. Immersed in the sea of rearing young children, diving in a little deeper would make more sense than treading water in an exhausting, futile attempt to keep at least one limb above the surface at all times.

Apparently Didier can't see this. His sisters, the ultimate working mothers, make juggling a career and family look like a piece of cake, a mere scheduling issue void of emotional conflicts such as the longing to stay close to your children or to cocoon at home. France's generous child-care system reinforces this, as does the ease with which nannies or grandparents will watch kids for entire weeks, or more, so couples can go away on extended business trips or second honeymoons. As a result, Didier believes in the illusion that from nine to five—or six, or seven—a woman can forget that she's a mom.

A second cup of coffee accelerates Veronica's pulse, fuels her wrath. Back in the States, who would dare ask a young mother *what, exactly, she wants to do?* Certainly not the husbands of the women she has seen sipping caramel lattes at Starbucks in Manhattan at ten in the morning while their infants doze in detachable car seats beside them, or those strolling their toddlers through New Jersey malls in the middle of the afternoon toting bags stuffed with merchandise from Saks. Certainly not the husbands of the moms Veronica has spotted in her parents' neighborhood, either, waiting for the school bus with their kids. While living with her parents after college, she drove past those bus stops each weekday morning on her way to work. From afar, the gatherings there always looked like some sort of impromptu party. Swarms of women wearing sweatshirts and jeans, thermoses of coffee in hand, stood chatting about where they bought their daughters' Power Puff backpacks or pink-and-white polka-dotted tights. Several times, running late, Veronica drove past the same street corners after the bus had collected the kids, only to find the moms still there, still chatting, still sipping coffee, smiling, laughing, happy, and carefree. Their hard-earned hour of liberty had arrived. Soon they would pick their way home to surf the Web, send off a few unrushed e-mails about a PTA meeting or school fundraiser, walk the dog, read a chapter of their book club's latest novel, or go to the gym. Later, they'd run a few errands, picking up a frozen pizza for dinner along the way, and then stop by the school to volunteer in the library for an hour. Veronica knows this because once, driving through the neighborhood on her way to work, she spotted an acquaintance from high school in the crowd. She pulled her hand-me-down sedan up beside the line of spanking new minivans, rolled down the window, and joined the conversation, basking in the fantasy that her own days began with easy chitchat and a long stretch of liberty ahead.

These young mothers have no qualms whatsoever about how they spend their days. Rather than incriminating them by asking *what they want to do*, their husbands probably thank them, at least silently, for handling all the minutiae of socks and soccer and schedules crucial to their children's lives that they personally have no time or desire to get involved with. They probably get a huge ego boost from running off to important commitments while their wives hold down the fort at home, and from financially supporting the whole brood. And they're surely grateful for the scraps of reheated frozen pizza waiting for them when they get home, ravenous, from work. Never mind whether the meal is kosher or the kids are using forks.

Even Stella, the big-shot corporate lawyer, resigned from her firm when her third son was born. It's the normal course of things. And Stella still has a nanny helping her, giving her loads of free time to do nothing more enterprising than take spinning classes with her trainer and shop.

A sharp glint of sunlight cuts through the kitchen window. Oddly, for this time of day, Veronica's body hasn't yet downshifted in anticipation of a nap. In fact, smoldering with outrage and jittery from caffeine, she feels more like weeding the yard, reseeding its bald spots, and digging up the lavender bushes growing in an unpropitious spot of shade, hauling them to the other side of the house, and replanting them, than crawling into bed.

She starts with the weeding. By late afternoon, her cheeks are sunburned and angry, red blisters splay her hands. Sacks of weeds and compost obstruct the front gate, and not a scrap of moss remains on the ancient stone well in the middle of the yard. But it isn't enough. The scraping, the digging, the shoveling, the heaving, and hoeing have done nothing to purge Didier's question from her system or to free her of the fury and the raw, reverberating pain. At least there's a manicured lawn to show for her toil, a neatly tilled bed of daffodil bulbs along the stone wall to admire, and plenty of dirt caked beneath her fingernails to prove that she's been busy and productive, awake, all afternoon.

Chapter Twelve

"Sleep deprivation's wretched," says Trish Guillot, host of the Anglo-American playgroup's March gathering. Her words, crisp with an Outback accent, lilt and then snap to attention, salute. "Have you tried Valerian? What about *passiflore*? It's a bit stronger."

Veronica manages a meek smile of appreciation. She's tried everything from Lexomil, the miraculous French sedative that got her through her wedding, to tapes of New Age music, but she has not been able to drift off to sleep after lunch since her frenzy last Sunday to dig up the yard. For some people a nap may be as frivolous and easy to skip as dessert, but the loss of those two precious, afternoon hours of slumber has made the crown of her head burn and the junction of her retina and her eyelids sting. Groggy and grouchy, she briefly considered opting out of today's gathering and sending Luc and Céleste to Maria's as usual. But she wouldn't miss a session of the Anglo-American playgroup for the world.

"Could you bring the kids into bed with you?" asks Abigail Letourneur from Concord, Massachusetts, seated yoga-style on the floor. "They'll settle down faster that way after waking, and you'll all get a better night's sleep." Her three-year-old, Camille, the youngest in a trio of girls, emerges from the bedroom where the children are watching a DVD and crawls into her lap. Stroking Camille's home-cut, straw-blonde bangs, she whispers, "Right?"

Veronica blushes, lowering her head to inspect the strange assortment of brown and burgundy tiles on Trish's floor, as mismatched yet oddly harmonious as the women gathered here today: Trish, a former classical dancer from Australia; Abigail, a yoga and organic food buff with a deconstructive literature degree; and Lorena Rannou, who left home at seventeen to scratch out a living waiting tables and dancing topless in Atlanta. Veronica announced earlier that she was short on sleep because her kids had woken her dozens of times each night this past week. Mentioning her nap didn't seem like the right thing to do. Some of the playgroup moms nap from time to time, especially those with infants and toddlers, but others have jobs and can't, or simply don't. The night-waking story was a harmless fib, the sort of little white lie you sometimes need to fabricate to express yourself without offending anybody.

Lorena—dark-haired, plump, and buxom, eerily sedate— slips her pinky between her bare nipple and the pink lips, delicate as rose petals, of her newborn dozing at her breast. "My whole gang sleeps with me every night," she says with a shrug. She met her husband, Pascal, while living in Atlanta. When Pascal left his position there as flight attendant for Air France to work at the ticketing counter in Marseille, she went with him, pregnant with their oldest son. At twenty-five she's the youngest member of the group, but, with four children under the age of six, she's the most experienced in matters of early motherhood.

"So that leaves Pascal ... where?" asks Abigail, a devious glint illuminating her pale blue eyes.

"Where husbands belong," says Lorena. "On the couch."

Abigail beams. Trish howls with laughter. Veronica snorts. This is exactly why she loves the playgroup gatherings. They're a rare chance to sit around and shoot the breeze with the girls once a month and giggle at the sort of jokes that just don't translate into French.

Trish springs on the balls of her toes into the kitchen—a windowless nook off the family room capped with a stucco stove hood stained by a century's worth of grease. "More coffee, anyone?" she asks, shaking her head of copper hair as if trying to shake away the image of her lanky husband, Jean-Luc, sprawled out on the couch in the middle of the night. She met him while apprenticing with a ballet outside London, where he worked at the time for a French software firm. Soon after that she broke her knee, ending her dancing career. "How about some biscuits? Veronica, you're sleep-deprived. You need protein. Would you like an egg?"

Veronica smiles, touched by Trish's maternal hovering and by the other women's supportive nods. She would've liked to steer the conversation back to husbands. Does Lorena really kick Pascal out of bed each night so the kids can sleep beside her? If so, does he mind? Have they gone for countless weeks, as Veronica and Didier have, without making love? But the conversation has already meandered to the topic of Trish's home, an awkward agglomeration of conjoined apartments rambling through sections of a townhouse circa 1650 in the hilltop village of Eguilles. It's much easier—and safer—to weigh in on how Trish can purge the ancient odor of moisture and mildew, of sautéed onions and stewed beef, embedded in her house's warped stone walls than to ask whether anybody else longs to have their beds to themselves from time to time rather than face, night after night, a six-inch space between two bodies that feels like a thousand miles. Asking such a question would only invite other inquiries in return, and Veronica might find herself letting all the facts pooled in her heart like water pent up behind a dam come gushing out, though they're nobody's business but her own. Then, when Didier's outlook improves, and the momentary chasm between them closes, her embarrassing troubles will live on needlessly in the playgroup moms' minds.

Trish, done ferrying out a plate of biscuits and one hard-boiled egg, squats beside Lorena to stroke her baby's silky head. "Will you go back to work when your maternity leave's up?" she asks.

Like Abigail and a handful of others not here today, Lorena teaches English part-time for a private company offering language training to adults. "At the latest," she says, tucking her braless breast into her husband's hand-me-down Oxford shirt. A wet circle forms where the fabric touches her nipple. "We need every Euro we can get."

"I've been begging Lorena to get back as soon as she can," says Abigail, the assistant director of the school. After dropping out of a graduate program in her twenties, Abigail headed with a knapsack for Paris, where she took a job teaching English at Berlitz. She was young. She was bored. She loved French. So she came. In Paris she met Philippe Letourneur, the comptroller of a European technology firm enrolled in her advanced conversation class. "It didn't take us long to cut past the conversation," she likes to say, her expression frozen in neutral despite the glint in her eyes. Six years later, Philippe accepted a transfer to Aix. Abigail hated to leave Paris, but the move would boost Philippe's salary and career. And in Aix the family could have a house with a yard, a pool. What could she say? She's helped manage the school where she now teaches ever since.

"We're short about four teachers," Lorena explains, lifting her baby, half-asleep, to her shoulder and patting his soft bump of a back. "One just moved to Italy. Another, an archaeologist, got called off to a dig right after I started my leave."

Abigail's square, mannish jaw twitches as she locks gazes first with Veronica, then with Trish. "We'll take anyone with working papers at this point, American accent or not."

Trish's face turns bright red. "Don't look at me! I'm staying right here at home." Still squatting, she hugs her knees and rocks front to back, her eyes dewy. "Not that I don't think it would be nice to have a job, mind you. And we sure could use the cash. I just don't know if I've got the constitution for it. I mean, it's hard enough having both Grégoire and Stéphanie off in school now, all grown up and out of sight. But Gabrielle's still so little. I like having her near. They're only little for so long."

"That's why I keep having more," says Lorena.

"That's why Philippe got a vasectomy," Abigail replies.

Lorena shrugs. "He's not the only fish in the sea."

"You're horrible!" Trish proclaims, bounding to her feet. "Absolutely horrible." She throws up her arms in mock dismay. "And to think an entire population of French men and women are learning their English from *you*!" Glancing at Veronica's half-eaten egg and the array of empty coffee cups on the floor, she sighs. "Teaching could be fun, I suppose. I might consider it later on, when my children are all a bit older. But not English—I'd rather teach ballet. That is, if I can get my bod back into shape."

Veronica straightens in her rickety, flea-market chair, struck by the accuracy of something Trish just said. "Later sounds good," she pipes up, giving a strong, Shirley Berg-style thrust of the chin. "I mean, what's the rush if things are fine the way they are? Juggling's not for everyone. And one day, the kids *will* be big."

Trish returns Veronica's chin thrust. "Not that I wouldn't love to be an artist, either, mind you. Work from home, make your own hours. It doesn't get much better than that!"

"Oh, it's not all it's cracked up to be," Veronica sputters, waving dismissively and willing her cheeks not to turn bright pink. "Believe me."

"Hmmm. Sounds to me like you could definitely use a little teaching gig on the side," Abigail persists.

Despite this comment's weighty implications, Veronica is seized with an inexplicable urge to laugh. Abigail has that distinct, earthy-crunchy "Cambridge, Massachusetts" look that Veronica remembers well from her college days living in Boston: gray smattering her fuzzy brown hair, stringy holes gaping at the knees of her faded jeans, Birkenstock clogs. Cut from clashing molds, she and Veronica—whom Abigail once described as a "New Jersey mall cruiser"—would never have exchanged a word back in the States. But differences vanish when you've followed your husband to a life in Provence, a world away from home. Abigail's dry spark of hilarity leaves Veronica weak with giddiness, just as Lorena's cool, compassionate demeanor, her ability to nurse a newborn and dole out snacks to her older children while conversing with adults, fills her with sanguine, New Year's-style resolutions to have more patience, more endurance, herself. And whenever Trish's mint-green eyes cloud over with abstract concern, as they often do, Veronica longs to throw her arms around her neck and give her a compassionate squeeze.

"Thanks anyway," she says, her urge to laugh swallowed up by an urge to cry. Just as she'd never dare ask whether anybody else longs to have their beds to themselves from time to time, she'd never dare let on just how touchy, how painful, any question related to *What She Wants to Do* is right now. Or spill the beans about the fact that stuffing herself into a pair of coveralls or cracking open an easel seems no less daunting these days than getting all gussied up in business clothes and rushing off to lead a week-long seminar on the present perfect tense. Taking the lid off such personal cans of worms only makes you look and feel like a fool.

Exhaustion descends upon her all of a sudden like fog. Limbs and eyelids heavy, she glances at her watch and murmurs, "Wow, time flies. I'd better get going or the kids'll fall asleep in the car."

"You can put them down here if you'd like," Trish offers. "I've got a couple of toddler's mattresses we can set up on a bedroom floor."

"Maybe next time, when I'm feeling a hundred percent." It's what she usually says. These intense gatherings tire her out, so she likes to keep them short and sweet. "Today I'm too zonked to deal with a change of routine."

Strange, she thinks, maneuvering her car through Eguilles' steep, alley-thin streets, how from a distance the village looks like a fairy-tale kingdom glowing enchanted shades of gold and fuschia in the sun. But within the invisible line of its long-gone, Gallo-Roman ramparts, deep potholes mire its pavement. Its houses and storefronts, gray as a chain smoker's teeth, seem to cling together on the verge of crumbling, threatening to come crashing down in a thundering, apocalyptic collapse. Yet its exterior, immortalized on postcards of Provence, betrays nothing of this ugliness. Nothing of the chaotic tangle of telephone and electric wires strung between its rooftops, of the sagging clothing lines dangling from its cracked windows, or the contingency of bedraggled, toothless elders with swollen ankles sitting on its stoops waiting for a passing neighbor with whom to exchange a few words or for the mistral to die down.

At home, she wrestles Luc and Céleste out of the car and lets them eat granola bars for lunch. Why not? Today's a special day, a stay-home day. And in the spirit of simplicity, she lies down beside them in her bed at nap time. Day or night, it's true that they settle down faster that way. She observes their translucent eyelids drooping shut, their bodies mollifying, and their clenched fists unfolding. White stripes of light pour through the slits in the shutters, elucidating the soft curve of their miniature shoulders, the pudgy creases in the folds of their elbows, the gentle rise and fall of their chests. Trish was right: it's nice having them near. Their warm, powdery scent and the downy sensation of their flesh against hers when she lifts them, carries them, dresses them, even when she changes them, is as sensual as a lover's caress. Yet, free of the immense spectrum of insecurities and fears that inevitably taint adult cuddling, it fulfills her more profoundly. Before she knows it, though, their arms and legs, still mere twigs, will burgeon into capable, muscled limbs. They'll become too busy, too independent, and too restless to snuggle and will squirm away, embarrassed, when kissed. How cold—how empty— that will feel.

Of course, Mother Nature has provided the perfect remedy, which Lorena clearly understands: having more. And no matter how glad Veronica is to have moved past sleepless nights, round-the-clock nursing, colicky crying, or the suctioning of mucus from a congested infant's nose, what people say is true: it all flies by so quickly. Knowing this, she could easily do it again. What a scrumptious treat it would be to sense the intimate tickling of a creature squirming once again in her womb, to await news of its gender, and then retrieve a few choice items from Luc and Céleste's old layettes while planning for new furniture, a stencil for a new nursery, a big change. She and Didier would chatter every evening about where to set the nursery up, when to schedule the ultrasounds so he could be there, and whether to book a C-section in advance as she did last time, wary of the risks of giving birth to twins, or to try to do things more naturally, as he would have preferred. Just thinking about it fills her with a longing as sweet yet insistent as a craving for chocolate.

Shutting her eyes, she lets the twins' rhythmic breathing lull her to the edge of slumber. Between moving to France, going through pregnancy, recovering from it, and contending with a double dose of infants and toddlers, it's been a rough couple of years, but maybe the hardest part has passed now, she thinks. Caught up in her futile attempts to paint and reliant on the luxury of a nanny, she's missed so much of their lives. Since they're the only thing she's able to focus on these days, perhaps she should. A year from September, they'll start school. In the meantime, she should stop sending them to Maria's every day, giving the family's budget a break. And she should explain to Didier, plain and simple, that this is *What She Wants to Do*, at least for now. Life will become more even and predictable—no more disruptive surprises—and will feel almost *normal* again, like the nice, neat piece of some divine scheme that it used to feel like all the time.

But the very notion of how life could be, how it should be—and what it is not—rams into her brain like a car slamming into a telephone pole. Disruptive surprises lurk everywhere, no matter how carefully you plan. For the umpteenth afternoon in a row, the electric buzz of nerves usurps her drowsiness. She tries to sleep, but the buzz just rises to a deafening crescendo. Her heart jolts, cutting her breath. She rises, makes her way downstairs, and flicks on the TV to empty her mind.

Now here's a can of worms she would gladly have dug into with the playgroup moms, she thinks, flipping to the news. Not her own can of worms, not Trish's, Lorena's, or Abigail's, but France's! She turns up the volume. According to TF1's Washington correspondent, there's some sort of a protest going on in the U.S. Congress over France's opposition to military action in Iraq. And it's playing itself out over what sounds like … French fries! In a culinary rebuke of France, the House of Representatives has removed the word "French" from the items "French fries" and "French toast" on its cafeteria menus. And they've replaced it with "Freedom."

"Freedom fries!" Veronica laughs. "I'll toast to that!" She would have loved to hear the playgroup moms' reaction to this sidesplitting tidbit of news, which, from an expatriate's perspective, seems less about Iraq than it does about giving the French a taste of their own medicine. She's spent many hours with Abigail, Trish, and Lorena lambasting the French habit of letting blunt or negative thoughts spew right out, point blank. Didier's ruthlessly candid reaction to her summer plans was a perfect example. So was Guylaine LeMaître's response to Didier and Veronica's impromptu wedding invitation four years back. During one of Veronica's trips here to finalize arrangements, she and Didier bumped into Guylaine at a café on the Cours Mirabeau. "We're getting married next month!" Veronica bubbled, squeezing Didier's arm. "You should come!"

"*Ah, ben, non*!" Guylaine huffed. "*Ça me dit rien du tout*!" Meaning, roughly, "No way. Not interested at all."

"Well, that was rude," Veronica said to Didier after Guylaine had gone her separate way.

Didier flicked a wrist, shrugged. "It is understandable. She has her reasons," he said.

Such brutal honesty has since become a fact of life. When Veronica struggles for her words in the *boulangerie* down the street or fumbles to count out her Euro coins, the baker scowls, taps his foot. It took three tries to find a pediatrician who doesn't huff indignantly when Veronica asks for explanations with prescriptions. At the local pool club, Le Set Club, her arrival is inevitably greeted by an overt, head-to-toe once-over by every topless sun goddess on the premises. That's why she just stopped going and prefers instead to hang out at her parents' pool club in New Jersey when she's there. But growing accustomed to bluntness and finding ways around it doesn't mean you have to accept it. God bless Freedom fries! It's about time someone took a stand.

Chapter Thirteen

Didier leads the way down the Cours Mirabeau toward Mireille's apartment, where the Benhamou clan will gather shortly for Shabbat lunch. On this cheery March morning, Aix bustles like a carnival with shoppers and tourists vying for space beside market stalls laden with hand-sculpted wooden cicadas, loaves of artisanal spice bread, and sachets of dried lavender, three Euros apiece. Luc and Céleste doze in their double stroller, oblivious to the gruff banter of vendors barking out prices and chanting numbers while counting out change. Didier, at the stroller's helm, elbows through the line stretching from the door of Béchard's—the Tiffany's of pastry shops—where Veronica's mouth waters at the scent of passion-fruit mousse cakes topped with white chocolate shavings and marzipan pear tarts in a caramelized sugar veneer.

She should venture into central Aix more often, she thinks, pausing to admire a tablecloth patterned with saffron sunflowers on a backdrop of olive green. The branches of plane trees rise above the streets like fireworks frozen in midair, releasing a festive profusion of fuzz balls that loop and swirl in slow motion on their way to the ground. The tantalizing display of eggshell linen suits and Hermès bags in store windows, the rows of sidewalk cafés packed with students and tourists, and the proliferation of ageless stone fountains burbling water fresh from the source make her limbs tingle with the same mysterious sense of anticipation and promise that drove her, years ago, to sign up for a painting vacation in Provence. Even the banners tacked to balconies today protesting *Pas de Guerre en Iraq* and *Non à l'Agression Américaine* are eclipsed by the beauty, the merriment.

Since the twins' birth she's shied away from the heart of Aix, leery of maneuvering their double stroller around tight corners and over cobblestones. And during the hours they spend at Maria's, her anxiety about painting—or not—and what to do instead, has made her stomach lurch with guilt at the thought of treating herself to a leisurely stroll. But her new vision of how she'll spend the next few years, which emerged after the playgroup meeting this past week, is exempt from such guilt. She's thought it over carefully and can't wait to tell Didier that, rather than canvas and coveralls, she sees herself donning coloring books, crayons, and … maternity wear. That she's already planned out the finger-painting projects she'll entertain the kids with in the studio, which she'll convert into a multipurpose art room, and the clay pots she'll teach them to throw. It won't further her career or her earning potential, but it will enrich the family in other ways. Then, in the spirit of Freedom fries, she'll give herself permission to join the playgroup moms for a quick coffee at Le Grillon from time to time, to window-shop, and otherwise enjoy this thriving, clay-and-tangerine hued town.

Didier cocks his head to the left, signaling that it's time to cross the Cours Mirabeau and duck through the Passage

Agard—a narrow thread of a street covered like a Florentine bridge. He's less tense than he's been in ages, perhaps because spring has settled in, hoisting temperatures into the seventies most days and coaxing roses, periwinkle, gorse, and Spanish broom into full, abundant bloom. Or maybe because Veronica hasn't chided him about his recent habit of coming home after ten each night: all things considered, it's only fair to give him space to do his job. Nor has she resumed their argument about July. As he'll understand in just a moment, there's no need.

"Hey," she burbles, pulse racing, as they start across the Place de Verdun, home to France's second-largest court of appeal. Given Didier's placid expression—forehead smooth, face alight at the scent of garlic and tomatoes wafting from a restaurant nearby—now seems like a very good time. "I've been thinking."

Didier raises an eyebrow. "Well. That is big news."

"No fair! At least hear me out." She fakes a pout, elbows him in the gut.

He continues walking, his eyes darting over the open-air antiques market that brings the sleepy square at the foot of the court to life on Saturday mornings. "Yes, of course." His tone borders on sarcastic, as it has for quite some time—a sign that he's still angry.

Veronica takes a few giant steps to keep pace and lifts her chest. This conversation should help clear the air. "I've figured out what's at the root of my painting rut."

"*Ah, bon!*" Sarcasm gone, he pauses before a stall displaying random 1970s memorabilia: bubble-shaped, orange lighting fixtures and drinking glasses embossed with overlapping brown and powder-blue spheres reminiscent of the Jetsons. His brows slide up a few notches as he catches

Veronica's glance in a round, frameless mirror. "What?"

"Motherhood!"

Didier's brows jump even higher.

"No, no, no. Don't get me wrong." She sticks out a hand, flaps it back and forth. "I don't mean that motherhood's a problem. It's painting that's the problem now that I'm a mom!"

His jaw tightens. He pulls his expression into neutral, professional. Blank.

"Trying to focus on anything other than Luc and Céleste is a total disaster. That's why my painting's going nowhere."

"But Vero." The tension in his jaw spreads to the rest of his face. "For about eight hours each weekday Luc and Céleste are not with you."

"I know, I know. But it makes no difference. It's even worse when they're not around. Then my mind starts wandering off to all the things I need to do to keep their lives and ours running smoothly. You know, the kitchen, the laundry, things we're running low on in the medicine chest, clothes they've outgrown. I can't just let those things slide. They have to get done. And the days go by so quickly. Knowing that it's never really long till they come home, I just can't seem to switch gears and concentrate on something as demanding as painting, something that takes me so far away."

His features wilt from neutral to glum, darkened by the same look of abandonment he wore the afternoon a few weeks back when Veronica opted out of a walk at Les Calenques. Perhaps she was too straightforward, too dry and abrupt, she thinks. Her confession caught him off guard. A dose of silliness would have helped him take it in. She sucks down her lips to keep from smiling as the perfect remedy of a phrase spills out: "Think of it this way: the day the kids were born, I … I … had a gigantic brain fart!"

He gapes at her in disbelief. "A *brain fart?*"

"So to speak." Veronica giggles.

"A brain fart," he echoes. "And this is funny?"

She rolls her eyes. "Loosen up! You make it sound like we're talking about some sort of disease!"

"Yes, Vero. That is exactly how I feel. Like this is … pathological."

"You are *so* overreacting!" she snaps. "Maybe 'brain fart' was the wrong way to put it. But geez, cut me some slack! Do you think this is easy? What I mean is, when the kids were born, my maternal instinct kicked in and took over the rest of my brain. It's natural. It happens to tons of moms. Not every single one, I know, but …" She pauses, searching for a tactful way to imply that Didier's superhuman sisters are exceptions to the rule. "But most. They think they wanna do all these amazing things: produce movies, trade commodities, help the homeless, end global warming. But when it comes right down to it, their kids are born, and they suddenly realize that deep down inside, the only thing that really matters, the only thing they really want to focus on, is them. And by association, their family and home. Just look at Stella: the big-shot corporate lawyer turned stay-at-home mom. It's taken a while for this to sink in, but as it turns out, I'm hardwired to be a stay-at-home mom, too."

Didier stares past the Jetsons memorabilia to some indiscernible spot beyond the square. The creases in his forehead deepen, his lips press into a thin, impermeable line.

"Look," she continues, before he can speak. She curls her fingers around the stroller's handle, rocks it. "It's been a really tough few years for me. You know that. Moving to France.

Having twins. Maria has been a godsend. With my mom so far away, I have no clue how else I would have survived. The thing is, though, I'm feeling more settled now. And more on top of things with the kids. So there's no need for them to be at Maria's all week anymore. Maybe a couple of mornings—you know, like a preschool schedule in the States. Then I can get some chores done and take a little ... break. But as long as I'm hardwired to focus on the kids, I should go for it. A hundred percent. Right?"

He nods at the spot in the distance. "So you are not hardwired to paint."

A short gust of wind blows in from the east, lifting Veronica's hair from her shoulders, spreading it out like a fan. She shivers and hunches over the stroller to tuck the twins' cotton blankets around their shoulders and under their chins. "Of course I am!" she clucks, standing back up. "But right now, the kids are little, and my maternal instinct's on high. They won't be little forever. I can always paint later."

"When, exactly, is later?"

Céleste stirs in her reclined seat. Veronica rocks the stroller a bit faster while jiggling it side to side: her special "shake-em-and-bake-em" stroke that never fails to put them to sleep or add a few minutes onto a snooze.

"Exactly?" she repeats, trying not to sound irked. "With little kids, who can ever say 'exactly?' I'll just have to take things one day at a time. So much could happen. A year from September, they'll start school. Maybe that'll be a good time. Maybe not." There's a lot she could add to this, but it wouldn't be productive right now to bombard Didier with all the details. The school schedule in France makes it hard to find the kind of long blocks of time painting would require. And just like in the States, school comes with all sorts of opportunities to get involved. On top of this, the chocolaty craving for another baby that seized her after the last playgroup gathering has deepened into a void akin to hunger, as if she'd opened the cupboard late at night for that one square of chocolate that would take the edge off, only to find that there was none left. She can feel it even now, cold and nagging, in the pit of her womb. With this mind-set, she might find herself pregnant again before she knows it. While she's eventually bound to figure out how to fit all these pieces together into a picture that includes time for painting, she can't say when.

Didier's nostrils flare. He glances askew at the merchant overseeing the Jetsons stand, a portly, sixty-something man with ruddy, wine-stained cheeks clad in a rumpled, gray suit, no tie. Grabbing hold of the stroller's helm with one hand and Veronica's elbow with the other, he advances a few yards, pushing the whole family out of the merchant's earshot. After a stealthy survey of the square for familiar faces to avoid, he lowers his head and says, "Vero, it is difficult to be a painter, I know. Any meaningful career is a challenge, but artists, creators, they work alone in a void, with no colleagues, no structure, few parameters." His words stream out like a filament of smoke, vaporous and muted yet pervasive. "The structure and parameters, they must come from within. It can be frightening and discouraging, I know, but surmounting the fear, finding the confidence to do what you believe in, this is perhaps the most important part of the work. Just like taking a step out into the world when you have spent so much time alone at home. You must overcome your fear, Vero. The sooner the better. The more time passes, the harder it will be. Do not hide behind the kids."

"Hello-o! Earth to Didier!" Her hands fall to her sides

and thud against the heavy black denim of her skirt. "Did you hear a thing I said? This isn't about colleagues or parameters or fear or confidence or even about art. It's about motherhood! Being a mom!"

"*Chhuut!*" Didier hisses, shushing her. "Do not make a scene." The tendons in his neck strain. Fury blazes in his eyes. "Having strong parental instincts is normal. It is a fact of life. I have them, too. But now you are telling me that perhaps you do not have strong *painting* instincts."

Sucking in her breath, she turns away and absorbs the spectacle of a pair of Italian tourists at a nearby stand haggling for a couple of more Euros off the price of a tarnished silverware collection. Their arms flail in spirited gesticulation while the antiques dealer puffs up her cheeks and folds her arms over her chest: final offer, take it or leave it. Céleste stirs in her seat again, and Veronica knows that in a few minutes at most, this conversation will have to alternate with snacks and diaper changes and toddler babble, or end. And she hasn't even made her point. So much is riding on it.

"Look," she says, as calmly as she can. "My painting instinct is on hold for right now. That's all. It's on hold so I can focus on our kids. It'll come back when the time is right. No big deal."

"Such instincts never stay on hold for very long. This, I know." He pauses, stares at her hard as though trying to zap over some secret message via telepathy. When he resumes, his voice splinters with impatience. "Your painting instinct, it has been on hold for so much time that I wonder if it was ever really there."

She stares at him, tears singeing her eyes, prickling her nose.

"Artists—creators, *si tu veux*—they feel a driving need to

do their work. Just like anybody with a passion or a sense of commitment to something outside of themselves. They fight the doubt, the fear, the obstacles, and find a way. So of course it is normal for me to wonder how passionate, how dedicated or committed, you have ever really been. You have had many chances to paint, starting long before Luc and Céleste were born. And yet you have not found a way."

"What if you're right?" she blurts out, too upset to try to refute him. How thoughtless of him to let his blasted French honesty rip when she's only trying to work with him to make their family happier. "What if, just what if, I'm actually not a painter at heart, but a mom? What if everything I've done over the past decade, including art school, coming to Aix on vacation, and meeting you have all been leading up to the discovery that *What I Want to Do*—what I *really* want to do—is raise my kids? Would there be anything wrong with that? Would it be such a crime for me to just want to take care of my children? Our children? *Your* children?"

Didier purses his lips and rubs his chin. He glances at Céleste, whose eyes have popped open. Round with awe, they soak in the busy market scene. "In principle, no," he replies, stroking Céleste's head. "But you are forgetting one thing."

She has a hunch about what he's thinking: something he has every right to question, and she has no real right to defend. "I know," she sighs, relieved. She's been saving this concession as a last resort but will gladly make it to help keep the peace at home. "Maria. We can stop sending the kids altogether if you want. Not even a few hours a week. I mean, if I'm gonna go for it and focus on the kids, I should go all the way. Not one, but two hundred percent. Right, doc?" A wave of tenderness rocks her. Didier may be demanding and fastidious, but it's always in the name of doing things well. It's a fine example to follow. From now on, she'll try.

"*Comment?*" Didier screeches, to her astonishment. He jerks his head side to side as if dodging flies. "I am not speaking about Maria! I am speaking about *me!*" He pounds his chest.

"I … you … you've lost me there." she whispers, her mind blank.

"Five years ago," Didier snaps, "I met and fell in love with a passionate artist." He narrows his eyes, stabs his gaze right into her soul. "Remember? She knew what she wanted and was determined to get it. Her energy, her enthusiasm, her drive, and her belief that if you just persist, even the craziest dreams can come true, they were contagious. I began to dream, too. I dreamed about a partnership with my wife. I dreamed about us working together to make a life where we could *both* pursue our creative ideas. In this dream, my wife, she wanted to do her best to contribute financially, through her art or through other initiatives she wanted to take. And I, perhaps, could have slowed down a bit at work eventually. I could have found some time for my family, which I am very sorry to have no time for now, and for my research. Remember? This research, I thought you knew how important it was to me. So can you imagine how it feels to do everything I can to offer *you* the option of pursuing *your* creative vision only to hear that, well, as it turns out, you are not interested in it anymore? Or to realize that personally, I have no options left except to continue working seventy hours a week so that you may have the opportunity to grow lazy and dependent and lose your mind to brain farts and potties and juice?"

Sunlight bounces off the sweet, cotton-candy pink walls

of a court annex to the left, slaps Veronica's back, bangs her head. A couple of shoppers turn to stare at what has now escalated into an official, full-fledged scene. From the stroller, Céleste yelps, "Papa, Papa!" She waves her arms, demanding liberation. Luc sobs mutedly, his eyes squeezed shut, as though struggling through the thick of some private, inner torment. Forget dreams: this is a nightmare. Of course she remembers all the fantasies she and Didier once brewed up. How could she forget? She was going to sell paintings to her parents' and Stella's rich friends for gobs of cash. She and Didier would build a cushy nest egg. They'd lead a life straddling two continents, filled with travel between Aix, Boca Raton, and New York. They'd expand their house. They'd invest in Didier's research. He wanted to design some sort of disposable, plastic scope for opening patients' throats during surgery, more hygienic and cost-effective than the reusable metal devices on the market now. Sooner or later, they'd sell it for a hefty profit, too.

But that was ages ago! Everybody fantasizes when they're young and in love. They conjure up far-fetched scenarios about taking two years off to sail around the world, about buying a town house in Greenwich Village or growing all their produce in a sustainable, organic garden in Vermont. Eventually, though, reality sets in. For ninety-nine percent of the human population, reality means wiping butts and paying bills. You don't have to let go of dreams, but you do have to keep them in perspective. The nerve of Didier to take all the romantic ideals they once entertained so seriously when in fact, they'd simply been tossing these ideals around like coins into a fountain. The nerve of him to hold Veronica to them, right down to the tiniest detail, like some sort of doctrine or law. But then again, "serious" is Didier's middle name. Veronica should have seen this coming all along.

"Well, we've both hit up against a whole slew of unpleasant surprises, then, haven't we?" she lashes out, practically spitting as if to rid her mouth of her words' bitter taste. This conversation has become so severely derailed it no longer matters what she says or how, and she's too hurt to care. "Five years ago, when you fell head over heels for a passionate artist, I fell head over heels for a promising young physician who said his priority would always be to support a family. Remember? Huh? Oh, and by the way, where I come from, physicians are well paid."

"Papa!" Céleste screams, shaking the stroller.

"I suppose that is why you Americans say—what is it? 'For richer or for poorer? For better or for worse?'" Didier sneers. "That is the vow, *non?*"

"But you and I didn't say that vow, did we?" She lunges for the stroller and unstraps Céleste. "No, we said it in French, just like you wanted. When the rabbi asked if we'd take each other for husband and wife, we just said "*Oui.*" Whatever that means."

In silence, Didier leans down to unstrap Luc, also now fully awake. His back is rigid, his eyes are glassy, tinged with resentment and disgust.

He's not the only one who's disgusted, Veronica fumes silently, swinging Céleste onto her hip so that with her free hand, she can feel around inside the diaper bag for the ziplock bag of crackers she's packed. His monologue about the passionate artist he fell in love with implied that he doesn't love her anymore. That he doesn't know her anymore. That he never did.

Anger and disgust aside, however, she must now collaborate with him to change Luc's diaper and find Céleste a public rest room so she can practice wriggling out of the pull-up she's already wet and then pretend to go pee. They'll have to act like everything is normal as they make their way through the antiques market, as they push the stroller past the Église de la Madeleine, where Cézanne was baptized, and head toward Mireille's street, the rue Epinaux. They'll have to coat their expressions with a sheath of sunlight as brilliant as the one enveloping this glorious day, lacquer their demeanor mint green and periwinkle blue like the shutters overhead, and add a touch of embellishment as lush and natural as the potted geraniums spilling from windows, the ivy crawling over doors. Can such beauty possibly be skin deep?

Briefly, she considers turning around and heading back to the house. But she'd be better off getting lost in the crowd at Mireille's than wallowing in self-pity alone at home. Besides, a good *dafina* and a few rounds of jokes with Gilles and Uriel might help Didier cool down. Together, the three are like a troop of wannabe stand-up comics competing to deliver the best punch line to a litany of well-worn jokes about Jewish guys named Moishe, Samuel, and David. The names alone, with their absurd pronunciations—"MOY-shuh," "Sam-yoo-EL," "Dah-VEED"—provoke raucous howls and sniggers. If a little dose of family and laughter can bring lightheartedness, it can bring reconciliation, too. When couples are at odds, family tends to bring them back together by roping them in. Then Didier will loosen up and realize how harsh he's been, how out of line. He and Veronica will return home with their elbows linked, and she will tell him her own punch line, the crucial point she wanted to make this afternoon: that with the money they'd save by reducing or eliminating the twins' hours with Maria, they could afford to send Veronica, Luc, and Céleste to New Jersey in July every year.

146

Chapter Fourteen

"*Ehh, la belle-doche Américaine!*" hoots Mireille's husband, Uriel Sarfati. He wipes his hands on his apron and leans over the kitchen counter to kiss Veronica on each cheek. The apartment smells of food: chick peas, beef, and rice stewing in a broth thick with curry and cumin, steamed string beans, and the acrid paste that forms when red wine vinegar and Dijon mustard are mixed.

"Yeah, that's me," Veronica mutters, a twin in each arm. The American sister-in-law. Despite Uriel's sunny welcome, she's unable to muster a smile.

"*Ooh là.* Something is not right." Uriel contemplates the three of them and then tweaks Luc's ear while Céleste squirms out of Veronica's arms and scampers off to join her consortium of cousins bouncing on the master bed down the hall. Didier lingers in the lobby four flights down, folding up the stroller. "Tell me. What is the problem?" To Luc, he adds, "*Allez*, you can tell *tonton* Uriel."

Veronica shakes her head, sucks back tears. It would feel so good to spill her guts to Uriel, unloading her sorrow and frustration. But that would be like telling the playgroup moms that she sometimes longs to have her bed to herself and hasn't painted in years.

"Ah!" he exclaims, giving a quick wave as if to dismiss her grief. "I know, I know." He thuds her shoulder. "You must need to do some vinaigrette. You have arrived at just the right moment. Come." He ushers her to the counter to cheer her up with his old routine of teaching her how to make the French national salad dressing. At every gathering, Didier's family offers unsolicited but enthusiastic cooking lessons, urging her to try her hand at local staples like ratatouille or roast chicken with garlic and potatoes, or Moroccan specialties such as *dafina* and stuffed sardines. Usually she humors them, observing their demonstrations the way a child accepts a peck on the cheek from an elderly grandmother with prickly facial hairs and leathery skin. Today she's grateful for the distraction.

"*Tiens,*" Uriel says. The frames of his thick glasses, round as the top of his balding head, magnify his mischievous regard and make him look more like a mad scientist than a pharmacist who studies the Torah by night. He pours her a glass of wine. "Medicine. Drink, drink." He clinks his glass against hers. "*L'chaim.*"

"*L'chaim,*" she repeats, taking a sip. Luc, perched on her hip, twirls a lock of her hair around his finger the way he does with his blanket at bedtime.

"Now." Uriel extricates Luc's fingers from Veronica's hair and takes him. "This is the difficult part. We have the mustard-vinegar paste, yes? You must add olive oil bit by bit and keep mixing, not too hard, so that it incorporates perfectly, no bubbles, just smooth, like the paste. *Hien? Vas-y.* You try."

Glad for this task to focus on, she begins trickling olive

oil from a bottle into the small, metallic bowl.

"*Et voilà! Bravo!*" Uriel exclaims. "See? You can teach something to Americans after all!" He elbows her in the ribs.

Didier, huddled now with Anne's husband, Gilles, by the living room window and engrossed in a hushed but animated conversation, purses his lips.

"*Alors?*" Gilles says a bit too pertly when he spots her. Six feet tall and thin as a praying mantis, he springs from the corner to kiss her cheeks. "How's our favorite saint?"

The children have started gathering at the table beside a tall goblet filled with wine and a challah displayed like a memento in a shrine upon an elaborate silver plate. As the adults take their seats, Veronica tosses an awkward glance from Gilles to Didier. If this is one of Gilles' jokes, she doesn't get it.

Jacques Benhamou, the family's seventy-five-year-old patriarch, places his forefinger on his lips. Silence spreads through the room. Rising, he chants the Hebrew blessings over the wine and challah in a dissonant, Sephardic aria evoking visions of belly dancers chiming finger cymbals, of mullahs kneeling on mosque floors. For a moment all else is forgotten, lost to this ancient ritual and its insinuations of unity and peace. But soon the children grow impatient. They begin to whisper and giggle, to elbow each other and jiggle their outstretched hands, slapping each other, pushing, pinching, as Jacques Benhamou tears off fluffy chunks of challah and dips each in a shallow dish of salt before tossing it across the table to whomever catches it first. Human nature always returns as soon as prayers subside.

"Saint Veronica," Gilles continues when conversation resumes. His bristly eyebrows waver mockingly. "She was very, very special. Do you know?"

Shaking her head, from the corner of her eye she catches Didier's face, darkening with rage as if she'd just disappointed him all over again because she doesn't know the history of obscure Catholic saints.

"She was a woman from Jerusalem who walked behind Christ while he carried his cross. She offered him her veil to wipe the dirt and sweat from his brow, and when he did, the image of his face appeared on it like a perfect reproduction, or painting, of his face. The face, some say, of God."

Veronica searches for something clever to say, something smart and sassy about an artist's power to reveal what's true and sublime. But she's embarrassed now by her own private vision of God's milky face, broad as the sky, and his benevolent, sapphire blue eyes—a vision as intimate yet potentially false as believing that life comes with a guarantee of serenity and fulfillment. And the fear that Gilles, always joking, always dropping complex innuendos between the lines, is somehow making fun of her, paralyzes her mind. Didier must have told him about their conflict or complained about her, as spouses tend to, grossly exaggerating her flaws. The word must have spread through the apartment in quiet snippets while she cooked pasta for Luc and Céleste, who don't like *dafina*, and learned to make vinaigrette. What do they see when they look at her now, passing on a first course of baba ghanoush that she wouldn't be able to swallow if she tried? What have they seen all along? The quirky, comical *belle-doche Américaine*, imperfect but loved, an awkward yet accepted member of the clan? Or an oddball, a pathetic misfit, a fool?

"Say, *belle-doche*," Uriel chimes in, changing the subject. "What is all this noise we hear about Iraq? Bush, he is not really serious about a war, no?"

Luc climbs out of his seat at the living room coffee table,

set for the younger children, and onto Veronica's lap. She hugs him, shrouding herself in his body's blanket of warmth. The French consider politics a neutral topic, more polite and respectful than gab about ambitions, money, or jobs. But with the entire country wrapped in banners flashing anti-American slogans, this particular political debate seems more like a minefield right now.

"Who knows." She shrugs.

"I know," Gilles declares as Mireille ladles a portion of *daf* into his bowl. "Bush is very serious indeed. He will invade Iraq, and it will be one big disaster of a mess."

Despite herself, Veronica stiffens and asks, "Why do you say that?"

"Just look! There are no clear reasons for an invasion, and the whole world, it is opposed! Except the British, of course. The Iraqis, most of them, they are innocent and cannot defend themselves against American missiles and M-14s. And who else will suffer? Who?" He sweeps his hand in a circle indicating everybody at the table: the adults, Mireille's thirteen-year-old son, Alain, and her eleven-year-old daughter, Sylvie. "*We* will!"

"We?" Veronica echoes, cutting meat from the *daf* to add to Céleste's bowl of pasta, her regard fixed on the gouge her knife opens in each sinewy morsel of overcooked flesh. Céleste, standing beside her, twirls her arms like the blades of a windmill, impatient to return to her spot at the kids' table where the youngest of her gaggle of cousins are eating with remarkable poise and restraint.

Anne, seated to Veronica's left, places a hand on her wrist. "We Jews. The Jews of France."

Veronica shakes her head, puzzled.

"The situation, it is very complicated," Anne says. "Iraq

is an Arab country. A Muslim country. No? And France, it has something like four million Muslims, mostly Arabs. The Arab Muslims here, they are very angry and frustrated. They are not accepted by the French, they do not get good jobs, they have not enough money, they live in the bad *banlieues* and the *HLM*s. When something happens to their brothers anywhere in the world—for example, when Israel uses force to defend against the Intifada—their anger and frustration are triggered. We Jews, we are their easiest target. We have come to France from many of the same countries as they have, but we have integrated here. We get good educations. We have risen to the top in many fields, like cinema and fashion. We have nice apartments and take nice vacations. And we have a conflict with them that is many thousands of years old. So they use us to let their anger out by bombing our synagogues, destroying our cars, spraying graffiti onto the walls of our schools. Last year they put fire in the hair of a Jewish teacher in Paris! If the U.S. enters Iraq, this anger, it will intensify. The attacks will multiply and will become very ugly, very violent."

"And of course," Uriel intervenes, "it is all made harder in a way by America's friendship with Israel, which the Arabs deplore."

"*Oui, c'est vrai,*" agrees Anne, switching to French to point out that this raises another issue: whether an attack on Iraq might, in fact, be a U.S. ploy to protect and fortify Israel, as some believe. Mireille jumps in, contending that the French press has spread this rumor to vilify both Israel and America, and Jacques Benhamou declares that the debate is multifaceted, with no single right answer. Soon the entire Benhamou clan, including Didier, is deliberating its myriad angles.

Veronica, awash with relief at having drifted to the outskirts of this conversation, swallows some *daf* and feeds a few pieces of cold pasta to Luc, still seated on her lap. Facts and opinions fly across the table like ping-pong balls. Of the substance, she retains little; she's struck mainly by the debate's feverish pitch, its urgency, which seems futile, given that all the arguments in the world add up to nothing that the lofty politicians determining the fate of nations will ever hear. With so little power and so many more immediate, mundane problems to solve, what difference does it make that Anne feels the Palestinians deserve a fair chance at sovereignty, that personally, Gilles would nuke them, or that, consequences aside, Veronica intends to stand faithfully behind the Bush administration's Iraq policy out of sheer nostalgia for home, even though she voted for Gore?

In fact, the only point worth stating right now is that clearly, everybody—everybody—would be much better off living in the States. But right now, she wouldn't dare say so. Instead, she continues feeding Luc, glad for the excuse to hide her watery eyes by looking down.

While Mireille collects dirty plates from the table and serves the rhubarb purée, the conversation shifts back to the French press and whether its bias against Israel should be construed as anti-Semitic or simply as a government-sponsored strategy for keeping the restless Muslim population calm. By now, though, wine glasses are empty and bellies are full. Voices have grown sluggish, tones have subdued, and one by one, Anne, Gilles, Uriel, Didier, and Jacques Benhamou rise from the table to ferry a token dish or two to the kitchen. The older kids retreat to Alain's room, where they'll read or play board games. The younger kids resume bouncing on the master bed down the hall. Uriel clears the coffee table and then sets down a large, silver platter bearing an assortment of marzipan pastries, along with seven hand-painted glasses and a heavy Berber kettle of mint tea. After easing Jacques Benhamou into an armchair, he joins Gilles and Didier by the open window at the far end of the living room. Anne and Mireille sink into the sofa behind the dining table; Veronica remains seated at the table with Luc, back turned, head low, as the conversation drifts from coverage of the Middle East to coverage of the French national soccer team, on a winning streak again.

For a while she tunes out, allowing her eyes to droop to half mast and words to blur. Anne and Mireille speak in a near whisper while the men talk more boisterously, belting out an occasional, "*Sérieux?*" or "*Tu déconnes!*" Even tuned out, though, Veronica catches these phrases, carried closer by the breeze lapping in through the window, as effortlessly as she'd catch any phrase in English. With a sudden flare of pride, she realizes that she can't recall when French started sounding so familiar, so crystal clear. In fact, paying deliberate attention, she can understand both conversations at once—a skill she thought she'd never master. She can hear Mireille telling Anne about the sparse, wiry hairs sprouting under her daughter Sylvie's arms and on her pubis, Uriel muttering that Aix's rabbi has grown severely hard of hearing and Didier agreeing.

"So is that why you haven't shown up at morning minyan for at least two years?" Uriel teases.

A rush of fight-or-flight adrenaline floods Veronica's veins. For as long as she and Didier have lived together, he has risen at five forty-five each weekday morning to make it to the minyan prayer group by six thirty. Fully alert now, she holds her breath to catch each muted word. Didier lowers his voice. He fumbles for excuses and attempts to change the subject. Finally, buckling under the pressure of Uriel's relentless prodding, he confesses that he's had something more important to do.

"Ah, yes. Like taking breakfast with a blonde?" Uriel chuckles.

A spasm rips through Veronica's neck. Her face burns, and the pervasive scent of hot, wet mint makes her want to vomit. She clutches Luc's shoulders like a guard rail to refrain from leaping up and pouncing on Didier.

"That morning—" Didier whispers. "When you passed by Le Grillon, I was meeting with a lawyer."

"A beautiful lawyer!"

"A patent lawyer."

"Not a divorce lawyer?"

"*Tchk.*"

"Ah. So then, a patent lawyer. Of course. They are very smart, patent lawyers." Veronica can practically hear Uriel wink. He's probably also elbowing Didier in the ribs.

Didier sighs. "There is a blueprint I would like to patent," he whispers. "A medical blueprint. *Voilà.* But it is too soon to talk about it."

"*Génial*! So you are Louis Pasteur! Why not? It is a good story. Very good." With a hollow thwack, Uriel clops Didier on the shoulder. "So, Louis, have you heard the one about how women are different than pearls?"

Mint tears stream down Veronica's cheeks. Mint snot drips from her nose. She stands, kicks back her chair, lowers Luc to the floor and turns around to face the cluster of men slouched into the window's threshold. A shaft of sunlight cascades over them, elucidating their smirks as they shift to astonished, oafish gapes. French words spilling from her lips as easily as they penetrated her consciousness, she snarls, "We know that one, Uriel. You've told it already. A thousand times."

Minutes later, practically jogging across the Place de Verdun, she hears Didier calling her name. Of this morning's antiques market, only a few banged-up vans loaded with worthless relics of another era remain. Vendors and drivers clang rear doors shut, shout instructions, and an occasional swear. The courthouse's alabaster exterior has transmuted to silver in the afternoon sunlight. Veronica hurries past it, ignoring Didier until he catches up with her and grabs her arm.

"Vero," he pleads.

"Leave me alone. *Fous-moi la paix!* Understand?" She wrestles her arm free, done with sunny-side-up deliveries. Done bending over backward to coax him into a better mood.

"It is you who must understand. Please listen."

"Don't waste your breath." She keeps walking, her skirt slapping her calves, perspiration gathering at her hairline and between her shoulder blades.

"I should have told you about this before, I know. Forgive me. It's just that, well, I did not feel we could speak about it together. It is about medicine and technology and work."

"Work. Yeah. I guess I'm just not up to speed. But your cute blonde lawyer sure is."

"My lawyer, she is only doing her job."

"Her job hasn't made a dent in our budget. Are you paying her in kind?"

"I have not paid her yet. It is too soon." He reaches for her arm again, but she jerks it away and accelerates, ducking through the Passage Agard and turning onto the Cours Mirabeau. "Listen, I know it was wrong for me to say nothing about this. You have always supported my ideas to develop a product. But our day-to-day priorities have become so different. It is like we live on different planets. I felt that even if I told you about this, you wouldn't quite grasp what it meant, or what it meant *to me*, so it was not something we could truly share. At least not now."

Before the moss-carpeted fountain where, years ago, Didier held her hand in a cascading rivulet and explained that Aix sits atop ancient thermal springs, Veronica stops. Its water still flows in shimmering, twisted ribbons, exactly as it did that day, exactly as it always has and always will, with no illusions of change. She contemplates Didier. He looks contrite and repentant, yet still as bitter as he did this morning. There are a million different things she could say. She could insist that he flesh out all the sketchy facts he's just divulged. She could cross-examine him, scrutinizing each tidbit of data for cracks and contradictions, proof of dishonesty. She could threaten him until he fesses up point blank, or just skip the facts altogether and berate him, insult him, humiliate him for having misled her, an unforgivable betrayal under any circumstances. But how can she? She tips back her head, rolls her eyes to the sapphire sky, now tinged with the bronze sheen of late afternoon. She's guilty in her own way. And when you omit information, tweak details, and edit the picture of how you spend your days, you're only really lying to yourself.

Chapter Fifteen

Garlands of blinking holiday lights left over from Christmas perk up the gray skeletons of New Jersey's oak and maple trees in March, adding a dapper flare to evenings when the sun sets at five. Shiny new vehicles with seating for eight stream down highways, their sleek, metallic silhouettes effacing endless miles of cracked asphalt. Yards, hard and brown as frozen hamburger patties, boast big, bright houses covered in vinyl siding, mustard yellow and ketchup red. Indoors, thick, store-scented carpeting, home theaters, giant, quilted throw pillows and impressive toy koala bears make it easy to nest at home all day. Puffy, fluffy, cushy, and inviting, they erase all evidence that outside, it's damn cold.

While her plane circled over Newark last Sunday before landing, Veronica braced herself for only mud, sleet, and an inevitable case of cabin fever. She prepared Luc and Céleste with descriptions of hailstorms and half-melted snowbanks too wet and dirty to play on, and the itchy coats they'd have to wear if they dared venture outside. She warned them that there'd be no swinging on swing sets or eating lunch at a picnic table in the yard as they'd been doing at Maria's. That no roses would blossom, no almond leaves would rustle in the wind. She forgot, though, that in New Jersey, the television gets about two hundred channels, there's space in Rich and Shirley's enormous, freshly renovated basement for running races, playing basketball, and bouncing on a minitrampoline and that all over the house lie colorful, life-sized toys that count, burp, recite the alphabet, and sing.

She also forgot about the mall. Aside from its vast collection of shops—a veritable Disneyland of merchandise to peruse and dream of owning—the mall hosts at least three separate indoor playgrounds, each equipped with monkey bars, jungle gyms, tunnels, slides, and bucking horse rides in every vivid color of the rainbow. Luc and Céleste can't get enough of it. Since arriving nine days ago, Veronica has spent each morning there with Shirley and the kids, letting the dynamic duo, as Shirley calls them, choose which play area to start at, which one to finish at, and which ice cream, cookie, or pretzel vendor to snack at in between. With Shirley supervising them, Veronica has cruised the shops, staving off the potential monotony of the mall routine by checking out the throngs of women flaunting dyed lashes and stiffly sprayed hair.

Acres of parking lots filled with wide, available spaces flank the mall, and beyond them, a universe of pancake houses, pizza parlors, sporting goods superstores, Blockbuster Videos, Wal-Marts, and Targets unfolds along roads and local highways. Veronica forgot about those, too, before coming, and about the endless possibilities they offer for entertainment and diversion. Each day so far, the kids have come home with something new to play with. They've devoured Happy Meals for lunch. It's no use trying to keep kosher while staying in someone else's home. After collapsing beside Veronica on Rich and Shirley's California king-sized bed at nap time, they've spent afternoons watching *Diego, Dora the Explorer,* and *The Land Before Time.* Satiation and bewilderment have made them delightfully complacent. The relative ease of caring for them in these conditions, along with the simple pleasures of state-of-the-art central heating, take-out Chinese food, and the option of a long shower in the morning while Shirley hangs out with the kids have made this awkward, unforeseen decampment to New Jersey seem more like a honeymoon. And it helps keep Veronica's mind from wandering to what she's left behind.

On her last day in Aix, after hearing Didier out in the middle of the Cours Mirabeau, she returned to the house alone. Didier went back to Mireille's to collect the kids and the stroller. Veronica told him not to bother rushing home. While he was gone, she called Air France. For a small fortune, she booked three one-way tickets to Newark for the following morning using the credit card number her mother had given her a few weeks before.

It took her no time to empty drawers into a suitcase and load a carry-on bag with juice boxes, diapers, and wipes. There was nothing else worth taking. She experienced a sharp twang of regret only when she thought of Anne and Mireille, of Gilles and Uriel, who had leapt to their feet and followed her in a clump to the door of Mireille's apartment as she'd left, groping for her wrists, her shoulders, anything they could grab, pleading with her to come back and let them help mediate what was surely a gross misunderstanding. "We are all married, we have all been through this before," Anne called out as Veronica freed herself from their grip and slammed the door. And she experienced a sinking feeling of dread only when she thought of Maria, to whom both she and the kids would have to say good-bye.

That night she slept in the pull-out guest bed in the office upstairs. The sight of Didier's medical books and reviews in a neat stack on the desk, illuminated by the glow of the computer's galactic screen saver, fueled her anger and suspicion each time she rolled over and opened her eyes. Didier left her alone. He didn't try to coax her back into their room and said nothing until the following morning, when she and the kids piled into a taxi headed for the Marseille airport. Then, he muttered, "See you soon?" Though this made her heart ache, the bitterness still miring his gaze, and her own frame of mind, confirmed that getting away, at least for now, was the right—the only—thing to do.

Airborne over the Atlantic after boarding a connecting flight in Paris, she stared for a long time at the fuzzy intersection of the sky around her and the sea below. Not a cloud specked the heavens. As the twins slept, curled like puppies into their respective seats on either side of her, she recalled the other occasions in her lifetime when she'd dared to shake a situation up, to instigate change by giving circumstances a little nudge. Each and every one of those instances, including signing up for a painting vacation in Aix and striding into Didier's office to introduce herself, had been a small, tentative first step offering plenty of chances to stop, test the waters, and, if necessary, turn around. This time, however, she had made an abrupt and decisive, irreversible choice. The minute she realized in the streets of Aix that she had nothing left to say to Didier, something broke inside her. Nothing, not even a return to the life they'd shared following a short break in New Jersey could restore things to the way they'd been before. Nor would she want them restored. That would be like putting a

Band-Aid on a patch of cancerous skin.

While she peered down at the gash where the World Trade Center used to stand as the plane commenced its descent into Newark, she recalled the day five years ago when Didier had dropped everything and caught a last-minute flight to New Jersey to talk her out of canceling the wedding. She understood now what he must have gone through that day: how devastating, how disconcerting, it must have felt to face the prospect of a completely unexpected reality—one that surges all of a sudden, yet, like the news that the Twin Towers had collapsed, takes a very long time to sink in. She knew how it must have felt when he plucked himself from his surroundings, hurled himself across the planet at a moment's notice with no chance to prepare mentally. And she knew just how dearly it had cost.

Luckily she doesn't need to worry about anything right now other than the kids. Their meals, their naps, teaching them to take turns shooting baskets in the basement and changing the sheets on their new, toddler-sized beds: Rich and Shirley's latest gift. Nor does she want to. After all she's been through, she deserves a little break from reality. A chance to purge her system of the tension and anxiety that's been building up forever, it seems. By the time the news leaked about Didier's so-called medical device and his so-called patent lawyer, her head was already reeling, splitting from the repetitive blows of one unpleasant surprise after another. The device and the lawyer were just the final straw. She needs this time to relax, to heal, to let the pain subside.

She also needs this time to reflect on what went wrong. Did motherhood really erase her ambitions and transform her from a spirited, determined artist to a dependent wife content to keep busy and relevant folding laundry and painting her own four walls? Or did she, in fact, mislead Didier from the start by dropping hints that she wanted to succeed when, deep down inside, she didn't really know what she wanted? Even back in college—incubator of dreams, training ground for glory—she found the thought of venturing one day from her cozy dorm room into the frightening world of galleries and brokers, clients and public scrutiny, absolutely daunting. She pushed the fear away by telling herself that eventually things would fall miraculously into place as they always had. That she'd somehow manage to avoid criticism, rejection, and the struggle to make ends meet. Was this because, lacking the drive and dedication, she'd mentally opted out of trying before she'd even begun? In class, whenever she'd compare the baroque curlicues on her canvases with the bold and angular, grabbing abstractions her peers produced, a lump would form in her throat. With so many fields to choose from, why had she rushed into art? Perhaps she should have explored other, less competitive majors first, like psychology or education, which she took a couple of classes in. The fields they'd lead to, she remembers thinking now with a shudder, would have gone well with family life, allowing a smooth juggle of work and kids. But she knew what she *didn't* want. The preparation seemed too rigorous, too academic. She couldn't see herself spending years with her nose in a book. And only art offered the total flexibility she craved, the freedom to work at her own pace, to take orders from no one, and execute her own ideas in the comfort and privacy, the delicious seclusion, of her own home.

Here in Tenafly, where she's now spent nine days, she also wants to enjoy—no matter how briefly—the chance she didn't give herself back in Aix to be a real stay-at-home mom. To take the kids to story hour at the Tenafly public library on Wednesday afternoons, lingering afterward to thumb through books with them, do puzzles and play with hand puppets, seated criss-cross-apple-sauce on the carpeted floor. To skip around the basement with them singing "*Un Poisson au Fond d'un Étang*" and "*Au Feu les Pompiers*"— whose catchy tunes they all learned from Maria. To liven up these otherwise uneventful days by leading them in art projects: creating ghoulish face masks made of feathers and bangles glued to paper plates with holes cut out for the eyes, impressing their paint-slathered hands onto poster boards and helping them string beads onto bracelets and weave gimp. She wants to crawl into bed with them at nap time if she has the urge or walk unhurried laps around the block at random times of day wearing floppy, formless sweats while Shirley babysits, nodding in solidarity at other women out jogging or walking their dogs. To choose willingly the slight, dull twinge of boredom that comes from spending hours on end with toddlers and having no particular goals over the stress of trying juggle too many things, and never to think about the bigger picture or the future—things you just can't control.

Rich and Shirley have made this all so easy. When Veronica called them from Aix the night before she left to explain that she and Didier were going through a rough patch, and she was coming home for a break, Shirley reassured her that it happens all the time. "Marriage is a never-ending dance," Shirley reminded her. "Everybody needs a little break now and then to catch their breath, rest their legs." At the news that she'd charged the tickets to their credit card, Rich and Shirley answered in unison, "Good for you." They greeted her at the arrival gate in Newark with sunny smiles and cheerful hugs as if she'd just arrived for her regular July vacation. They didn't ask any thorny questions, like how long she planned to stay, and haven't since. Nor have they mentioned any inconveniences this impromptu visit might have caused.

A few times, Rich has sneered with disapproval—like when Shirley insisted on doing everybody's laundry twice a week. But a single, sharp glance from Shirley wipes the sneer off his face. He lets Shirley answer when Didier calls at eight each morning. At Veronica's behest, Shirley exchanges a few words with Didier and then hands the phone to the kids. Rich also makes sure the heating in the house is set properly, that all three cars are running smoothly, and that they always have a full tank of gas. On the day when President Bush announced that the United States had started bombing Iraq, Rich gave Veronica a sympathetic noogie as she fretted about the consequences for her Jewish friends and family in France. He then slunk away so she could watch the full story alone. He's even made a generous deposit to her local bank account to spare her the embarrassment of asking for cash.

Though she sometimes wakes at night confused and dispirited by the emptiness of her bed, and her heart squeezes when she spots e-mails from Didier in her inbox—which she deletes, unread—or hears Shirley pick up the phone each morning at eight, for the most part, she is so focused on the here and now, on each small task at hand, she can even forget that she misses Didier. That he's not here. Sometimes it feels like he's simply off at work as usual. As a result, she can easily imagine that this sojourn in Tenafly is her real life. Often— like now, as she lays out pipe cleaner and crêpe paper on the crafts table she's set up in the basement where she'll create replicas of daffodils and sunflowers with Luc and Céleste this afternoon—she indulges in the fantasy that her parents' plush, spacious house is hers, that she stays home with her children, that her mother lives nearby, and that she doesn't have to worry about how, exactly, to keep money flowing into the bank. That her husband is here but busy with other things, as husbands tend to be, and that one of these days, like Stella and Ray, he and Veronica will make a date to spend some time together. And that in exchange for her devotion to the house and the kids, in exchange for her role tending to the heap of laborious details that make up the foundation of their lives, he supports her morally and provides for her materially, just like her parents.

Chapter Sixteen

What a relief it is to have some time away from the kids, Veronica thinks as she drives into Manhattan to meet Terry for lunch. Earlier this morning, day twelve in Tenafly, Céleste woke her by waving colored popsicle sticks in her face and demanding that she help her glue them together into a castle right away. Veronica wanted to snap the sticks in half. Luc followed her around as she showered and dressed, asking "Why?" before she finished—"Why?"—each sentence— "Why?" She wanted to scream. When the two tugged her toward the crafts table in the basement to string beads onto yet another pair of bracelets and weave yet another length of gimp, the slight, dull twinge of boredom she'd embraced until now mushroomed into a sickening, sinking feeling spreading through her stomach and chest. Didier was right about one thing: every mother needs time to be a woman.

It's a relief, too, to have some time away from her parents and their house. For the past few days, prickly details she forgot about while living in Aix have leaped out and smacked her in the face. Catching glimpses of her old, framed collages of unicorns and cherubs on the living room walls, she's cringed. Their childish frills and loopy curls strike a squeamishly intimate chord. What was she thinking when she let her mother put them on display for the whole world to see? She may as well have hung her own naked body up there, flaws shamefully exposed. While scrapbooking at the desk in Stella's old room beneath a shelf full of track trophies and Harvard pennants, she's relived the humiliating sense of inferiority that Stella's mere existence has always triggered. And when her father's been in a crabby mood, she's braced herself for a barrage of disparaging questions the way she used to as a kid: "Why don't you stand up straight like a mensch?" Or, "What's this C in chemistry? Does a daughter of mine bring home Cs?"

Rich, she has noticed, is often in a crabby mood. He turns his back when Veronica or Shirley approach, averts eye contact, or keeps a newspaper open before him like a shield. Though sometimes he defrosts spontaneously, rolls his paper up into a tube, and bops it on her head, more often he smirks, mutters under his breath, rolls his eyes. Just this morning, after breakfast, Veronica asked Shirley to watch the kids while she dried her hair. She then came downstairs to find Rich waiting for her, pacing. Shirley had asked him to take over so she could go for a walk on the treadmill in the basement. He raised a bristly eyebrow at his watch and called out, "Shirl! I'm off duty here and headed for my next shift!" Then, without a word to Veronica, he left for work.

Meanwhile, Shirley's glossy optimism never cracks. A few minutes after Rich left, she came panting up the basement stairs. Hands on hips, chest heaving, she surveyed the scene: Veronica, refilling cups of chocolate milk for Luc and Céleste as they watched *Sagwa the Siamese Cat* sprawled out on their backs on the family room floor. "Well, this worked out nicely!" she declared, dabbing her sweaty forehead with the terry cloth band on her wrist. "Maybe tomorrow if your father has no early appointments we can both sleep in."

This perennial sunny outlook has irked Veronica lately, though she can't quite say why. Maybe it's envy: she'd give an arm or a leg to be so happy and upbeat all the time.

Up ahead, New York City's steel silhouette looms on the far side of the George Washington Bridge, and behind it, the city's towering agglomeration of buildings and skyscrapers radiates a frenetic energy Veronica has also forgotten all about. Millions upon millions of windows squeeze together into a thriving mosaic presenting endless, overwhelming possibilities of what to eat, what to buy, who to be. Rickety steel slabs covering potholes clang beneath the car's tires. As the city reaches down and scoops her in, a choking stench of exhaust and uncollected garbage assaults her nose. A businessman in a designer suit crossing Ninety-fifth Street barks orders into a cell phone. Back in Aix, Veronica often longed for Manhattan's bagel shops, its ten-minute nail-salon massages, and her weekly lunch dates with Terry at Au Bon Pain. But she blocked out memories of the barking voices, the stench, the jolt of potholes, and the intimidation: reminders of reality's darker side.

Instead of Au Bon Pain, Terry has reserved a table for today at I Tre Merli, a trendy Italian spot in SoHo near her new office. Sometime last year, she moved to a big-name PR firm with clients all over the world. "Lunch is on me," she told Veronica when they set the date. "I'll expense it."

Standing on West Broadway, car parked, Veronica steadies herself in the mayhem, her pulse quickening to match the street's frenzied throb. Droves of pedestrians wired to Blackberries and iPods elbow for space on the sidewalk. Taxis dart like angry bees through the traffic, weaving past buses farting brown exhaust, past delivery people on wobbly bikes, and obnoxiously long stretch limousines. A tall, slender woman in a fashionable wool swing coat strides toward her, and it takes a moment to recognize her old college roommate known on campus for the holes in the butt of her jeans. She doesn't recall Terry as so stylish, so sleek. But then, she hasn't seen her in nearly two years. Last July, Terry was out of town on business, so the two missed their annual date. Has her bony figure always appeared so svelte? When did she let her hair's black ringlets, once cropped to her earlobes, grow out to cascade past her pointed chin? And her fingernails, which she used to lament biting down to frayed stubs, now look perfect in their crimson manicure, as if they'd found their true length and color at last.

"Look at you!" Veronica gushes, squeezing her and then giving her an exaggerated once-over. Terry's always had an all-black wardrobe, but now, instead of the turtlenecks and pleated pants she used to wear to work, she has on a silk blouse unbuttoned to the cleavage and a tight, hip-hugging skirt. "You're so … chic! *Ohh là là.* I can't get over it!"

"Yeah, well. The office uniform." Her coarse, baritone voice hasn't changed. "And you! You're the same as ever."

"Gee, thanks," Veronica smirks. The last time she saw Terry, the twins were five months old. Her breasts, double their usual volume, were leaking milk. Her midriff sagged like a semideflated inner tube, and the only decent outfit she could manage was a formless maternity dress handed down from Stella.

Inside the restaurant, Terry slides her shades to the crown of her head and promenades her regard from one corner of the dimly lit dining room to the next, absorbing each detail between its polished brick walls. Veronica smoothes her denim skirt, wondering if she looks as frumpy as she feels. She should have bought something new for the occasion or worn one of the old blazers in her closet rather than the cotton sweater she has on.

Seated, she studies the menu while Terry studies the diners packing the mezzanine, striking debonair poses as if for an invisible camera, assessing the bouquet of their wine. "Whadd'ya think? Salmon carpaccio to start with and then penne in a vodka cream sauce? Or maybe—ooh, check it out! How about the gnocci?"

Terry exchanges nods with a blonde woman in an audacious, paisley halter top a few tables away. "I'll have my usual. Spinach salad."

"Out of this whole Italian feast, you're getting a pile of leaves?"

"I've tried everything else. It's all overrated. And I've had to starve it off." She pats her thigh.

"Gimme a break!" Veronica squeals. "You're a stick!"

"If I'm not careful, I'll turn into a tree trunk."

Veronica stares wistfully at a waiter balancing a platter heaped with portions of linguine al mare and orders a spinach salad, too.

In her new job, Terry manages a team of publicists who pitch news stories about fashion houses and designers to the press. She talks about it for a while and then about her new apartment—a one-bedroom in the East 90s, a real step up from the studio she rented before on the seedy side of Prospect Park. Now she's looking to buy. "Nothing fancy," she explains, pushing the cheese in her salad aside. "I just want to get a foot in the real estate market so that a few years down the line I can sell at a profit and buy something nicer. The market's moving so fast." She also tells Veronica about the bonuses her company offers, which motivate her to bust her ass.

Veronica puts on her best listening face to mask her apathy and stupefaction: narrow eyes; a sharp, inquisitive regard. Back in the days of croissant sandwiches at Au Bon Pain, Terry would start talking about art before the two had even said hello, eager as a teenager bursting to confide that she's in love. She'd prattle on about the all-nighters she pulled trying to finish her latest sculpture of writhing hands before leaving in the morning for work. She'd bring photos of her canvases in progress for Veronica to critique. Sometimes she'd get so wrapped up in describing the gallery openings she'd crashed and the cocktails she'd finagled invitations to so she could sidle up to all the right dealers and agents, that she'd forget to order food. Art was the raison d'être for everything else she did, including her job, which she viewed as a convenient but meaningless cash cow. Now the subject's glaring absence feels as awkward, as wrong, as Veronica's ignoring Didier's phone calls every morning.

"Good thing we've got art degrees, huh?" Veronica ventures. Maybe with a little reminder, the real Terry will reemerge.

"That degree set me on my path! Without it, I'd never have landed my first PR job. And I've given art my best shot, I really have. But it's always been one step forward, two steps back. How many times have I heard, 'Come back next week?' Or, 'What if you tweaked this or tweaked that or tried a different medium?' Meanwhile, at work, I've taken three giant steps forward every day. What can I do? Stop going into the office and hang around waiting for a miracle?"

Veronica snorts.

"At one point I considered it. You know, quitting work so I could take a shot at sculpting and painting twenty-four seven. But I needed the money. And work just kept … happening. Moving forward. Progressing. For the most part, I've really liked it, too. Then, somewhere along the line, it occurred to me: maybe this work *is* my miracle! Not exactly the one I've been hoping for, but then, miracles never are."

"Yeah. I know exactly what you mean."

"Oh, really?" Terry straightens, fingers her earring. Anger flickers briefly in her pale blue eyes.

Veronica looks down at her plate and its impoverished portion of spinach leaves and walnuts. She should have changed the subject when she had the chance, moved on from miracles to a harmless topic like where Terry shops. But it's too late now, and she can't bear to let her friend imagine, with resentment, that she, Veronica, has it easy because she found a man to bankroll her life. "It takes way more than time, believe me," she breathes, her gaze sliding to her hands and their maze of soothsaying lines. "As a matter of fact, you and I are pretty much in the same boat."

Terry makes a guttural sound, a combination of a snigger and a grunt.

"I'm serious! You've got your job, I've got my kids. They're happening every day, like work, progressing and moving forward. It turns out that my art, well, it's not." She shovels the remains of her salad into her mouth and shrugs. She's said enough. "No biggie, though. Things change. And here we are, finally. I can't get over how amazing you look!"

"Idiot!" Veronica shouts to herself, sitting in the bumper-to-bumper traffic clogging the Hudson River Parkway. She bangs the steering wheel until her fists ache and lets tears stream down her cheeks, safe in the isolation of her car.

Lunch ended abruptly, with Terry checking her watch and announcing that she had a meeting to race off to. She gave Veronica a circumspect peck on the cheek and then clicked away on her pointy heels. Veronica stared at her until she was gone, numb with the certainty that she'd never see Terry again.

Why should she? she bristles silently. They have nothing obvious in common. They no longer share a college dorm room, a major, or a need to commiserate about thwarted expectations and muse about glamorous dreams. Terry has no husband—she still careens from one date to the next, disgusted with the shortcomings of every man she meets— and has no children. The two can't compare stories of pregnancy and breastfeeding, of managing temper tantrums and picky eaters. Nor can Veronica relate to the latest tactics in schmoozing or how the Internet is changing the press.

Yet when a chance arose to bridge these gaps, she chose to let it slip away. She said just enough to give the impression that she's put her art on hold to raise her kids, but, like a coward, presented only half the truth. Confiding in Terry about the mess she's in—the rocky state of her marriage, the dead end her mind skids into whenever she tries to think about solutions and the future—would have shed light on the profoundly human things that the two do share: frustration, conflicting desires, loneliness, and disappointment. The bittersweet legacy of having moved forward yet having left a big part of themselves behind. Instead of hurrying back to their separate lives, they might have reveled in a lengthy, bonding heart-to-heart.

Of course, opening the floodgates to her heart would

have been as terrifying as trying to sell a painting. Veronica hasn't even peeked behind those gates yet. When she does, she might drown.

Traffic inches forward. A dented blue van to the right turns into Veronica's lane without signaling, cutting her off. She slams on the breaks and bangs the steering wheel again, jerking her hand back at the startling blare of her horn. A driver to the left—a ruddy-faced man in a greasy undershirt—gives her the finger, shoving it high into the air. *Yeah*, she thinks. *Insult me. I've had it coming all along.* Did she honestly believe that by delivering only the sunny side of her story she could somehow make the dark side go away? Or that she could mask it without sounding shallow and insincere? How exasperating Terry must have found her. How dull.

Back in Aix, did she really think that she could hide herself from the playgroup moms? She always scurried off from their get-togethers after barely an hour, abuzz with excuses about the twins' nap time, their mealtime, or someplace else she had to be. Could they sense that, in fact, despite her desire for kinship, the strain of looking chipper while carefully selecting just a few good things to say left her feeling drained? At the mere thought of Abigail, Lorena, and Trish, who might have otherwise become the dearest friends she's ever had, she convulses with sobs. They've continued copying her on e-mails about playgroup meetings and coffee dates at Le Grillon. A real pro at ignoring messages in her inbox that she doesn't want to read, like Didier's, she's never answered them. She never told them she was gone.

Up ahead, dense lines of vehicles snake toward the George Washington Bridge. Its arched silver beams stretch upward like the gates to heaven, pulling her forward. But where do they lead? Beyond them, in Tenafly, Shirley will greet her with a pert account of the books she read to Luc and Céleste, the hot dogs and Tater Tots they shared at lunchtime, the songs they sang together, and how the twins sat as still as angels in the bath while she washed their hair. She'll list Luc's new vocabulary words and the number of times Céleste used the potty. She won't mention any of the nettlesome details: meltdowns, time-outs, or new chocolate stains on the white living room sofas. And this will make Veronica's blood boil. It's boiling now. Because, come to think of it, what irks her about Shirley's glossy outlook on everything, including the shit she cleans up, is that it rings as idiotically hollow as the half truths she fed Terry today.

Shirley always shines a great big spotlight on everything she wants to see, wants to show, leaving the rest to languish in the shadows. Yet who knows what toxic mass of emotions lurks, undetected, in those shadows? Embedded in a mind and heart, such a mass can sprawl and rot, corrode the health. And her father: surely his acidic grouchiness has a source. But Rich, who loathes risk and confrontation, would never dare reveal it, perhaps not even to himself.

Shame rages through Veronica's neck, burns her ears. She has bought into the illusion, hook, line, and sinker. Worse yet, she has tried to mimic it. Could she really marry a man who lives in France? Of course! He's a doctor—a surgeon! Besides, no town in the world is more beautiful than Aix-en-Provence. When the kids ask her these days about Didier—when they'll see him, when they're going home—she says, "Aren't you having loads of fun right here?" No wonder Didier, who digs down so deeply into every moment he experiences, felt unable to confide his innermost hopes to her, his fragile ambitions and plans. Perhaps he wanted to.

Perhaps he tried. And while his confidence in another woman remains a painful enigma, Veronica understands, suddenly, that by questioning her choices and desires he was simply attempting to reach into her soul and grab onto something substantive, something he could hold.

Chapter Seventeen

On April Fool's Day it rains and then snows and then rains again. The walls of Rich and Shirley's house clamp down like the sides of an enormous vice, squeezing the breath from Veronica's lungs. She's rummaged through the bin of DVDs in search of a movie she can watch with Luc and Céleste, one they haven't all seen a hundred times, but the sickeningly familiar characters and cartoonish colors on their covers made her stomach turn. She's stacked the dishwasher, dressed the kids, changed their sheets, added their laundry to Shirley's hamper, and organized their newest art supplies. There's nothing else to do. She needs to walk, to run, to get out for some air but can't bear the thought of another morning at the library or the mall and has nowhere else to go.

She'd rather not spend another day with Shirley, either, but here they are, on the living room sofa listening to the rain. Shirley's sipping coffee from her thermos, always full. Luc and Céleste are attempting somersaults on the floor, and each time Shirley cheers, "Good job! Way to go!" Veronica grits her teeth. The somersaults go nowhere, flopping off to the side and ending before they begin.

After a while, Luc has had enough. He wanders toward the glass bookshelves flanking the fireplace.

"Hey, where's my acrobat going?" Shirley croons, coaxing him back. "Your sister just did her best one yet! How about you?"

"Baba!" He thrusts a chubby index finger toward the bookshelves.

"Ba … ba …" repeats Shirley, glancing at Veronica, who shrugs. She's not in the mood for playing guess-that-word with her mother, who prefers to insert her own word instead of really listening to the kids.

"Ba, ba … bread?" Shirley ventures.

"Nooo!" Luc marches closer to the shelves and points again. "Baba! Baba!"

A confused frown pulls Shirley's fleshy jowls into her neck, then suddenly her eyes light. "Ba, ba, brownie!" She hoists herself from the sofa, disappears into the kitchen then returns with a Tupperware container of brownies. "Tada!" She opens it and holds it under Luc's nose.

Luc jerks his head to the side without a glance at the brownies. "*Baba!*" he pleads, his brown eyes pools of desperation. Planting himself before the shelves, he flexes his knees, bounces in place, and points, waggling his arm. "*Baba! Baba! Regarde!*"

"I don't think he wants food, Mom." Veronica wills the tension splintering her voice to drop down her limbs and into the clenched knots of her fists.

"Well, he shouldn't be eyeing those shelves." Shirley raises an eyebrow at the portrait they boast, front and center, of Veronica and Didier on their wedding day.

"Ignoring them won't make them go away," Veronica hisses. She squats beside Luc and traces the imaginary line extending from his fingertip. It aims roughly at the portrait, in which Didier holds her in his arms like a baby. Her head is tipped back in staged glee, engulfed by her misty veil, her beaded gown drips to the grass.

Goose bumps erupt on her arms and back. "Papa?" she whispers, caught off guard by the specter of Didier's face among them, staring straight ahead and wearing a disarmingly frank expression brimming with that day's rich soup of love and fear and anxiety and anticipation. "Is that what you want?" A wave of tenderness ripples through her chest. She never noticed before how Didier's essence, pure and unaffected, projects from that portrait to fill the room.

"No!" Luc insists, thrusting his finger with renewed agitation. "*Baba!*"

Céleste shakes Veronica's shoulder. "Mommy, Shabbat!" Chocolate cakes her fingertips and mouth. "Luc wants Shabbat! See?"

Veronica turns to her daughter, examines her copper hair and, beneath the hem of her overgrown bangs, her lucid, hazel eyes. Like Luc's, they transfix the shelves, drilling straight past the portrait, straight past a collection of glass elephants and other fine gift-shop tchotchkes beside it to a row of glossy atlases and leather-bound encyclopedias, never used. Tucked like an afterthought in a space between two volumes stand a silver kiddush cup and a matching pair of Shabbat candlesticks, black with decades of tarnish.

"Oh, Duke!" Veronica squeezes her son, tears pooling in her eyes. Hopping to her feet, she removes the silver pieces from the shelf.

"Cah we light *baba?*" he asks, turning them over in his hands, his eyes round with awe.

Veronica beams and shoots Shirley a vindicative look.

"We'll light the candles tomorrow," she promises, kissing the top of his head. Sensitivity rises like steam from his solid little sternum, wrapping her in its sultry warmth. "That's Friday. Friday's Shabbat."

While Luc and Céleste nap after lunch, she scours the kitchen cupboards, fueled by the prospect of having something—anything—to do. Over time, even a slight twinge of boredom can begin to feel like full-fledged emptiness: there's such a fine line between the two. Projects as simple as preparing a Shabbat dinner stop the twinge, at least for a while.

And Shabbat, in particular—what better cause to throw herself into? She should have guessed that the kids missed it. It's been woven into the fabric of their lives as tightly as bedtime stories and baths. Back in Aix, they'd whoop with joy whenever she announced on Friday afternoons that it was time to put the candles on the table. When she lit them, they'd gape, mesmerized, at the luminous white and amber patches flickering on the walls. They'd ask repeatedly during the week how many days until they'd see their cousins at Mireille's house for *la daf*. Occasionally, they've asked her the same thing here. Each time, she's had to swallow back tears.

On Friday afternoons, Didier would come home early to transition from a week of frenzied pressure to twenty-four hours of intensive family time—the time that holds them all together, he'd say, like glue. He'd massage Veronica's shoulders while she sang the blessing over the candles. After dinner, he'd draw Luc and Céleste onto his lap and nuzzle their heads. Later, he'd hum in Veronica's ear and whisper that they had an important mitzvah, or prescribed good deed, to take care of. Lovemaking is considered a mitzvah on Shabbat.

Shabbat can be special even without him, she thinks now,

ignoring the pinch in her gut. She'll polish the neglected candlesticks and kiddush cup. She'll buy a nice bottle of wine and make a healthy, home-cooked meal. Enough with foods that do nothing to help a family bond, like frozen pizza and Lean Cuisine! In fact, she'll use the "*archi-simple*" recipe for roast chicken with garlic and potatoes Uriel once gave her, urging her with a nudge in the ribs to give it a shot. She never did, but the recipe was indeed so simple that she memorized it on the spot: chicken legs in a pan sprinkled with olive oil, lemon juice, coarse salt, pepper, and rosemary. Potato cubes around them, a garlic clove here and there. Bake for forty-five minutes at the equivalent of four hundred, and *voilà*! Recalling how she and Uriel tried to calculate what temperature in Fahrenheit would equal the imprecise French oven setting of "medium-high," she smiles. He'd give her a hearty high-five right now if he knew she was planning to attempt it, hooting, "*Ouaaii! Bravo!*"

Uriel, of course, would use kosher meat—not a bad idea at all. For the past few weeks, Veronica has found herself missing the nearly sacred sense of bonding that comes from sharing kosher, home-cooked food. Indeed, tradition reinforces identity. It weaves families together and connects them with something far greater than anyone can fathom. Didier was right about this, too. So she'll buy the right ingredients, and, in keeping with tradition, will serve it all kosher-style, excluding dairy products from this meat-based meal. And if it comes out well, she might just do it again.

Humming, she scans the cabinets' contents and notes the things she'll need to buy: candles, silver polish, a challah, the chicken, the wine. Shirley wanders into the kitchen and peers over her shoulder, standing so close that Veronica can feel the repulsive, prickly heat of her musk-and-Wint-O-Green breath.

"Whadd'ya need?" Shirley asks, reaching past Veronica's neck to pull out a box of Oreos to nosh from.

How about a little elbow room? Veronica thinks.

"Coffee? A Coke?"

"A bunch of things. For tomorrow night. You know, if we're gonna light the candles, we may as well do the whole shebang and have Shabbat dinner, too. The kids'll get a kick out of it. I'll cook."

"Save the leftovers. Your dad and I are going out."

Veronica places a mental bookmark in the checklist she's been building. "Oh. With who?"

"Just us. A date. It's high time."

The bookmark and checklist vanish like balloons popping in her face. Does Shirley mean it's high time she and Rich finally got out to a dinner date together that they'd had on the calendar last month, perhaps, but had to cancel when Veronica showed up like a vagrant on their doorstep? Do they still dine out every week after all these years, Shirley gussied up in hairspray, silk, and velvet, Rich in a dreaded tie? Or did they decide just this morning that it was high time they got out for some air because with their daughter and grandchildren overrunning the house, the walls were closing in on them, too?

Shirley takes a seat at the table and breaks an Oreo in half. The haughty glint in her eyes makes Veronica seethe. Rich and Shirley had no date on the calendar at all: Shirley decided on it herself in a vengeful power play as soon as Veronica told her that, on Friday night, she'd do things her way.

"Great." Veronica gnaws the inside of her lower lip, tensing against an incipient ache in her jaw. Her left eye twitches as she forces herself not to glower. "Enjoy. The kids and I'll have fun. We're having chicken—kosher. I might stock up on some while I'm shopping if you don't mind."

Shirley raises an eyebrow and laughs. "As long as you don't mind if I throw the scraps into a sandwich with a big slice of cheese!"

Veronica considers her mother, reclining imperially in her chair, chin settled in her neck like a hen in its nest, arms crossed upon her corpulent bosom. She can't tell whether Shirley's trying to be humorous or means business, but there's an edge to her voice, a slight, uppity pitch that says, "Bite your tongue. This kitchen is mine."

In the dim, purple shadows of her childhood bedroom late that night, Veronica paces in circles as tight as a noose. The ache in her jaw has amplified into an acute knot of pain spreading down her neck and into the marrow of her bones. She's taken three Advils. She's held a dozen imaginary conversations with her mother, negotiating ways to share the house without resentment, but with each imaginary word her own resentment builds.

Down the hall, her father snores. The brass clock on the living room mantle clicks like Didier's tongue against his teeth—"*tchk*"—as it ticks. "Dammit!" she mutters, shoving her hands under her hair and clutching her scalp. Like the mistral wind, this incessant noise, *tchk, tchk, tchk*, can drive a person insane! She needs silence. She needs fresh air and space. Loads of it. Space to think.

The spaces in Rich and Shirley's house that appeared as vast as football fields when she arrived one month ago have collapsed into boxes, coffins, where the slightest movement slams you up against a splintery plank. Turn left, you bump into Shirley, gaze lofty with the pride of petty triumph. Turn right, and there's Rich, skulking, glaring at the floor. Look up, and faces on school portraits from kindergarten through the seventh grade leer from shelves, larger than life, mocking the fruitlessness of attempts to preserve what was, what might have been.

Even back in Aix, beneath the infinite blue expanse of the Provençal sky, there's no space to think. The mistral's howl, the swallows' twittering, the nasal drone of French, and the edgy puffs of air wafting from Didier's pursed lips invade Veronica's mind as insidiously as Rich and Shirley's ubiquitous voices do here. Even when alone, she never really is.

At her window, she turns back an edge of the shade and peers into the starless night. Pale, smoky light from an invisible moon illuminates the crescent-shaped street and the stately brick and clapboard homes that line it. Tidy and uniform, they beckon like midrange hotels glimpsed from the highway when you're driving, bleary-eyed, late at night. What a relief it would be to check into a hotel like that right now. To stay for a couple of days in a standard room with a standard double bed, industrial carpeting, and a compact coffee maker on the counter over the minifridge. Anonymous in a place where she has no memories, no acquaintances or ties, she could reason at last about the past and the present and find an answer to the question rolling in her stomach like a swallowed sob: what next?

A cackle escapes down the back of her throat. A couple of days? She needs weeks. Months. Many. Months alone to lift the layers of obscurity. Months to hang around in overalls and her penguin slippers if she wants to with no silent accusations flying about how sloppy and unfeminine she looks. To sing her kids "*Un Poisson au Fond d'un Étang*" or "*Au Feu les Pompiers*" without anybody snapping, "We're in America! Don't stunt their English!" Months to help herself to the kids' art supplies at night as she's yearned to lately, experimenting just for fun with new forms and figures that no one else will ever see. Months of freedom—yes, freedom!—to sleep in her very own bed, to buy her own groceries, and wash her own dirty clothes.

Chapter Eighteen

At dawn she pulls on sweats and drives to the gas station to pick up a copy of the *Bergen Record* and, just for the heck of it, the *New York Times*. Armed with a giant coffee and a pair of glazed donuts for Luc and Céleste, she spreads out the newspapers on her parents' dining room table and sets to work combing through the "Rentals" section of the real estate pages. Jittery from a sleepless night and too much caffeine, she circles ads for furnished rentals and sublets in towns as far north as Montvale and as seedy as Newark—any place where prices are low.

Over the next couple of weeks, this becomes her routine: an early rise, the gas station, a giant coffee, and the real estate pages. Quickly, before her children and her parents wake, she makes lists of the rentals that look most realistic and, on an occasional whim, the ones that seem ideal. Then the kids call for their milk. Her parents shuffle down the stairs. The house snaps into motion with coffee brewing, waffles toasting, and disputes erupting over who gets the prize from the cereal box. The old, familiar feeling of drowning in motherhood, of treading water desperately just to stay afloat, returns, making her want to throw in the towel, quit treading, and end her ridiculous search. But that would leave her right back where she started: stuck between a protracted adolescence and the stagnant, incomplete adulthood she slackened into in marriage.

This notion sends a cold burst of panic through her veins, followed by a rush of fight-or-flight adrenaline. Like a drill sergeant, she pushes doubt aside and orders Luc and Céleste to quit whining, eat their breakfast, and stay still while she gets them dressed so she can hurry on to the next logical step each day: phoning the numbers on her lists for more information. Her firmness, her absolute conviction that other priorities matter and that she, not the children, is the boss, has the surprising effect of convincing them, too.

Never before has she thrown herself into a task with such unfailing energy or determination. But then, never before has it seemed that her very soul, her survival, depended on her actions. Grateful for the comfort of a house to cocoon in, she's accepted the constraints of letting someone else provide it. And secure in the knowledge that she could always fall back on Didier or Rich and Shirley for the things she needs, she's felt no real impetus to act. Now, if she doesn't, she'll suffocate. Her spirit will die.

She's not even sure what she's looking for. A place to rent for a couple of months? A place to settle down in and call home? Or simply a starting point, a random endeavor to spark ideas, break the stalemate she's in, and generate momentum? Because without momentum, nothing will happen. This, at least, she knows.

Back in art school, Terry used to call the conception phase of any new project the "gray matter" phase. Mushy and amorphous like the gray matter in a brain, it served a similar purpose: channeling a hodgepodge of stimuli into something coherent. At that early phase, vision still muddy, she had to sift through a big blob of confusion in order to excavate the seed of her inspiration and then cultivate it into a balanced ensemble of colors and forms. Whether painting or sculpting, she always began with a very long series of aborted attempts— brush stroke after brush stroke, blobs of color splattered down then wiped away, piles of metal scraps banged and hammered paper-thin and then crushed wrathfully in her callused hand. "You're not getting anywhere," Veronica would say. Terry would stare past her, eyes murky, as if possessed. "Are you kidding? I'm cutting through the gray matter to the heart of the matter. Clearing away the superfluous shit."

The rental ads are Veronica's gray-matter phase, and her first foray ever into such a mushy, amorphous place. Her own artistic process always used to start with a swift sketch of something familiar, something she'd seen or done a thousand times before. She'd then tweak it until distinguishing features emerged. Similarly, her broader choices have always sprung from an instant vision of an end point or a clear reference point: a bachelor's degree to take pride in, a wedding under a chuppah, Antibes' chalk-white cliffs. In checking out ads for two-bedroom apartments, she's sifting through the gray, pounding metal strips, and dropping dollops of random color onto a canvas, testing to see what's viable—or not—in this seed of an idea that has popped into her head.

Scouring the ads, she learns the jargon of "eiks," "hwfs," security deposits, and heating bills. Within days she figures out how to glean from a two-line description whether or not a place is a dump. Though seemingly trivial, these new skills boost her confidence and spur her on. She forgot how good it can feel to wrap her mind around something new. She also trains herself to pick up the phone and recite her questions, regardless of how pathetic or embarrassed she feels, going out on a limb as she's never dared to before. After all, the strangers she's calling don't have to know her reasons. They don't have to know that she has no income and only several thousand dollars to her name.

In the middle of her second week of searching, she ventures off on a couple of visits, schlepping Luc and Céleste along. Shirley, back to her usual routine of spending half the day at the health club and the hair salon, can't always watch them. The frustration of having to stop every few miles to find a bathroom for Céleste or to search for a binky that fell from a yelping mouth makes her want to tear out her hair—or theirs—every time. Yet the urgency of her mission transforms her stress into will power. It sharpens her mind, enabling her to concoct spontaneous solutions to each new dilemma that arises. One afternoon, running very late on her way to a visit, she pulled into a Verizon shop and bought herself a cell phone so she could call the landlord she was meeting. On another visit a few days later, she asked the realtor to stand by her car and keep an eye on the kids, who fell asleep during the drive, while she did a quick walk-through alone. Situations that used to seem like immovable mountains have become trivial, laughable, just another new twist to another crazy new day. And with each challenge she overcomes, her stamina increases. She can hardly remember how it felt to crave the languor of her bed each afternoon.

Shirley has pretended not to notice when Veronica combs the ads or races out the door. In fact, since this search began, she hasn't said much at all. When Veronica enters a room, she scuttles away. Rich, on the other hand, has shown signs of an inexplicable thaw. Two weekends in a row, he's brought Veronica a copy of the Sunday paper. One morning, he peered over her shoulder as she circled ads and asked, "So what are you up to, anyway, kiddo?" Her explanation drew a respectful nod. The next day, when she told him that she'd just spotted an underpriced gem of an apartment in Hackensack, he looked at her square in the eye and said, "If you need any help, just say the word."

The rare tinge of empathy in his voice made her long to gush, *I do!* and to confess how frightened, how daunted, she's felt by the uncertainty looming ahead even as she's continued pushing toward it. But—wary of repeating old mistakes and landing right back at square one—she steadied herself instead and answered, "Thanks, but I don't think so." This earned her a two-fisted noogie.

On a Thursday morning toward the middle of April, she pulls into the lot of Homestead Manor, a sprawling apartment complex in Hackensack, New Jersey: the address of the underpriced gem. Seeing the complex's half-acre manicured lawn and its serene, two-story, brick exterior resembling an enlarged version of a regular, single-family home, her heart clenches the way it did the day she showed up at Didier's office unannounced five years ago. Tidy rows of shrubs edge the brick. White colonial-style shutters flank the windows and a pillared portico frames the entrance, beckoning her to come in and kick off her shoes. Like the bronze plaque on the façade of 73 rue Espariat in Aix, it stirs a latent yearning yet intimidates her slightly, frightens her: it's probably out of her league, too good to be true.

A slender, sixty-something woman dressed in gardening overalls and a purple fleece jacket opens the door. "Now who have we here?" she asks, squatting to face Luc and Céleste who, to Veronica's embarrassment, are busy swinging around on the portico's pillars like tetherballs circling poles.

Luc and Céleste dash ahead as the woman, Rose, leads them down the carpeted hallway lined with identical red doors. In an articulate accent that sounds as if it's from someplace wholesome like Connecticut, or Vermont, she explains that the apartment belongs to her son, a hotel manager who's just been transferred to Cleveland on a yearly, renewable contract. He has a wife and two small children not far in age from Veronica's twins. They'll eventually come back to New Jersey, but they don't know when. "So we can only commit to one year at a time," Rose says. "That's why we've priced it on the low side."

Veronica nods and steps into the living room, freshly carpeted and furnished with a new, pine futon and matching end tables. A year is the shortest lease she's come across, yet it's far longer than she banked on when she started this search. At the same time, given the sliding glass door in the back, the spanking-clean kitchenette beside it, flooded in an entire Provençal summer's worth of sunshine and the scent of Windex and rug shampoo, a year seems like nothing.

To the left of the living room, two bedrooms, identical in size, each have a roomy closet and a window looking out onto a cluster of maples. The beds, like the futon in the living room, appear new. She can easily picture herself tucking Luc and Céleste in at night and then sitting down at the kitchen table to experiment with colored pencils and a sketch pad. The maple leaves outside must explode with shades of orange, red, and yellow as vivid as Provence's firethorn berries in the fall. She lifts her chest. "One year at a time is fine with me."

Beyond the sliding glass door, a picket fence encircles a square of grass the size of a porch, just right for a compact swing set and a bouncaline or a blow-up pool. Spotting it, Luc and Céleste press their fists and noses to the door. "Hey, off the glass, pronto!" Veronica orders, glancing apologetically at Rose.

"Can't blame them," Rose laughs. "They've found the best part. Well—almost." She squats beside them and steers their shoulders to the left so that they face three shallow steps leading down to an unfurnished, rectangular space. "The playroom."

The kids race down the steps and throw themselves to the carpeted floor, shrieking with glee as they attempt somersaults and wave their feet in the air. Veronica frowns, smiles, frowns again. All the other apartments she's visited have had warped linoleum floors. The kitchens have been dingy and ill equipped, the furniture stained with God knows what, the windows scant or nonexistent. There's been no space for somersaults, no space for shrieks of glee. Some landlords or realtors have turned her away immediately upon seeing that she has toddlers.

She's always left with a sigh of relief. No good, won't do, she can continue searching without having to worry about next steps, which she hasn't yet considered. Now, however, the yearning that clawed at her chest when she rang the doorbell has expanded into hope, galloping alongside apprehension: how can she possibly pull this off?

"These ground-floor units are the best," says Rose, sitting down on the steps and rubbing her dry hands together. "Great for children. All wrong without them, in fact." A side of her mouth curls upward in satisfaction. "And it looks like these two feel right at home. Don't you think?"

Veronica paces the room's perimeter, at a loss for what to say. She could try to buy some time by answering that she likes it but has a few other visits lined up and will call back in a couple of days, but that would leave the door wide open for Rose to show the apartment to who knows how many other people. Some lucky family would rent it in a heartbeat. Another pair of children would move their train set into the playroom, build snowmen in the yard in the winter, and play duck-duck-goose in the grass in the spring. Meanwhile, Veronica would find herself back at the drawing board, making lists in her parents' dining room. At a certain point, lists of phone numbers to call become just like lists of Things to Do around the house: an excuse for doing nothing else.

"I love it," she blurts out. "It's just that …" She clears her throat, opens her clammy fists, and examines the half moons that have appeared where her fingernails dug in. "I'd be moving in alone. With the kids, that is, but you know, just the three of us. So I need a couple of days to figure everything out."

"That's all right," Rose stands and touches Veronica's shoulder. "The right choice is always worth the wait. Think it over. Call me next week. Meantime, I'll let you know if anybody else comes along—that is, anybody else I wouldn't mind seeing move in here."

"Are we gonna live there, Mommy, are we?" Céleste clamors through a mouthful of pizza. They've stopped at Papa Gino's for lunch on the way back to Tenafly. Veronica's also hungry, but too worked up to eat.

"Daddy too?" Luc pipes in.

"I don't know, guys," she says, cutting a rubbery strand of cheese on Luc's pizza slice. Her hunger pangs sharpen into sickening pangs of guilt. All this time she's led Luc and

Céleste along to prospective apartments as if playing a game, pumping up their expectations with embellished scenarios of riding an elevator to their new front door, of trick-or-treating in the corridors at Halloween. At this young age, anything new makes the past so easy to forget. She's turned the prickly questions Céleste has articulated about their real house and Didier into exclamations about how much fun it would be to live right next to a public playground, or to have a balcony off their living room with a bird's-eye view of the neighborhood below, never letting on that these scenarios don't include their father. Or that they may not see him for quite some time.

Nor has she revealed the dark dilemma each visit raises, the dilemma twisting her stomach into knots right now: how in the world is she going to afford this? She has no significant savings, no income, no art to sell. When the desire seized her late one night to live on her own in order to sort out her life, she shut her eyes to practical matters. Take theengs one at a time, she told herself. Start with the rental lists and somehow, sooner or later, the rest will work itself out. She forgot, though, that taking things one at a time can mean losing sight of the bigger picture, losing sight of reality and of yourself.

Swallowing back a nauseating rush of saliva, she turns her focus to the kids. Luc is chomping the crust of his pizza slice, his gaze riveted on a bead of grease rolling down his pinkie. Céleste, done eating, has lain down on the booth's shiny, red plastic seat and is sliding back and forth, one foot against the wall, contemplating the large photos of hot cheesy pizza pies and turkey subs on the menu board above the cash registers. Her skirt has flopped up above her belly, revealing a bulky pull-up encased in pink tights. Luc's probably planning to lick the bead of grease from his pinkie, while Céleste is undoubtedly choosing a dessert. Such is their field of vision, the scope of their attention and concerns. Veronica, however, knows what they are thinking before they do. Her own, adult field of vision is infinitely broader, the scope of her attention and abilities far more powerful and multifaceted.

"C'mon, guys," she says, rising to collect the paper plates and tray.

"But I want one of those!" Céleste protests, sliding to her knees and pointing at the photo of cinnamon sticks.

"I'm sure you do," Veronica sighs, taking her wrist. "But we've got lots to do if you'd like to live in the apartment we just saw."

"Like what? Whadda we hafta do?" Céleste steps double-time to keep up with Veronica as she exits Papa Gino's, Luc on her hip.

"For starters, we have to go someplace where I can put on my thinking cap." She pats Luc's head.

"Me too?" he asks.

"Sure!" She laughs. She squeezes him, relishing the sensation of his warm body, so fragile and so small.

Chapter Nineteen

After driving north, then south, for forty minutes, unsure of where to go, Veronica heads for the Tenafly Public Library. Though not quite the ideal private refuge she pines for, its floor-to-ceiling windows ushering in rivers of sunshine and its spacious, silent halls lined with books and works of art make it the best place she knows of in this neck of the woods to put her thinking cap on.

It also has a state-of-the-art children's room complete with games, toys, computers, and a mesmerizing fish tank that she hopes will keep Luc and Céleste occupied long enough for her to not only reflect on the puzzle she needs to piece together, but also to browse the community job board in the lobby and reference books about résumés and careers. Because with no savings, no artwork to sell, and the prospect of outside help nothing but a slippery slope, she needs to work.

On past visits, she's glanced briefly at the job board, noting its eclectic announcements for everything from housework, babysitting, dog-walking, and elder care to freelance film editing and local theater set design. Set design sounds right up her alley, she thinks, her heart skipping with hope. Certainly better than a dull office job where she'd stare at the clock all day waiting to bolt at five, or a job teaching the present perfect tense, which she barely understands herself, to befuddled adults. If she'd wanted that job, she would have taken it on the spot.

Oil paintings of rugged battles frozen in time, of pioneers toiling in great Western prairies or pausing in gardens decorate the library's lobby; behind it, exhibits of eclectic work by local painters hang among the main-floor book stacks. Pushing the double stroller up the handicapped ramp and in the door, she absorbs the peaceful echo of silence reverberating from these elegant tributes to the mind and the imagination. Luc and Céleste, who fell asleep during the car ride and didn't wake when she transferred them to the stroller, begin to stir. She jiggles the handle with the old "shake-em-and-bake-em" stroke that she prays will add at least another ten minutes on to their precariously short nap.

In the lobby, her hopefulness collapses into a thick lump of despair: Luc wakes and starts whining for his cuddly, which she doesn't have, and the job board is gone. Summoning the dregs of the adrenaline rush that has propelled her, lately, past so many other spur-of-the-moment obstacles, she whispers, "We don't need your blankie, Duke. We're at the library. Let's go read some books."

How much easier it is to pursue something you'd like to own, to buy, or to rent, she thinks, crossing the library's main floor, than to figure out how the heck you'll use your own two hands and brain to generate the income to pay for it. The simple disappearance of the job board in the lobby has left her reeling with anxiety and doubt: can she possibly find a job that won't feel like a set of shackles, that won't make her want to call in sick every day so she can stay home to watch TV and nap? How long will it take? Who'd want to employ her? She has nothing but rudimentary office skills, rusty at best.

In the children's section, Céleste's eyes pop open beneath the bright fluorescent light. Unstrapped, she scampers across the room to bang on the keyboard of a computer and wiggle its mouse. Bouncing a disconsolate Luc on her hip, Veronica paces alongside the bookcase displaying this month's "Librarian's Picks," reading aloud the titles of the half dozen or so featured books to calm him down. Their vivid cover illustrations remind her of the editorial meetings she once sat in on, the production checklists she ticked off under tight deadline pressure, and all the other harrowing steps she helped coordinate to turn an illustration's final proof into a finished product, pages bound. The lump of despair in her chest thickens, obstructing her breath. Meetings, checklists, deadlines, and harrowing steps are part of almost every job. If she'd given herself the chance simply to stay home with her kids, she might have battled twinges of boredom and emptiness, but she'd have risen above the drudgery of employment to become the CEO of her own private world.

Rounding the corner of the bookcase, she spots a familiar style gracing the jacket of a book bearing a round, gold sticker in one corner: the emblem of a prestigious literary prize. Her ribcage squeezes. Beneath the title, in an inconspicuous, blocky font, is the name Brenda Gray.

Impossible, she thinks, struggling to reconcile this name with her former boss's pale, narrow face. There must be another author-illustrator by the same name. She snatches the book, flips it over and scans the back cover's inner flap. An unmistakable thumbnail shot of Brenda, giving a pensive smile from behind the same old horn-rimmed glasses and sleek, platinum-blonde bob, sits in the bottom-right corner. She wants to scream, to cry, to turn and run. In the past five years, while she has floundered, her old boss has become a literary luminary. Brenda's probably touring the country right now, signing autographs in schools while Veronica's on the verge of applying for jobs cleaning other people's toilets.

The book is called *The Stonecutter's Gift*. Its jacket illustration shows a timeless, European village of thatched-roof cottages. In the foreground, a young girl dressed in a tattered burlap dress belted at the waist stares at a pile of rocks. Her expression oozes with melancholia so palpable it seems to rise like mist from the page, with spellbinding undertones of the stoic lucidity that comes from battling hardship. If Veronica saw her in the street, she'd want to scoop her up, kiss her cheeks, and take her home.

"How 'bout this one?" she says to Luc, taking it to the sofa, wishing she had the steel nerves required to pretend she never saw it. Céleste scurries over, and both kids listen, mesmerized, as Veronica reads them the story of Liora, a young girl who lives alone with her father, Peter, a stonecutter. Peter can't afford to buy Liora gifts or toys, but instead offers her stones, which she keeps in a growing pile. Though dispirited by the pile, which reminds her of the things she doesn't have, Liora learns over time to appreciate the stones' hidden virtues, including their many entertaining uses, and to cherish the hope they embody that if she becomes skilled in carving through their hard surface, one day, she might uncover a nugget of gold.

"Read it again, Mommy, read it again," Céleste begs.

Tears spring to Veronica's eyes. "Wait. There's more." She opens the back cover and taps a finger beneath the thumbnail photo of Brenda. "This lady wrote the book and drew the pictures. Let's hear who she is."

"A lady wrote it?" Céleste asks.

"Yeah," Veronica breathes. "All by herself. Books are made by people." She peruses the short blurb about the author. "It says here that the lady who made this book is named Brenda Gray, that she lives in Rhode Island with her family, and that *The Stonecutter's Gift* is her second book for children."

Céleste yawns. "Now read it again."

Veronica hands the book to Luc. "How about if we go find the other book this lady wrote instead?" Before leaving her publishing job, she saw the galleys of Brenda's first book but never read it. She can't even remember what it's called.

She walks to the librarian's desk and rings the bell, mind whirring. Brenda lives in Rhode Island. She must have stepped down from the corporate ladder years ago. She probably earns a comfortable living from advances on her books, including fancy add-ons like movie rights and licensing agreements. To think Veronica used to scorn her dry, nose-to-the grind ways, when in fact, those very ways enabled her to stick it out through thick and thin and produce the art that she knew welled in her soul. Now her art's in full bloom, and she has a husband, a family. She has it all.

Despite socking Veronica in the gut right where it hurts the most, however, this realization also uplifts her. Brenda's only human, like everybody else. She may have talent, but above all, she knew how to cultivate it through relentless hard work. Veronica's talent may not match Brenda's, but if she sets her mind to it, she, too, can surely find a way to do something gratifying that also makes a meaningful contribution to the world beyond her own four walls. If she didn't believe in her ability to do so, she'd have filed for a divorce long ago, blaming her lack of satisfaction on Didier. Or booked a flight back to Marseille.

A heavy-set, bearded man wearing a smoke-blue cardigan emerges from the office behind the librarian's desk, breathing as though he'd just climbed a flight of stairs. Veronica has seen him here before, reading to groups of children at story hour.

"Can you tell me where I can find Brenda Gray's first book? I'm not sure of the title."

The man adjusts his glasses. "Good choice. It's even better than the second one, if you ask me. Don't know why it never made it off the short list." He turns his head to wheeze into cupped hands and then indicates the book's location. "Enjoy."

"Thanks." She clears her throat. Blushing and forcing herself to keep looking him straight in the eye, she adds, "By the way, what happened to the job board that used to hang in the lobby?"

He slouches, shakes his head. "Shame, huh? There were a few too many complaints about abuses. You know, people getting hold of the numbers up there and using them for marketing and, well … entertainment. We can't even post our own openings on the premises now. And those Internet want ads bring in so many résumés. Who has time to go through them all? My own slush pile's this high." He holds a hand beside his ear, palm down. "I'll probably be combing through it till I retire."

"Are you—is the library hiring?"

He nods and begins thumbing through a return on the desk.

Pulse racing, Veronica draws herself up as straight as she can and lifts her chin, hoping to look confident, competent.

Professional. At least she's still dressed in the wool pants and sweater she chose for this morning's apartment visit rather than overalls or jeans. "What sorts of openings do you have?"

"Just this one." He opens a drawer and pulls out a sheet of paper. Turning it toward her on the desk, he jabs his index finger into the headline: Project Assistant, Children's Room. "Vacant since my assistant moved to Florida last month. She'd been with us nearly twenty years." He wheezes again and then slides a knuckle beneath his glasses to rub an eye.

Veronica leans forward and scans the series of typed bullet points: Plan and lead story hours. Screen books for "Monthly Pick." Coordinate birthday parties and fund-raising events. Edit newsletter. Assist with orders, inventory, and circulation. Sweat drips down her inner arms. Forget set design. She could put her heart into a job like this! Her publishing experience would transfer seamlessly, and, with children everywhere, she'd feel perfectly natural, right at home. She'd be great at reading to them, leading them in sing-alongs, and helping them find misplaced toys. She's had plenty of training, hands-on. The schedule is manageable, too—ten to four Monday through Friday plus two Saturday mornings a month—and the hourly pay would add up to a little more than what she earned back when she was working in Manhattan. With that, she could squeak by.

"Sounds interesting," she says, trying to infuse her voice with the same confidence and competence that she hopes her appearance exudes. Yet inside, she's shaking like a leaf. Suddenly, this dusty librarian is no longer a kind stranger, but her judge. And the cheery, welcoming children's room now abounds with potential traps and hurdles: learning curves to climb, responsibilities to assume, and commitments to make. Biting the inside of her lower lip, she reminds herself that, for now, she's just exploring, and that if she changes her mind or if this man laughs in her face she doesn't ever have to set foot in the Tenafly Public Library again. "How can I apply?"

"Bring your résumé on in with a cover letter. I'll add it to the pile." He raises his hand to his ear again to indicate his growing slush pile. "But hurry up."

She thanks him, folds the job description into neat thirds, and slips it inside the diaper bag that doubles as her purse. Voilà. What was so hard about that? Yet as she fumbles to snap shut the only bag she's carried for the past two years, it occurs to her that she has overlooked a very important detail. This job, however, may just offer a simple way to work it out.

"The position," she starts, fidgeting with the strap of her bag. "Being that it's in the children's room, could the person who fills it bring their kids to work?"

"I'm afraid not. We do have a list of child-care resources in the area, though. Centers, nanny agencies, home day cares and the likes." He points his chin toward a table at the front of the room and coughs. "Right over there."

More lists, Veronica thinks, thanking him again. More numbers to call. There must be an easier solution. In fact, she may have one right at her fingertips. It's worth a try. Mouth dry, stomach cramping with anxiety and past-due hunger, she returns to Luc and Céleste, busy yanking books down from a shelf.

"Time to go, guys." She squats to gather the books on the floor into a tidy pile. As she gathers, Luc yanks others down.

"Nooo!" Céleste whines.

Veronica takes a slow, deep breath. Suddenly, she can't wait to get back to her parents' house. She'll plunk the kids in front of a video or let Shirley color with them while she retreats to her room for a good, long cry.

"Princess," she says, rubbing her nose. "We're on a scavenger hunt. We need to go because we have lots of things to find."

"A Power Ranger hunt?" asks Luc.

She laughs through her impending tears. "No, silly, a scavenger hunt. That means that we have to go from one place to the next looking for clues about where to find a hidden prize."

"What's the prize?" chimes Céleste.

"Well, that's the whole thing about scavenger hunts. We won't know until we find it. But we have to look, or we won't find a thing."

"I wanna stay here!" Céleste grumbles, screwing her face up into an angry pout portending a howl. "I wanna read that other book you said."

"We'll read it. Just not here. We'll go buy our own copy. Of that one, and the one we've already read."

"Why?" asks Luc.

"To have for keeps." Quickly, while the twins are still busy digesting the exciting idea of a new purchase and a trip to the store, Veronica lifts them each into the stroller. She then steers her load out of the children's room, out of the library, and back down the handicapped ramp. As a gust of April wind wet with raindrops hits her cheeks, she shouts out, to nobody in particular, "And to show the lady who wrote them that we care."

Chapter Twenty

"My fingers are crossed for you, hon," says Shirley, phone to her ear. She's in the living room, deep in conversation, when Veronica, Luc, and Céleste come home. "Can I spread the word?"

A pause. Shirley glances at Veronica and nods. Her hair, freshly sculpted and sprayed into a poofier-than-than-usual cycling helmet shape, glints a metallic shade of ruby. "All right. Gotta go. Hugs and smooches to the boys."

"Stella?" Veronica asks, unzipping the kids' coats and hanging them in the front hall closet. Freed, Luc and Céleste sprint into the living room and twirl around.

"Mmm hmm." Shirley gets up and flicks on a cartoon. "These two look wired."

"They skipped their nap."

"Uh-oh. Red alert. Big day?"

"Yeah," Veronica sighs. "Really big. How's Stella?"

Shirley draws her chest up and thrusts out her lower back like a peacock about to strut its feathers. "Stella's doing great! You should give her a call."

The urge for a good, long cry, which Veronica put on

hold in the library, resurges. Stella's always doing great. She should have known. She rubs her hands together and stares at her mother, who's staring at the kids as they stare at the TV. "Can we talk?" she asks. "Someplace quieter?"

In the kitchen, Veronica describes the apartment she saw this morning, her trip to the library, and the vacant children's room position. "I've gotta give it a shot," she says. "But there's a glitch. And you and Dad, well, you've been amazing. You've done so much since I got here. I'm just wondering if maybe you can lend a hand with one last thing."

Shirley contorts her mouth into a frown and draws her chin into the folds of her neck. "Your father told me he offered to help. But he said you turned him down. I figured that meant you'd never go through with this meshuga idea of living on your own. What sort of existence would that be, locked up in some roach-infested rental with the kids when you have a fine husband who misses you to death and can offer you so much more?"

"What do you know about how much he misses me?" Veronica snaps.

"For God's sake, I hear his voice every morning on the phone! Do you think Luc and Céleste answer by themselves when he calls?"

Veronica turns away. For the past five weeks she's steeled herself against longing and pity by imagining Didier seated at Le Grillon with a sexy patent lawyer, leaning close to her across the table, touching her arm. That he might in fact spend his days wallowing in grief hasn't crossed her mind. Now she pictures him, alone in Aix, peering despondently through the steam on the mirror as he shaves each morning, inspecting the stubble on his slackened jaw for new grays. Does he still radiate contentment and slap his knees at

Uriel's jokes when he gathers with his family on Saturday afternoons or does he pick at his *daf* and leave early? She wishes, suddenly, that she could reach out and touch him, stand beside him for a moment to assuage their pain. She'd bury her face in the soft pocket of flesh between his neck and his jaw, inhale the trace scent of oil in his skin mingling with the tangy residue of his Eau Sauvage aftershave and feel his breath in her ear as he murmurs the nickname that used to make her cringe: "Vero."

Lately, peering into Luc's date-brown eyes, she's seen Didier's. When did Luc start looking so much like his father? His cheeks, though soft with baby fat, have begun to show signs of a prominent sharpening above the jaw. His overgrown, espresso-colored hair hangs practically to his eyes, mimicking the banglike slab Didier often pushes back from his forehead. The mere sight of him has also made her wish she could stand beside her husband for a moment and watch their children run into his arms.

But to join him for a moment is impossible, and to return to him for any length of time would require a sacrifice far more depleting than separation. For the impetus to strive for change that she's discovered over the past few weeks has developed a life of its own. Each new step she takes, albeit frightening, sends a buzz of excitement through her veins, reminding her that, yes, she can do this: she can grow. Ideas fly through her mind night and day like sparks ready to ignite. If she returned to Aix, to the comfort of a livelihood provided by her husband, the sparks would fizzle. She'd slip right back into the older, easier habit of putting initiatives off until tomorrow, every day. Didier would resent her, and she'd resent herself.

"I miss him, too," she says. "But our problems haven't

disappeared. If I just turn around and go back now, we'll wind up hating each other. Before you know it, I'll be here again, banging on your door."

"So wait," Shirley shrugs. "There's no rush."

"Wait for what? For our problems to evaporate? For something to come along and gloss them over? This isn't Disneyland!"

"If you lock yourself up in some rental and leave your kids all day so you can go off and—what? Sort books?—you'll be the new Cinderella!"

"Oh, please. So the job has no fancy pedigree. Big deal. I *need* it. Even the kids will be happier to see me focused and together, in control of my life, instead of falling apart and faking it at home. They already are. And by the way, I'm not asking for your blessing. Just a hand."

"This is breaking my heart." Shirley's nostrils flare as she regards Veronica for a few long seconds, then throws up her hands. "But what can I say? How much do you need?"

"I'm not asking for money, Mom. I'm getting a job. I'm just wondering if you can watch the kids."

Shirley roars with laughter as though finally spotting the proof she's been expecting that this entire conversation is a joke. "Why didn't you say so in the first place? Of course I'll watch the kids! When?"

Veronica lists the hours of the library job. "Hopefully this one will work out and end of story."

"Monday to Friday," Shirley repeats. "Ten to four. And every other Saturday morning. I thought you meant tomorrow. Or this afternoon. But a weekly schedule, for what, a year? Two? More? That's a full-time job!" She contemplates her fingertips for a moment, turning them at different angles as if critiquing her pink manicure, then sighs. "How about this: I take them the Saturday mornings, and weekdays when I get home from the hairdresser at one o'clock, give or take. Except when I have appointments or lunch dates. And except when I'm in Florida helping Stella."

"Helping her?" Veronica echoes, frowning so hard she can feel the faint lines she's detected recently on her forehead deepening into wrinkles. Stella has a live-in housekeeper and nanny. She no longer works. A visit from Shirley is one thing, but what help could she possibly need?

Shirley beams, her chest puffing with pride. "It's not official yet," she whispers with forbidden delight. "But Stella's pregnant again."

"*What*? She's having a fourth?" Veronica sputters. She's ready for that solitary sob now. Engrossed in other things, she's forgotten lately about the hunger for another baby that clawed at her during her final months in Aix. How delicious it would have felt to indulge in it, carefree.

"Well, you know Stella," Shirley declares. "And you know how badly she's wanted a girl. But let her tell you herself." She nudges her chin in the direction of the phone. "Give her a call."

"Later." Veronica rolls her eyes and trudges out of the kitchen. "For now I need to start looking into child care. All day, year round."

With enough repetition, disappointment eventually shrinks from a steel nail in the heart to a thumbtack pinning up a reminder to just keep going, keep trying, without looking back. So when Veronica flops belly-down onto her bed convulsing with sobs, it's not out of despair, nor out of envy of her sister, nor even out of fury at her mother, unable—or unwilling—to commit. Caring for kids too young for school really is a full-time job. She sobs, simply, to release the tension that's built up in her bones during this energetic race down a dozen different streets only to arrive with a screeching halt at a dozen dead ends. She sobs to mourn the myriad possibilities that won't pan out, to relieve the anguish of uncertainty, and to purge the self-defeating ruminations that ensue so she can pick herself up and continue.

As she works through the library's child-care list over the next several days, she sobs to buffer the shock. Nanny agencies have a prohibitive upfront fee. Home day-care centers, originally her top choice, are grim and run-down. At the first one she visits, four children, noses running, sit riveted to the TV in an unheated basement while, upstairs, the woman in charge nurses her own infant. Another reeks of stale, embedded smoke. Dog hair mats the furniture, and two aging golden retrievers scrounge among the children at snack time, licking their faces and lapping up the contents of their plates. The bigger, more organized centers have an unnerving, corporate feel. Their polished corridors smell of Lysol, which just barely overpowers the stench of poop-filled diapers in the trash. Large groups of children stand in line like soldiers to march from one activity to the next on schedules maintained by buzzers that blare like fire alarms. In some centers, the children don name badges or ID bracelets in case they get lost. And the few smaller, homier places that Veronica visits have waiting lists of up to a year.

Face buried in her pillow each evening, she weeps for Maria, for her vivid black eyes radiating as warmly as the Mediterranean sun. In her best imitation of Maria's Portuguese-twanged accent, she murmurs, "*C'est bee-ayng, mon petit chou,*" and nearly chokes on her tears. The morning she left Aix, she asked the taxi driver to stop at the pink stucco house at the bottom of the street—the one with the dapper, pine-green shutters that make the living room so cozy-dark at nap time—and to wait while she, Luc, and Céleste knocked on the door. At the news of their departure, Maria shuddered with sorrow, knelt, and pulled the kids into her arms. "*Vous revenez bientôt, oui?*" she said, imploring them to come back soon. She vowed that there'd always be space for them in her home and a spot for them in her heart and begged Veronica to send news from time to time, to write or to call.

That Veronica never did, and that she'll never again find a caregiver like Maria, makes her want to kick herself for having taken so much for granted. Dropping the kids off at Maria's was as painless as having a relative come watch them at home. If she forgot to send them over with a swimsuit or an extra stack of diapers, she could run back home and get them. If they didn't like the lunch she'd packed, she could swing by with a peanut butter sandwich. And if they got sick, she could drop everything and go pick them up right away. With no billable hours, no clients to impress, and no colleagues raising eyebrows, she was as free as the wind—on her own, yet near her children and available to them at a moment's notice.

Such delicious flexibility also meant setting her own agenda and planning her days however she liked, and she weeps for the loss of this privilege, too. Yet every privilege has its cost, and this one cost her vitality and self-esteem. At least now she has a chance to pick a different set of trade-offs.

After three days she exhausts the day-care options in Tenafly and moves on to other towns, bringing Luc and Céleste along wherever she goes. Their reactions teach her that kids see long, polished corridors as great places to run, that name tags remind them of cool sheriff's badges, and that they consider lining up a great opportunity to get to the front. They don't see dog hair at all. If they break loose from her side and join the other children in a circle-time discussion of whether it's sunny, cloudy, warm, or windy out today, she knows they haven't registered the smell of poop and Lysol or don't care. When they become so engrossed in a game or story that they don't notice when she turns her back, she understands that they'll adapt far more easily than she will to the right new situation. And that she should worry more about finding what suits her than what suits them.

Between visits, she works on her résumé, still stored in her parents' computer from the days when she lived with them after college. Reading it is as mortifying as looking in the mirror first thing in the morning. Did this jumble of clichés really land her a job in publishing? No wonder she hated the job! And what on earth made her think that volunteering as a dormitory decorator or taking private art classes in high school counted as "experience?" Negotiating mergers and acquisitions like Stella used to counts as experience. So does perfecting new surgical techniques to correct a deviated septum. Organizing a kosher kitchen and raising bilingual twins does not, so aside from answering e-mails and sorting through slush piles for Brenda Gray, Veronica has nothing to list. But a résumé needs fluff and fillers, and the mere thought of spinning old endeavors that went nowhere into snazzy sentences implying skill and accomplishment makes her stomach turn.

Her disgust with the first few drafts gets flushed away every evening by her tears. By her sixth or seventh try, she's seeing each bullshit phrase she crafts as a portent of her future. She will conceive and implement new strategies for outreach. She will develop streamlined filing systems and leverage Internet tools for improved communications from some desk in a stuffy back room. While gritting her teeth and praying for the day to hurry up and end, she will effectively identify new opportunities, define priorities, and meet deadlines. Maybe, if she's lucky, she will plan and supervise an event from time to time where people will have fun, or select a Title of the Month whose story and illustrations will win their hearts. More often, though, she will exercise her outstanding interpersonal skills to refrain from cringing or muttering a snide remark each time the librarian to whom she'll be sending this résumé irritates her with one of his loud, hacking coughs.

What a concept—spending more time each week with a hairy-faced stranger than she does with her children! That cough makes it sound like he's got chronic bronchitis. Maybe he does. God knows, Veronica might pick up some nasty bug and bring it home to the kids. What will she do then, if she, Luc and Céleste all get sick, one after the other, for weeks on end? How do working mothers manage with so many conflicting needs to balance and so much on their plates? Why didn't she ever find the verve, the flame, to paint?

One sunny morning late in the week she lingers at the bottom of the staircase until, promptly at eight, the telephone rings. Until now, she has always found a way to disappear into the shower or her bedroom before eight o'clock to avoid catching snippets of the kids' morning conversation with Didier. But today, having trashed her umpteenth draft, she aches with nostalgia for the soothing steadiness of Didier's voice when he used to talk her through dilemmas and doubts. Back when each new day brought one infuriating mistake after another by the work crew renovating their house, he would remind her that no finished product emerges perfectly on the first try and that success comes only at the price of failure and frustration. After each round of retching when she was pregnant, he'd say, "Now you are one step closer to the end of this phase. Just think how good you will feel when it is done." Then he'd brew her a refreshing cup of mint tea. In the aftermath of her attempt to cancel their wedding, he told her that surviving their first major crisis had left them well-prepared to face all the others life had in store.

Now, hearing her mother pick up the phone, the longing, the pity, and the loneliness she has steeled herself against for the past five weeks lurch in her chest like a time bomb about to explode. She braces herself to leap out from the stairwell, grab the receiver from Shirley, and cry, "It's me! I'm here!" She can't wait to tell Didier at last how desperately she misses him and how sorry she is to have hurt him. He was right, she'll say: her mind's abuzz with creativity and spunk. She just doesn't know yet how to channel it or what it will produce. But she hopes with all her heart that, once she does, their fledgling branch of the Benhamou family will reunite.

Reassured that he feels the same way, she'll then sit down and bang out a final, sparkling version of her résumé, which she'll send off without hesitation, confident that she has other options and that, as if by miracle, everything will turn out for the best.

"Mmm hmm," Shirley says. "I will."

Silence.

"Well, you never know, but I don't think so. I mean, how could anybody not like the south of France!" Shirley laughs.

Silence.

"Nah, I know my Veronica. She just needed a little vacation. You know, a change of scenery and some fresh ideas. She's getting the picture that it won't be easy. Give her another week or two, max."

Rage flares through her body. Every morning for the past five weeks Shirley has answered Didier's calls. How often have they spoken like this? What does Shirley believe? What does she know?

She sucks in a breath so deep that it seems to pull the heavens in their entirety, immense and cloudless, into her lungs. Their aura, blue as God's eyes, fuses with a boundless sapphire expanse unfolding to reveal itself inside her mind. She turns around and climbs the stairs to the study where the computer and her résumé await her. Miracles come from within. She'll talk with Didier when she has something to say.

Chapter Twenty-One

Clouds gather overhead the next morning in big, smoky bunches like linens crumpled on an unmade bed. As Veronica approaches the Over the Moon daycare center in Teaneck, a few fat raindrops splash onto the windshield; when she pulls into the parking lot, it begins to pour. "April showers bring May flowers," she chants, unbuckling Luc and Céleste's car seats and pulling up the hoods of their windbreakers. Funny how she's become inured to the endless tease of a New Jersey spring, when any given day can bring warm sunshine just as easily as passing thundershowers or feet of snow. The trick is to let go of expectations.

It takes a couple of seconds for her eyes to adjust to the dim lighting inside, which she notes as a potential drawback, like the daycare's location in a shopping center on a busy road. But Luc and Céleste don't seem to mind. They race toward a carnival-caliber rocket ship ride mounted on a stand in the center of the corridor. Céleste gets there first. She climbs aboard and claims the driver's seat. "Mine!" Luc cries, pounding its fluorescent, orange sides.

"You're next, Duke," Veronica says, picking him up.

"Check this out." She points to the ceiling, strung with globular replicas of the seven planets illuminated like lamps from within. A million silvery stars glimmer from the walls, and patterns of the big, swirling contours of the Milky Way skip across the carpet.

The center's director, Karen, a short woman with a frizzy, auburn perm and bulging eyes, waves from the end of the hall. She has on a goofy hat mimicking planetary rings. Patting it, she explains: "Today's Jupiter day. Next stop, Venus. Eventually, we'll come back to Earth!"

Small rooms, Veronica remarks as she heads down the zigzagging corridor barely wide enough for the impressive girth of Karen's hips. She crinkles her nose at the nauseating stench of burnt pizza cheese wafting from the kitchen and the mess of paper scraps and glitter covering the floors. Yet she also notices that the air buzzes with laughter and squeals of joy. In the preschool section, a little girl whose blonde ponytail springs from the top of her head like a fountain declares with endearing seriousness, "You get what you get, and you don't get upset." In the younger toddlers' section, a hush spreads over an assembly of peanut-sized children as a teacher tells them to put on their listening ears. Infants sleep in identical cribs in a room at the end of the hall. Beside them, a grandmotherly woman clucks and coos in Spanish at the tiny baby fussing in her arms. The tour ends at the older toddler's section, where Luc and Céleste would enroll. A group of kids their age have just taken seats at a knee-high table piled with scraps of glow-in-the-dark felt. The two immediately find a space among them and begin pasting scraps together into cosmic shapes.

Karen winks and excuses herself to greet another visitor. Alone, Veronica backs into a low futon sofa along one wall and observes her twins, squeezing Elmer's glue from its familiar, orange-capped bottle. She's gone through this drill a dozen times now: a meet-and-greet with a facility's director, a tour of its grounds, and twenty minutes or so watching her children play. Usually, they wail in disappointment when it's time to go. A dozen times she's promised they'll come back, and a dozen times she's silently reviewed the center's flaws after leaving, then crossed it off her list, letting the kids forget about it, as they always seem to, while telling herself that surely a better option awaits just around the corner.

The futon is firm and comfortable. She inches back, letting the corner brace her like a strong pair of masculine arms. She's so comfortable she could almost fall asleep. How decadent it would feel to continue drifting day in and day out from one prospect to the next in search of perfection, never committing, never locking herself in. With no choice made, she could muse forever about ideals: an entertaining, part-time job with no boss, no deadlines, no files, or phones—a job where she could make her own hours and leave at the drop of a hat to ferry the kids to soccer or ballet. A clone of herself to care for her kids in her absence. A winning lottery ticket or windfall inheritance. An epiphany of an idea, at last, for the single painting that will catapult her to instant success. The possibilities are endless when they aren't real.

Luc looks up briefly from his pasting as if searching for her. She blushes and snaps to attention, back straight as a wall, seeking his gaze in case he needs the reassurance of meeting hers. But his focus drifts right past her, absorbing its surroundings, lingering for a couple of seconds on a wooden toy chest painted with meteors trailing fat wakes of star dust before returning to the table where he's still busy, still intrigued. Beside him, Céleste giggles and waves a pom-pom made of yarn at a girl with bronze freckles cascading down her arms. Veronica's back muscles soften again. She could return to her daydream, doze off, and her kids wouldn't notice: they feel as at ease as she does among planetary rings, orbiting debris, and messy floors. She could rise and move toward the room's gate, unlatch it with a *click,* and walk down the hall—as she does now, swiftly—and it wouldn't faze them in the least. She could even exit the building and drive off to face the world, such as it is.

At the end of the hall, the door to Karen's office stands ajar. Veronica knocks on the threshold and then pokes her head in. Seeing Karen seated behind a cluttered desk speaking with the visitor she greeted earlier, she recoils. She hasn't bothered requesting enrollment information at the other day cares she's visited. Now she feels like a kid with a crush on the teacher: so excited and filled with yearning that she's weak in the knees, afraid to speak.

"Don't be shy!" Karen waves her in. The planetary rings encircling her head bob. "The more the merrier!" She gestures with her chin at an empty wooden chair standing amid the dissembled parts of a computer—a dead hard drive, coiled wires, a monitor.

"I just wanted to grab an enrollment package or … whatever you've got." It occurs to her that she's not really sure what enrollment entails.

"I do have several spaces in the younger toddler's section," Karen answers, nodding at the visitor in her office—a dark-haired woman holding a baby on her hip, flanked by two older children. She rummages through a tall pile of papers on her desk and produces a couple of sets of stapled sheets. "Here's the skinny on tuition and enrollment."

The dark-haired woman shifts her baby to her other hip.

Her oldest, a boy about four, is sitting on the ground behind her punching her calves. "Quit it, Con," she snaps, blowing at a fuzzy strand of hair that's escaped from the large barrette at the nape of her neck. She takes a set of papers and passes one to Veronica, whose hands tremble as she flips through the pages requesting emergency contact information, date of birth, eye color, height, and weight. She'll have these filled out in no time. Perhaps by tomorrow she'll have a new home, a job. On a scavenger hunt, sometimes one key clue can lead directly to the prize.

"Skinny's right!" the dark-haired woman clucks. "This tuition I could actually manage. How long do you think till a space frees up in the pre-K room?" There's a desperate squeak to her gravelly voice, a pleading in her misty brown eyes.

"I wish I had a crystal ball," Karen says. "But as I mentioned, I do have space for the littler ones right now. All of them." She jerks her chin toward Veronica in affirmation.

Veronica gapes at the information package in her hand. "Skinny? Even with the sibling discount, these rates are, like, four times what I paid for a nanny in France!" They're also twice the monthly rent on the apartment she liked in Hackensack, and practically the entire paycheck she'd net as a librarian's assistant—or in any other job she'd qualify for. The lump of despair she's so bravely remolded over the past few weeks into a steel nail of determination explodes into shrapnel scraping through her lungs, clogging her heart. This won't work out. Nothing will.

"France?" A brow slides up the dark-haired woman's forehead.

"Yeah." Veronica peruses the woman's round face, the puffy violet rings encasing her eyes. Nose prickling madly, she rolls the information package into a tube. "Well," she says, drumming it with a note of finality against her palm and glancing wistfully at Karen. "Thanks anyway." To the dark-haired woman, she adds, "Good luck."

In the hallway, she steels herself against the joyful clamor of babies' gurgles and nursery rhymes. She silently curses the mural of purple aurora borealis sprawling across the ceiling that, under other circumstances, might have inspired her to crack open her tubes of paint, dust off her pallet, and mix unprecedented, nameless colors late at night. No more fantasies, she chides. No more dreaming. The time to define herself, to come of age, is gone. She had her chance, a thousand times over, but opted instead for the path of least resistance, the path requiring minimal effort and risk. Now she's a bird with clipped wings.

At the gate to the older toddler's section, she contemplates Luc and Céleste, sharing a snack of apple slices and raisins with the children who might have become their classmates, their friends. Extracting them is going to be as painful as taking away a new toy. Heart raw and inflamed, she doesn't have the wherewithal to face Céleste's inevitable screaming fit, or, worse yet, Luc's silent beleaguerment, his muffled grief. And she dreads the prospect of returning to Rich and Shirley's house, tail between her legs.

A child's footsteps pound past her down the hall. A hand catches on her sleeve. Surprised, she spins around.

"Hey, Connor!" shouts the woman from Karen's office. She's striding in Veronica's direction, baby flailing on her hip, trying to catch up with her sprinting, four-year-old son. "Watch where you're going! And if you don't slow down and listen to me right now, there'll be no going to the playground!" Passing Veronica, she shakes her head and mutters, "Sorry."

"No problem," Veronica mutters back. Then the shrapnel

in her chest stirs, provoking an involuntary giggle. You can lose yourself just as easily to the bigger picture as you can to the minutiae of zooming in your focus tight and narrow to the little things that keep everybody sane. "Hey," she calls out as the woman recedes down the hall. "If you don't mind, we'll follow you to that playground!"

Chapter Twenty-Two

"The *south* of France?" gawks the dark-haired woman, standing by Veronica's side at the base of a swing set. She appeared relieved earlier when Veronica suggested joining her at a public playground. Now, as their children weave in and out the orifices of a mock fire engine a few yards away, she leans close, eyes wide with disbelief. "So what the devil are you doing *here*?"

The morning's cloud bunches have ironed out into diaphanous, ashen sheets pierced by a few random streaks of powdery blue. Wind-whipped puddles, murky and tremulous, dot the playground's rubber flooring. Veronica nibbles at the inside of her lower lip, twisting her mouth into one shape after another as phrases bubble inside it and then dissipate, unspoken. The woman—Angie Mazzola, from Englewood, New Jersey—has no idea how weighty and complicated her seemingly frivolous question is.

For a few brief weeks, Veronica thought she knew what she was *doing* here. Now, doubt leaps out at her, big and ugly as a billboard on a scenic country road. Perhaps all the lists she's compiled, the phone calls she's placed, and the snappy new words she's inserted into her résumé never will add up to anything but gray matter, that nebulous precursor to an idea that, at a certain point, just isn't worth probing any further.

As for why *here*, in eastern New Jersey rather than the sublime south of France, she could easily rattle off the thousand superficial things that made her pine for home: French people's irritating bluntness, the cramped size of homes, towns, cars, shops, and streets or the constant, maddening scream of the mistral wind. Lately, though, she's found herself missing the way the French touch your forearm during conversations or tell you frankly if they think you look good or bad, tired or distressed. And how, when you tell them the truth instead of glossing reality over with a smile, they understand. She's also realized that less space indoors and out just means less space between friends and family members, even strangers. More intimacy. Living in a quirky old house whose walls bear the scars of centuries past reminds you of the relative insignificance of the present. Even the mistral's drone is no more or less disturbing than today's random yet ferocious breeze.

A more sincere answer would require digging down into the real reasons she came to Tenafly last month, which, recently, have blinked in and out of focus, becoming crystal clear for a few brief seconds before fading away again, too fuzzy to grasp: her marriage to a man whose complexities seemed too much for her to handle until she started seeing her own. Provence's glorious yet deceptive beauty, which hijacked each of her senses, right down to taste and smell, and lured her into believing that her feelings matched the scenery—or should have. And the bittersweet realization that, at least for now, she must settle for carrying this beauty in her heart like a wallet photo of an estranged lover she still dreams of, the reminder of an ideal she hopes to attain.

A few drops of water blow off the swing set and splash her cheeks. She tucks her chin into the collar of her parka—a beige, hooded relic from her working days that looks much better on her now that her complexion bears the first scars of experience and her waist has narrowed from the exertion of striving toward a goal. "Some things were just too hard for me in the south of France," she says, shivering. "And everything else was—" She chuckles. "Too easy."

Angie throws her head back and howls so loudly that her baby, Emily, perched in a swing that looks like a red, plastic car seat, begins to howl, too. "Too easy? Oh, honey, bring it on!"

"You wouldn't want that, believe me," Veronica blurts out, embarrassed that the brief phrase she chose for its blandness could strike such a raw nerve. "When things are too easy, you may as well be—I don't know—dead!"

Angie wipes the corners of her eyes. Their puffy, violet contours have lightened a bit, blended somewhat into her cheeks, ruddy from the wind. She lifts Emily from the swing, whispers a few appeasing words in her ear, and nods, her gaze basking in a warm glow of acknowledgment. "You're so right. Let's just hope things really are so easy for the dead." Her voice drifts off, suddenly sounding more coarse than gravelly, as if battered from years of forced laughter or disconsolate tears. "I guess after a morning like the one we just spent, with insult piled on top of injury, I'll gobble up whatever little crumb of denial I can get. That person—Karen?—she may as well have said, 'You're a single mom with three kids? Whoa, don't wanna go there. Can't help.'"

Veronica glances at her, then turns away, face red. A single mom? With three kids, including a baby who looks barely twelve months old? "Oh!" she says, struggling to camouflage her stupefaction, to silence the thousand impertinent questions flooding her mind. "I didn't realize."

"Yeah," Angie sighs, bouncing Emily in one arm while fishing in her diaper bag with her other hand. "I haven't totally realized it yet myself." She raises her chin and inhales, nostrils constricting against the influx of chilly air.

Veronica snorts. "Sounds familiar."

Angie studies her, lips turned down, premature frown lines cupping her mouth like parentheses enclosing a fading reference to the past. "One year and seven months already." She turns to peer at the manicured park beyond the chain link fence encircling the playground, where oak tree branches percolate with leaf buds on the brink of unfurling. "One year, seven months and ..." She pauses, calculating. "Twelve days."

Like a videotape rewinding on a VCR, Veronica's mind spins backward past the twins' first foray into potty training, past their first words and their first steps, to one gloriously sunny, September day around the time they started crawling. The explosion of blood-orange berries on the firethorn bushes along her street in Aix took her breath away that morning as she returned from dropping the kids off at Maria's, sparking visions of a painting she might begin, she mused, that very afternoon. But around three fifteen, her mother's voice blared through the answering machine, wresting her from her nap, and prompting her to trudge downstairs, turn on the TV, then gape with horror at the news that would forever erase the firethorn berries from her imagination, replacing them with pictures of another blood-orange explosion, one mired in smoke and cinders, destruction and debris. "We're okay. Ray's okay. He isn't in Manhattan today," Shirley's message had said. Still, Veronica's limbs turned brittle with panic as she watched, again and again, the footage of indomitable steel edifices collapsing like a house of cards at the mercy of a sneeze. She raced down the street to pick up Luc and Céleste. For weeks she kept them home, close to her, safe, reluctant ever to bring them to Maria's again, riddled with anxiety and preemptive guilt should something, anything, happen to them in her absence. What's a little painting compared with your children's precious lives?

One year, seven months, and twelve days. Eventually her panic diminished to no more—yet no less—than what it had always been: a latent fear of her own fragility. The same fear made her feel safer flying home to New Jersey last month after U.S. troops rolled into Iraq than staying in France amid protesters brandishing anti-American banners and anti-Semitic ideas. Yet now, perusing Angie's stalwart brown eyes, it occurs to her that even right here, in this dapper, suburban playground equipped with swing sets galore, an impressive mock fire engine, and a collection of grinning, plastic ladybugs to ride and to climb on, safety exists only in the heart.

She opens her mouth, closes it again, shakes her head, then steps forward and loops her arms around Angie's shoulders. Angie hugs her back. Emily remains wedged between them, soft as a cotton ball.

"Wow," she manages after a couple of seconds, releasing Angie and shaking her head again. "I'm so sorry."

"I didn't even know I was pregnant with Emily yet," says Angie, plunging her hand back into her diaper bag to continue fishing for whatever she was trying to find earlier. "He … my Joey … wherever he is, God, I hope he knows about her."

Veronica lifts Emily from Angie's drooping arms, searching for an answer commensurate with the magnitude of this statement. When nothing comes to her, she murmurs, "At least you have her. What a gift."

Angie bobs her head aloofly and produces a sippy cup filled with milk. "Chow time," she whispers, extending the cup to Veronica and zipping up her navy blue down vest.

"Do you have family? To help out?"

"My folks," Angie nods. "The insurance policy has helped, too, even though I hate it. Who can put a dollar value on a life? But the funds won't last forever, so I've gotta get back to work."

"What do you do?"

"I'm a dental hygienist."

"My dad's a dentist. In Tenafly."

Angie smiles. "Bet you always floss."

Veronica laughs, grateful for the comic relief. "Twice a day."

"My old boss called a couple of weeks ago and practically begged me to come back. Ten years I worked for her and loved it. But after Joey died, I was in no state whatsoever. First I took a leave of absence. Then, when things just weren't improving, I decided it was only fair to resign. I'm doing better now—not great, but then, what ever is?—and it's time, really. So when she called, I told her I could start at the end of the month. Meanwhile, I figured I'd find child care. Didn't see a thing or person that I liked and could afford until today. And then, well, you heard it."

"Yeah." Veronica bounces Emily in her arms, nuzzling her silky head and inhaling her powdery baby scent. Funny how a baby pulls you in, making you forget everything else. For a moment, the details of Angie's tragedy blur surreally against the backdrop of Emily's cool cheeks and perfect, petal-shaped lips. The crushing weight of this morning's disappointment lifts from her chest, and the impulse it sparked to throw in the towel, crawl into a hole, and die gives way to a desire for stock-taking and quiet reflection. Even the muffled melody rising from her bag on the ground—her cell phone's ring—seems trivial, though it's rare.

Reluctant to hand Emily back over to Angie just yet, she crouches, perching Emily on a knee while supporting her in the crook of one arm, and dips her free hand into her bag. Better at least see who it is. *Out of area*, blinks the caller ID. She's never received that ID before, except ... she scours her memory, rewinds again ... when her parents used to call her French cell phone number from the States. Her heart rolls over like a rock in her rib cage. It's an overseas call. Only one person overseas would have this number—courtesy of Shirley, no doubt. Heat lashes through her torso and limbs. She silences the ringer.

"So what do you think you'll do?" she asks, eager to forget the phone and follow this conversation's thread, tugging impatiently at her heart, before Luc starts whining for her to come lift him onto a plastic ladybug or Céleste starts complaining that she's cold.

"Good question." Angie twists a loose lock of hair smattered with gray strands around her index finger and then lets her arms fall to her sides. They drag her shoulders into a defeated slouch. "My parents both still work, so they're out. I could put Connor in private school for the year, till he's old enough for kindergarten, but it would cost an arm and a leg, plus my sanity, since I'd have to drive all over the map twice a day to drop him in one town, drop Vance and Emily off in another town, and then get to work in a third town in rush-hour traffic both ways. What do I look like, a bus driver? You'd think someone would pay me for doing all that!"

"Tell me about it." A sardonic grin tweaks Veronica's lips. "What town's your office in?"

"Hackensack."

A few ascending notes of music—da-da-da-DA!—sound from Veronica's bag on the ground. A message. From *Out of area*. She tightens her jaw. Over at the mock fire engine, Luc is busy negotiating the hollow middle of an enormous rubber tire, but Céleste has had her fill. She toddles toward the structure in the playground's center—a suspended maze of corridors, bridges, and pagoda-shaped watch towers—then climbs up and positions herself at the top of an undulating slide. Its surface glistens with rainwater left over from this morning's downpour. Veronica braces herself to dash over and order her not to go down it. She'll get all wet. But suddenly, an epiphany washes over her, a deluge of coolness and clarity far more consequential than a toddler's damp derriere. She straightens her back, squares her shoulders, and arranges her face as she might have for a job interview: confident, competent, poised. Take theengs one at a time, she reminds herself. But keep stepping forward. Dare.

"I'll be moving to Hackensack soon," she bluffs, steadying her voice. "Just me and the kids. My husband, well, he's staying in France. So we're on our own." She fixes Angie with an intentional look to emphasize the solidarity, the kinship, this implies and then tells her about the apartment she found, her background in art, and the dilemma of her job hunt, going nowhere. "Truthfully, I can't think of anything I'd enjoy enough to do every day. But I'm happy as a clam doing art projects with my kids. You know, salt-dough, ceramics, water colors and acrylics, braiding, weaving, exploring what happens when you mix different colors and mediums. They love it, too." She takes a deep breath. "So I've been thinking: I should start a home day care and do just that, with Luc, Céleste, and whoever else is there. Like Connor, Vance, and Emily, maybe?"

Angie stares at Veronica for a moment, then, suddenly, a mystified expression spreads over her face. Her eyes dance with mirthful disbelief. "Oh my God!" She gushes. "Are you kidding? I mean, are you serious? Would you really do that?"

"I should have done it ages ago."

"Well then, let's talk!" Angie slaps her knee, and leans forward. "And hey, as long as you're at it, do you think you could teach them a little French?"

Emily opens her lips and burps. Undigested milk dribbles down her chin. Laughing, Angie takes her and wipes up the mess, while Veronica, head spinning giddily, scans the playground. Luc has managed to climb atop a ladybug on his own. Céleste is slithering down the slide for the umpteenth time—on her stomach. The wind-whipped puddles dotting the playground's rubber-mat surface have turned darker, murkier, in the shadow of a new batch of ominous clouds that just rolled in. Any minute now, it'll rain again, Veronica notes. It'll pour. But who cares? April showers bring May flowers. And with them, a whole new cycle of life will begin. She can see it now, vivid and clear, its details unfolding before her like the brush strokes of a startlingly honest self-portrait produced in a moment of absolute lucidity.

Tomorrow, she will sign the lease on the apartment in Hackensack, putting down her life's savings as a deposit. Drawing on an inner strength and stamina she never knew she had, she'll watch Luc, Céleste, Connor, Vance, and Emily by day, work as an intern a few hours a week at Over the

Moon, and take night classes in child development so she can qualify for a license to operate a home day-care center in the state of New Jersey. She'll structure her child-care services with a schedule, a program, goals, and themes like any professional would. She'll subscribe to trade magazines, stock up on cheap supplies, and lead the children in alphabet games, number games, and art projects ranging from simple drawings to Van Gogh-like watercolors of sunflowers, cypress trees, and starry nights. At circle-time each morning, she'll teach them to sing, "*Un Poisson au Fond d'un Étang*" and "*Au Feu les Pompiers.*" In the afternoons, she'll play Simon Says with them in French: "*Jacques a Dit.*" Each Friday, she'll type up summaries for their parents, and previews of the week ahead. Shirley will stop by from time to time to help her out, or to baby-sit on weekends while she catches a movie or browses the mall to relax and unwind. The income will cover her rent and expenses. Along with her clients' gratitude and the satisfaction of seeing her endeavor thrive, it will fill her with pride. Weeks and months will file by in a jumble of busy commotion.

At night, when Connor, Vance, and Emily have returned home with Angie, when Luc and Céleste have gone to bed, when Veronica has mopped the floors and sponged the counters and prepared snacks and supplies for the following day, she'll stay up late painting bold, abstract shapes suggesting monolithic limestone cliffs sprouting rosemary, thyme, and Spanish broom. Against backgrounds of rich, Mediterranean turquoise, she'll create silhouettes evoking bright red poppies and swallows circling over moss-coated, terra-cotta roof tiles. Some, she'll sell to friends and clients for a pocket full of change and loads of pride. In lieu of a signature, she'll place a trademark unicorn and cherub in the corner of each canvas, and just for fun, she'll replicate these creatures in a stencil and apply it to the walls. She'll use the same stencil to make a sign for the front door with her day care's name: *Les Cherubins.*

A couple of days from now she'll call Stella. She'll congratulate her on her pregnancy, too wrapped up in the momentum of her own plans and her vibrant To-Do list to recall the latent emptiness revived by Stella's news of an impending fourth. To her surprise, Stella will reverse the compliments, praising her for being lucky enough to know what she wants and having the chutzpah to go out and get it.

"Chutzpah?" Veronica will laugh. "That's a good one! I don't even know if I *want* this—I just don't have much of a choice!" After a brief pause, she will add, "I guess that's the real stroke of luck. And a blessing."

Over time, she will list *Les Cherubins* in directories of local child-care providers, build a Web site, expand enrollment, and hire an assistant. Having passed the child-care licensing tests with flying colors, she'll prepare, at her own unhurried pace, to become licensed to teach. When Luc and Céleste turn five and enter school, she'll join them, becoming an elementary school art teacher. For decades to come, she will love her job on good days, not mind it on bad days, and cherish having time with her kids and at the easel during school vacations and summer breaks.

Fat raindrops pummel her scalp, roll down her cheeks. For now, she thinks, as Angie, Connor, Vance, and Emily dash for the shelter of their car, she will listen to her husband's message and get ready to call him back. Pushing her matted hair out of her eyes, she lowers her buttocks into the rubber seat of the nearest swing. Elbows hooked around the chains that suspend it, feet off the ground, she punches in the password to her voice mail.

"Vero." The familiar, nasal pitch of Didier's voice, so close yet so distant, sends a shiver down her spine. She plays his message once, twice, three times, until his flat, creamy words fuse into a coherent story. The patent on his surgical device is pending. Because it appears Veronica has decided to remain the States with Luc and Céleste, he will market it there. In three weeks, he'll fly to Boston to meet with venture capital firms. If he receives an offer for funding, he'll take it, found a company, and stay, leaving France, leaving medicine and its perks, to embark down a far less certain yet infinitely more gratifying path.

Veronica tips her head back, face to the rain. Soaked hair clings to her forehead and jaw. Her jeans and parka stick like Saran Wrap to her skin. Luc and Céleste run toward her, wailing that they're wet, they're hungry, they wanna go home. She pumps her legs, astonished by the force they generate, the velocity at which they send the swing flying up and back, back and down. She is a child again, at her parents' pool club on a hot summer day, relishing the scent of charred burgers and chlorine. She is an art student throwing paint onto canvas in risky, experimental gobs, enamored with the nameless shapes that emerge of their own volition from an amorphous field of gray. She is a young woman on vacation in Aix-en-Provence standing before a handsome doctor's office door, wearing brand-new Capri jeans, snakeskin sandals, and an intoxicating dash of perfume in the deep, suggestive valley of her cleavage. Short wisps of pavement-colored hair frame the youthful face of her twenties like the edges of an open fan. Yet her complexion bears today's scars of experience; her voice, the accent of someone who has mastered the nuances of French over the course of many years. If only time could indeed reconfigure, shift, like the colored chips of glass inside a kaleidoscope, its finite set of elements forming and reforming unprecedented combinations of present and past. With a simple twist of the hand, she would reinstate that hot, June afternoon and relive it today. She'd enter, right now, on this dank New Jersey morning, the office of that handsome doctor whose date-brown eyes welling with sensitivity touched her soul the moment she first saw them. Dripping with rainwater, hair matted to her scalp, mascara streaming down her nose, muddy children jettisoned at her feet, she'd hold out a hand and—recognizing a moment ripe for an introduction—say, "*Je suis* Veronica Berg Benhamou."

Acknowledgements

My deepest gratitude to Han Nolan, Sophie Powell and Michelle Seaton for the generous support, encouragement and feedback that's helped keep my commitment to *Veronica's Nap* and to writing alive.

Heartfelt thanks to Therese Walsh and Kathleen Bolton, founders of the blog Writer Unboxed, and to all those who are part of it. More than just a priceless source of information, it's a community and a virtual family. I'm also fortunate to be connected with Grub Street Writers, which provides unparalleled mentorship.

Friends and family members have helped make juggling work, motherhood and writing possible. I'm humbled to acknowledge that there are too many to name. Yet one name warrants special mention: Bially (Ted, Phyllis, Ann, Janice and Allison). I'm proud to share it.

For the opportunity to work in a creative and flexible environment, special thanks to Farrell Kramer.

As the publication date of *Veronica's Nap* approached, intern DeAnna Jacobsen stepped in. I'm grateful for the talent, acumen, and initiatives she's brought to this phase where a book truly begins.

None of it would have come to be without my husband, Jacques Cohen, whose brave commitment to striving toward a vision has given me the courage to do the same. Thank you, Jacques, for sharing this destiny.

 Sharon Bially lived for twelve years in Paris and Aix-en-Provence before settling with her family in Massachusetts. A graduate of Columbia University's School of International and Public Affairs, she's a public relations professional and leads seminars for the Boston-based nonprofit literary arts organization Grub Street Writers. Visit Sharon's Web site and blog at www.veronicas-nap.com.

CPSIA information can be obtained at www.ICGtesting.com
Printed in the USA
BVOW02s0919021015

420737BV00004B/32/P